WICKED
LEAKS

WICKED LEAKS

A Thriller

MATT BENDORIS

Skyhorse Publishing

First North American Edition 2017

Originally published by Contraband in 2016

This is a work of fiction. Names, places, characters, and incidents are either the products of the author's imagination or are used fictitiously.

Skyhorse Publishing books may be purchased in bulk at special discounts for sales promotion, corporate gifts, fund-raising, or educational purposes. Special editions can also be created to specifications. For details, contact the Special Sales Department, Skyhorse Publishing, 307 West 36th Street, 11th Floor, New York, NY 10018 or info@skyhorsepublishing.com.

Skyhorse® and Skyhorse Publishing® are registered trademarks of Skyhorse Publishing, Inc.®, a Delaware corporation.

Visit our website at www.skyhorsepublishing.com.
Visit the author's website at www. http://mattbendoris.co.uk/.

10 9 8 7 6 5 4 3 2 1

Library of Congress Cataloging-in-Publication Data

Names: Bendoris, Matt, author.
Title: Wicked leaks : a thriller / Matt Bendoris.
Description: First North American edition. | New York, NY : Skyhorse Publishing, 2017. | "Originally published by Contraband in 2016."
Identifiers: LCCN 2017013063 (print) | LCCN 2017018406 (ebook) | ISBN 9781510725799 (ebook) | ISBN 9781510725782 (hardcover : alk. paper)
Subjects: LCSH: Conspiracies—Fiction. | Journalists—Fiction. | GSAFD: Mystery fiction. | Suspense fiction.
Classification: LCC PR6102.E53 (ebook) | LCC PR6102.E53 W53 2017 (print) | DDC 823/.92—dc23
LC record available at https://lccn.loc.gov/2017013063

Cover design by Erin Seaward-Hiatt
Cover photo: iStockphoto

Printed in the United States of America

To my wife, Amanda;
children, Andrew and Brooke;
my courageous mum, Annie;
and my brother, Sean.

Finally, this book is in memory of
my uncle, Allan McIntosh.

Prologue

Monahan took one look at the mangled features of one of the world's most famous and loved female icons, and knew instantly it was mission accomplished. What seemed like an improbable set of circumstances leading to a tragic road 'accident' had, in fact, been carried out with military precision: Monahan's attention to detail was legendary. Like a chess player he could work out in the blink of an eye every permutation, ten moves ahead of any opponent.

Her chauffeur had taken off like a Formula One driver from the Hôtel Ritz Paris, with the paparazzi in hot pursuit. The Mercedes she was travelling in could easily outrun the cameramen on their mopeds, but one powerful black motorcycle kept pace, switching from side to side with the car, like a lion harrying its prey, goading its driver to go faster and faster. All the time the bike's pillion passenger was taking pictures, the flash from his camera briefly illuminating the occupants even through the vehicle's darkened glass. Monahan saw a male passenger remonstrate with the driver, presumably telling him to lose their paparazzi pursuers.

Exactly at the moment the chase entered the Pont de l'Alma tunnel, the motorbike rider suddenly accelerated in front, with the pillion passenger throwing a switch on his camera. The next flash was an intense white light that momentarily blinded the Mercedes driver, who recovered his sight in time to see he was about to plough into a white car directly in front of him. He took evasive action, clipping the rear of the Fiat Uno, before losing control.

When the large, German-built vehicle struck a concrete pillar head-on inside the Parisian tunnel, it was travelling at nearly eighty miles per hour. There was just one survivor, a bodyguard—the only occupant wearing a seatbelt.

The Princess rarely wore hers. Monahan knew that.

He stood over the dying woman as she took her last breaths, watching impassively as her body shut down before his very eyes. He casually flipped back the switch on his camera and fired off a few frames of his eliminated target, this time using the normal flash once again.

Hearing the mosquito-like buzz of the real paparazzi approaching on their mopeds, Monahan jumped on the back of the motorcycle, which roared off into the late summer night—unseen and untraceable, just like the Fiat Uno, which had been driven by one of Monahan's men.

It didn't matter to Monahan who the target was, or the reasons given, as there rarely were any. It was just another confirmed kill in the long, lethal career of Mad Malky Monahan. The entire operation had gone like clockwork, perfectly predicted by a man who left nothing to chance.

But life had a very different plan ahead for Monahan—one that he had been unable to foresee. As the twentieth anniversary approached of the death that shocked the world, the Princess's assassin would be fighting for his own life . . .

1

Sausages

April had arrived extra early at her favourite café, the Peccadillo, to enjoy a full fry-up in peace, without the usual barbed comments about her dietary habits from her younger colleague, Connor 'Elvis' Presley. April truly loved her food, and liked to eat without being judged, so she was slightly miffed to see Connor already sitting at their regular table. Then she caught sight of the café's waitress, Martel, wearing a skimpier skirt than usual.

That's when it dawned on her . . .

April ordered her morning mountain of the various salty and high-fat foods that pass for a traditional British breakfast before Connor said, 'Actually, that sounds good. I'll have the same.'

In all their years dining at the Peccadillo, April had never seen the fitness-conscious Connor order a fry-up. The waitress was just as stunned.

'Really? Okay then, how do you like your eggs?' Martel asked.

'Unfertilised,' April smiled, as the waitress's face turned scarlet, before she scuttled off in the direction of the kitchen.

'Miss Lavender, I do believe you made a young lady blush.'

Connor and Martel had an on/off relationship. April figured they must be having an 'on' phase. Not much got past her.

'So, long night?' she asked mischievously.

'You should know I never kiss and tell, but yes, five times if you must know.'

'No wonder you're hungry. It's Martel I feel sorry for.'

'And how come? She got to spend the night with one of Scotland's top journalists,' Connor said loftily.

'Sure, but she's still got to serve us our fry-ups. I'd have thought she'd seen enough sausage.'

April enjoyed the moment, as it was normally Connor and Martel who took the mickey out of her. It was something she had got well used to, having developed a very thick skin after three decades in the rough and tumble world of newspapers.

'I think there's another round of redundancies coming,' Connor said gloomily, moving the conversation on to work.

The pair had become all too familiar with job losses over the last few years as their old-fashioned print industry continued its terminal spiral into oblivion. Online subscriptions had been a disaster, failing to replace the lost revenue that had fallen away with the plummeting circulation and advertising revenue. All of their rival publications were in the same boat. It was simply a case of who would sink first.

'Think this will be it? A tap on the shoulder?' April asked. A 'tap on the shoulder' was literally what happened to journalists before a senior manager told them they were at risk of redundancy.

'Could be. I'm told they're going after the high-earners this time.' They both fell into that category. 'So you work your arse off to get some causal shifts, then graft and beg and plead for a staff job, then work even harder to keep it. Show loyalty by staying with the company for decades, then end up a redundo target because you now earn too much,' Connor moaned.

'God, how times have changed. Remember the days of taking a flyer? Paraphrasing?' April recalled fondly.

'Yeah, then the *News Of The World* screwed it all up with their bloody phone-hacking. Idiots,' Connor seethed.

'Then there were the hospitals. Some journalists made a career from getting hold of medical records. Now they'd be locked up,' April said.

'I know. Shit, isn't it?' Connor replied with no hint of remorse.

They sat in silence until their breakfast was served. Martel instantly lightened their mood as she had playfully arranged Connor's sausage and two fried eggs to look like a cock and balls.

'I'd have thought a chipolata would have done?' April teased.

'She should have arranged yours into an old boot,' Connor retorted.

'I hope he's more charming in bed, love,' April said, directing her attention to Martel.

'Oh yeah, he's stopped holding my head under the covers when he farts,' the waitress smiled back.

'Jeez, you do that once and you never hear the end of it,' Connor said as he stabbed right into the sausages, fat and juice oozing around his fork's prongs.

The pair tucked into their breakfast, which contained at least half the daily calories required by an adult, and exceeded the recommended salt and fat intake probably for a whole week.

'See, this is the problem with healthy living, nothing tastes as good as this heart-attack-on-a-plate,' Connor said after finishing everything bar the fried tomato, which looked like a blood clot.

'Yet you've left the healthiest thing on the plate,' April observed through her customary mouthful of food. 'If you're not having your tomato . . .' And without waiting for an answer she scooped the slimy, red blob onto her plate.

Connor was always amazed at just how much April could shovel away. She adored eating and had hips 'wide as the Clyde' to prove it.

They had worked for the same newspaper, the *Daily Chronicle*, since the early nineties, but had only been thrown together in the last few years to head up the special investigations desk, from a windowless, converted broom cupboard, which passed as their office. The news editor at the time had hoped they would crash and burn so he could free up their salaries for new, younger, and cheaper staff. But, much to their own surprise, they had worked wonders on a string of high-profile cases, including the murder of a jewellery tycoon, Selina Seth, and the death of the US television presenter Bryce Horrigan, which had seen them both involved in the thick of the action in America and Scotland.

Connor had just turned forty, while April was old enough to be his mother at fifty-eight. He loved his social media and techie boy's toys, while April would break into a cold sweat even thinking about them.

'Another lord named,' Connor said, scrolling through some website on his iPhone.

'Named what?'

'On this site, beastshamer.com. It's like Wikipedia for pae-dophiles. They should call it Wikipaedo. They've just outed another judge. Lord Geoffrey Delphina. A particularly pious old bastard. Always liked to lecture about true family values in court.'

'How can they do that? Where are they getting their infor-mation?' April asked, finishing off Connor's unwanted fried tomato.

'They're apparently based in Russia. Some of it's stolen data from official files, others from survivors' testimonies, I guess.'

'Then why don't we just print it? Publish and be damned and all that.'

'Oh, we're very brave once they're dead. But otherwise we're scared shitless. Even retweeting just a hint of these alle-gations and they'll sue you. You are basically taking on the establishment.'

'If only there was solid, cast iron proof. Something to nail them before they die,' April seethed. She had interviewed enough victims throughout the years to know the utter devas-tation that sexual abuse can cause: broken and shattered lives.

'Yup, if only. Right, I'll pay for this. My "Help The Aged" good deed for the week,' he said as he settled up with Martel, giving her a cursory peck on the cheek and a promise to call her later. The truth is he rarely did, hence why their relationship was always in a constant state of flux. For Connor was a reporter first and foremost. Everything else came a dim and distant second in his life, as Martel had discovered.

April knew it too. 'I may be an old technophobe. But you're definitely a commitment-phobe,' she remarked as they walked the short distance to their office in Glasgow's city centre.

2

Sleep, glorious sleep

Kelly Carter arrived home at half eight in the morning, beyond tired. She had briefly fallen asleep behind the wheel yet again, only to be woken by the rumble strip when her car had drifted off the main highway onto the hard shoulder. She had wound the window down, with the cold, icy blast of air enough to keep her awake for the final stretch home. Kelly pulled into her drive to see her front door was already open, with her mum taking her children, William and Beth, to school.

'Morning, Mum,' Beth said, rushing to embrace Kelly. Her daughter was just nine and still free and easy with her hugs, but William had recently turned twelve and held back a bit, especially in public. 'Too cool to give your mother a kiss?' Kelly asked, gently chiding her son as she hugged him tightly.

'Hi, Mum,' William said, his cheeks reddening slightly.

'*Hi, Mum*,' Kelly mocked. 'Your voice is getting deeper. Oh no, I've got a tweenager!' she said, ruffling his hair.

'Mum, I've just brushed it,' William said, patting it down again.

'Worried in case one of your little high school girlfriends thinks you're a scruff?'

'Bye, Mum,' William said, his face now properly red.

'Everything okay?' Kelly asked her mum, Caroline.

'Yes, dear, they slept while I put the washing on and emptied the dishwasher. Now off you pop to bed,' she replied.

Kelly didn't need to be told twice. After a quick shower, she would be sound asleep before the clock struck 9 a.m., giving her precisely five and three-quarter hours of glorious sleep before her alarm went off, and she would pull on a pair of joggies to go and retrieve Beth from the school gates, feeling like a total slob amongst the other well-heeled mums. Then it would be snacks before she cooked the evening meal and afterwards hopefully she would grab a nap in her living room chair. Although it would be a short snooze, it was essential to get her through the twelve-hour night shift that lay ahead. William and Beth knew better than to wake her. On a good night Kelly could sometimes manage a whole hour and a half of shut-eye while her two ate their dinner. But the cacophony of noise would steadily rise along with their blood sugar levels as their food was digested. Kelly often thought that was the fundamental difference between 'them' and 'us'. While adults wanted to kick back and relax on a full belly, kids wanted to climb the walls.

Kelly had found out the hard way that it truly was exhausting being a single mum. Her husband, Brian, had left the previous year for no particular reason other than they'd fallen out of love. There was no row, no screaming matches, he'd just turned round one morning and said, 'Well, this isn't working out, is it?' and left.

Brian had moved into a flat just a few miles away, but it may as well have been on the moon for all the help he'd been with the kids. He hadn't been a total bastard about it—when it came to the divorce settlement he had signed over his half of the house without dispute. Brian was aiming for a clean break and Kelly understood that, but what she couldn't grasp was his total indifference towards his own children. He was a perfectly loving father on the weekends he did take them, but he never asked to see them. It was always at Kelly's instigation.

Kelly wasn't even angry, or sad. Truth was, she felt nothing at all. Her closest friend, Joanna, believed Kelly needed cheering up. She would arrive with a bottle of wine and warm hugs on the nights Kelly wasn't working. Although Kelly appreciated the sentiment, she found it all a bit tiresome. But, at thirty-nine years old and as a single working mother of two, everything seemed tiresome now. She was convinced that had been the downfall of her marriage. They had both simply run out of steam. Kelly didn't even have the strength to try to salvage it. She just let it go.

But that was then, and this was now, and she still had bills to pay. Her job was to nurse terminally ill patients through their final days, at home, instead of in the sterile surroundings of some generic hospital ward. Kelly had lost count of how many people she had seen die. One night she witnessed five deaths—a record for her unit—earning her the unkind nick-name of 'Nurse Dredd'.

She had a job most people couldn't comprehend, but Kelly didn't have a problem with death as it was never her focus: she always concentrated on her patients' lives. She loved getting to know them. Talking to these fading human beings about their families, before they were slowly erased. Seeing photos of where they'd been and what they'd done during their years on the planet. They were usually surrounded by love and warmth, and Kelly's job was to make their passing as comfortable and as pain-free as possible.

Those were good deaths.

Then there were the other kind. Mums and dads her own age, cut down in their prime by an illness they didn't deserve. Fit young men with lung cancer, who hadn't smoked a ciga-rette in their lives. A woman on her last legs with chronic heart failure, from some virus that ruins the organ you need most. Almost always supported by a partner with a haunted look and bewildered young children who were about to lose a parent.

Those were the hardest, because empathy can be a bitch. Kelly was often asked by her non-nursing pals how she coped. She coped simply because she had to. She was never in any way cold and she never, ever forgot a single patient she cared for. But, back at home, her mum would sleep over with the kids and get them ready for school in the morning. It was the only way Kelly could keep going to work since Brian left.

And Kelly guiltily acknowledged that work was actually the easiest part of her life. She enjoyed the randomness of the call sheet, which determined who she would be nursing through the night. There was the usual sadness, when a line had been drawn through yet another patient, but in the business of dying there are always plenty of customers.

That morning, as usual, sheer exhaustion kicked in as she slipped under her duvet, the previous night's shift being put to bed with her.

3

Back off

April and Connor walked into their office shortly after 10 a.m. In movies and TV shows the editorial floors of newspapers are always shown as hives of activity, with phones ringing and journalists hammering away at keyboards. That was true of the golden era of print. Nowadays the newsroom of the *Daily Chronicle* resembled a morgue. Constant job-cutting meant that reporters were down to a skeleton staff. The building didn't get busy until early afternoons when the sub-editors, who edited and made the words fit the boxes on the page, began their shifts.

'Look at that,' Connor said, pointing at the ceiling, 'half the lights aren't even on because no one has walked past the motion sensors.'

The low energy lighting flickered into life, illuminating the way for April and Connor as they walked to their converted broom cupboard office. Connor tossed a copy of the day's paper onto his desk in disgust. 'Princess bloody Diana. We were all happy to pour buckets of shit over her while she was alive, but now she's taken on sainthood status. And where do they get all this crap from anyway? Any ex-cop or failed journalist wanting to make a quick buck releases another Diana conspiracy book and we faithfully report their drivel.'

'Funny how people always think we're at the cutting edge and how our job is so action-packed and exciting. How little they know,' April said, chuckling as she went through the daily rigmarole of trying to get her PC to boot up and the numerous attempts to get her password right.

Then it was down to the most important part of the day—stories.

Connor despaired at the attitude of many reporters who would wait around to be given something to work on, believing that they were there solely to report the news. That may have been fine once upon a time, but these days news was what you made it. April felt the same, but in more simple terms; she liked to keep herself busy as it made the days fly by 'til she could be home again, snoring in her chair with her cat, Cheeka, curled up on her lap.

'Right, sod it. I'm going to call Lord Geoffrey, see what he's got to say about appearing on Beast Shamer,' Connor said.

'Do you have his number?'

'I think so, from years ago. Got him to do some first-person bollocks on changes to the Scottish judicial system or something. He's from one of the islands, although you'd never know it. Became quite the quintessential Englishman when he ended up in the House of Lords.'

'I hate when they do that. Cover up who they really are.'

'Get you with your peroxide blonde hair. Aren't you really a redhead?'

April regretted ever telling her colleague that. He often used it against her, but she had truly hated the carrot-top she'd been born with and spent most of her years disguising it.

Connor found the number for Lord Delphina on an old Microsoft Word file, one of the many incarnations of his contacts book that had originally started out as a Filofax before being transferred onto two generations of Psion organisers, which had become obsolete. Connor then had to copy and paste his thousands of numbers, emails and postal addresses onto a Word file, before painstakingly typing almost all the 5,000 entries one by one into his BlackBerry, which was eventually replaced by his current iPhone. Those he hadn't deemed worthy of migrating stayed on his Word file, which he was using now.

April still had the same bulging, fade to grey, tattered old diary she had faithfully lugged around for thirty-odd years and in which she'd used every colour of pen to scribble the names and numbers of everyone she had ever interviewed. Remarkably she could locate even the most mouldy of contacts almost as quickly as Connor could from his smartphone.

'Got it. It's the old bastard's home number too. Excellent,' Connor purred after locating Delphina's contact details. He popped a tiny Olympus microphone into his ear so that it could record the telephone conversation on his Panasonic digital recorder. He pressed the record button as the phone connected. It was picked up on the second ring by a woman.

'Lord Delphina's residence.'

'Hello, it's Connor Presley from the *Daily Chronicle* in Glasgow. Is the Lord available?'

'Can I have your number and email address?' the woman asked, politely enough.

'Sure, but can I speak to him now?' Connor pressed.

'Your number and email address, please?' she repeated, somewhat more forcibly this time.

Connor gave both before the lady thanked him and hung up. 'Weird. She didn't even ask me what I wanted him for. I wonder if I'll hear back.'

He didn't have long to wonder: an email arrived from the prominent London law firm McIlvanney and Mallicks. It stated:

Dear Mr. Presley

We act for Lord Justice Delphina, OBE. His Lordship has instructed us to contact all members of the press with regards to Internet rumours of historic sexual abuse.

His Lordship is currently undertaking a series of medical tests. He will not be making any comment on these unsubstantiated and unfounded allegations.

You are to cease and desist from any contact with Lord Delphina. As this is also a medical matter, we have copied your editor and your legal department into this email too as all information contained in this correspondence is confidential and not for publication.

Yours sincerely
Henry McIlvanney

'Fuck me,' Connor said, shaking his head, 'talk about heavy-handed. And you wonder why the mainstream media never report even the existence of these rumours? These bastards would happily shut us all down.'

Connor stared at the email for a long time. He wasn't in the mood to kowtow to a lord, or anyone else for that matter.

4

Mad Malky

'Got a new one for you tonight, Kelly. A Mr. Malcolm Monahan. Bone cancer. Forty-nine. Ex-forces, apparently,' said Kelly's boss, Sister McIntosh, reading from her computer screen.

'Bone cancer? What's the primary source?' Kelly asked. It was a legitimate question as cancer usually, but not always, spread to bones from the likes of the prostate or lungs.

Sister McIntosh scanned down her notes. 'Nope, doesn't say. Although, it doesn't say much. He was being treated by the army before being dumped on us. Must've wanted to come home to die in peace.'

'Any family?'

'Sorry. Name, age, and condition. That's your lot. Patients are like a box of chocolates, you know.'

'Alright, Sister Gump, I'll be on my way,' Kelly said, smiling as she collected her things to leave for yet another night of sitting.

• • •

Monahan's flat was on the top floor of a four-story, red-stone tenement block on Glasgow's Southside. Kelly lifted her heavy black nurse's bag from the trunk of her car and moaned, 'Why is it always the top floor?'

She lugged her case up the flight of stairs, passing the various lingering cooking smells that determined the nationality of each flat's inhabitants—from deep-fat, fried chips to mouth-watering Indian spices. Kelly reached the top landing and stared at one door, which looked like the entrance to a student flat, with scribbled surnames written on temporary

Post-its stuck to the framework. The door opposite was a steel affair, no doubt with reinforced locks. There was no name on the door, but it did have an expensive-looking entry system, complete with a camera lens that would undoubtedly be linked to a monitor inside.

'Ex-forces, my backside—bloody drug dealer more like,' Kelly sighed. She spoke from experience, having visited enough mini-fortresses, which were the trademarks of gangsters and drug pushers.

Kelly pressed the buzzer and was greeted with a very formal 'Who is it?' She stated her business, but was then asked a curious question: 'Are you alone?' Kelly stepped aside so that the camera lens could see the landing behind, and chortled, 'Yup, just little old me on my ownio.'

The door buzzed open and Kelly let herself in. A voice from far away beckoned, 'In here, please.'

Kelly followed the sound to a bedroom. What she saw next stopped her in her tracks. It looked like a private medical wing, with a fully adjustable hospital bed, various monitors, and a morphine syringe driver.

'Wow', she said with genuine amazement, 'Looks like you've robbed a medical suppliers.'

Monahan raised a smile below his military-style clipped moustache. 'I'd say the best piece of equipment just walked in the room.'

'Now, now, Mr. Monahan, keep that sort of patter for the officer's mess. We don't want to get off on the wrong foot. I'm Nurse Carter.' Kelly only ever went by her surname when patients were being inappropriate.

'You wouldn't catch me in the officer's mess with those inbred, chinless wonders. And I'm sorry, Nurse Carter. Wrong foot, indeed. I would blame the painkillers, but I've always chanced my arm,' Monahan replied.

He got the hint of a smile for his honesty, while Kelly took off her jacket and placed it over the back of a chair. She studied her patient momentarily. He was gaunt, underweight and with a jaundiced look and yellowing of the eyes, which suggested that his cancer had spread to his liver. She found Monahan's notes at the end of the bed and checked for confirmation, but there was no mention of any liver problems.

'Must say, I have never come across a set-up like this before in a patient's house,' she said, her eyes scanning through the pages of information. 'I'd guess I'm not the first medical professional to have been in here. So who was doing your care prior to the good old NHS night-sitting service?'

'My former employers,' Monahan replied without giving too much away. 'But dying can be an expensive business, so we've had a parting of the ways. I'm guessing they'll take all this stuff back when I'm gone. They shouldn't have too long to wait.'

'And who's been responsible for your syringe driver?' she said, pointing at the apparatus which dispensed the regular doses of morphine with a push-button 'top up' booster switch.

'Me. Don't worry, it's not the first time I've had to use one. But it was running out and it's easier to buy heroin than medical-grade morphine so I had to ask for help. Otherwise I'd have been quite happy to see myself out the door.'

'Out the door?' Kelly asked, incredulous at his nonchalance. 'Just die here alone?'

'Yeah, why not?' Monahan shrugged. 'We all die, right? I'd be quite happy to drift off in a morphine-induced haze.'

'Sadly, death doesn't always work out the way we planned,' Kelly replied.

'It does for me,' Monahan said through a faint grin. But his eyes weren't smiling.

'And yet you needed to call us,' Kelly said in a matronly manner that was alien to her as she was always a lot warmer than this with her charges. But she couldn't seem to help herself; this patient's coldness was beginning to irritate her.

'I guess you were Plan B,' Monahan said, looking at Kelly as if studying her.

She changed the subject. 'Do you have a primary source for the bone cancer? Prostate problems or something?'

'Not that I know of. Was having a little issue with the water-works, but my medicals all came up clear, and, believe me, they were very thorough. Anyway, doesn't matter now—same end result.'

'Any family? Friends? Support at all? Someone to do the shopping?'

Monahan just shook his head. 'Nope, lost contact a long time ago and my appetite disappeared a few weeks ago. Got plenty of protein shakes and all the water I need in the taps. That should be enough to see me through.'

'Can you still walk? Get up for the loo?'

'Walking is a bit tricky. I was using that,' he said, indicating towards a commode in the corner, 'but since I changed to a liquid-only diet, I'm just passing fluids. So I catheterise myself.'

'Well, you're certainly the first patient I've had who has been able to set up a syringe driver and catheterise themselves. There's hardly any need for me to be here,' she joked.

'Except for the morphine. I can't write a prescription for that. Believe me, I would if I could.'

'Where did you receive your medical training?' Kelly asked, unable to help her nosiness.

'In the field. It's pretty basic stuff, to be honest, but it has proved to be effective enough.'

'I will need to get a doctor called out to prescribe the morphine.'

'Who's the quack?' Monahan said suspiciously.

Kelly had never been asked that before. 'Just whoever's on duty. Might be Doctor Shabazi.'

'Ah, a towelhead.'

'Ah, a racist,' Kelly quickly replied.

'I'm not a racist. That's just what we called them. I know plenty of towelheads. One saved my life once.'

'Well, he's not Arabic, he's Persian. We really need to work on your out-of-date vocabulary.' Kelly was getting downright annoyed by this obstreperous new patient. However, she was intrigued at the same time, though loathed to admit it.

'Yeah, because I've got all the time in the world, haven't I?' he replied sarcastically. 'I think I'll just stay politically incorrect, if that's okay with you?'

Kelly said no more and instead got her mobile out to call GEMS—the Glasgow Emergency Medical Service—for the on-duty doctor. She could feel Monahan studying her body.

'No wedding ring, I see, but you still have an indent where you wore one. You could take it off before your shift, I guess, but somehow I don't think so. I'm going for recently separated.'

Kelly glared at him. She was pissed off now. 'Well done, Sherlock. You're full of hidden talents, aren't you?' Kelly finished making her call and while they waited for the doctor, she went about her business, charting the patient's heart rate, temperature and blood pressure.

Half an hour later the door buzzer went, and Monahan turned the flat-screen monitor by his bed towards Kelly.

'Is this your towel . . . I mean, your quack?' he said mischievously.

'Yes, that's Doctor Shabazi. I'd appreciate it if you were polite to him.'

Monahan grinned. 'You may have mistaken my directness for a lack of manners, but I'm always polite.'

Doctor Shabazi was as surprised as Nurse Carter when he walked into Monahan's bedroom. He raised his eyebrows. 'It's like Aladdin's cave in here.'

'*Salam*, Doctor. *Fekr mikonam parastar azman khoshesh namiad.*' (Hello, Doctor. I don't think the nurse likes me.)

Neither Kelly nor the doctor had expected their patient to speak perfect Farsi. Doctor Shabazi replied, '*Motmaenam shoma eshtebah mikonid, Parastar* Carter *hamara doost dareh,'* (I'm sure that's not the case. Nurse Carter likes everyone), before slipping back into English. 'Where did you learn Farsi? It's very good.'

'Thanks. Just through my line of work,' Monahan replied, saying no more than he needed to.

The doctor went through his various questions about Monahan's well-being, before hooking up a new syringe of morphine. He then wrote up a repeat prescription for the powerful pain relief.

'Okay, we're all sorted,' the doctor said reassuringly.

'I'll take it from here, Doc. I know how to set up my own drip,' Monahan assured him.

'Nice try. My morphine, my rules. The nursing service will set up and monitor the syringe driver. You're not in the field anymore, soldier.'

The doctor had never once asked Monahan what he had done for a living. He didn't have to. Growing up in Iran, he had experienced his fair share of military types.

'Nurse . . .' Doctor Shabazi beckoned as he made his way to the front door. Out of earshot he whispered, 'Just watch yourself with that one. I've found that Special Forces usually have special enemies. Don't tell him anything about yourself. His type use information like weapons. That's the reason I ended up in Scotland: to make sure I was far away from folk like that.'

Kelly thought about what the patient had already deduced about her marital status, and thanked the doctor for his advice. When she returned to the bedroom, Monahan was sleeping with a strange smile of satisfaction across his face as the morphine did its work. He remained like that for the rest of her shift.

• • •

By 7:30 a.m., Kelly found herself standing at a supermarket checkout, having grabbed some gammon steaks, eggs, and pineapple rings, which would do for tonight's dinner. It was as uninspired as she felt after coming off a mid-week night shift. Kelly viewed cooking as a daily battle. There were only certain foods the kids would eat and if you gave them the same too often, then they went off them.

She had left her patient still sleeping, making him one of his protein shakes, and leaving a sandwich and fresh water by his bed. He was a curious sort, for sure. And she'd never seen a set-up like it, like a private hospital room you see on an American medical drama. Some houses Kelly went to, you were lucky if the poor patient had a spare set of sheets.

Then there was Doctor Shabazi's strange warning about 'Special Forces having special enemies'. It was just weird. But now she was too tired to think. Kelly shuffled her way past a newspaper stand towards the checkout, staring vacantly at the headlines vying for attention. It was the *Daily Chronicle* that caught her attention with yet another front-page splash on the death of Princess Diana. They were obsessed. Kelly chucked to herself, thinking, *Nearly twenty years on, guys, and she's still dead.*

She picked up a copy and added it to her basket, not knowing when she would actually have time to read it.

5

How the mighty have fallen

Detective Chief Inspector David 'Bing' Crosbie had once been tipped for the very top. He ticked all the right boxes and was the epitome of a commanding police officer in the twenty-first century: part law enforcer, part social worker, part politician. But around two years ago he started to undergo a fundamental personality change, and he was scared to try to find out why. The last time he had sought professional advice someone ended up dead.

Part of this change was a sort of inner Tourette's syndrome, a torturous affliction for Crosbie, who abhorred bad language—a fact his alter ego seemed to revel in. His alternate self would trot out every swear word known to man, then some that weren't. It wasn't even restricted to his inner monologue anymore, with offensive obscenities frequently escaping his lips. It had earned him the new nickname of 'Boom' Crosbie, because almost every time he opened his mouth he dropped a swear bomb. It meant he was good fun to work with for the rank and file, but his bosses had had enough and he was moved sideways to one of Police Scotland's new high-tech call centres, in the hope that he would soon be up on a gross misconduct charge for inevitably swearing at a caller. He could then be dismissed from the force post-haste. In the meantime it was a case of out of sight, out of mind, as far as his superiors were concerned.

It had a devastating effect on Crosbie. He was having trouble enough battling his inner demons before being effectively demoted and demoralised. Now he didn't have the willpower to keep the bad Crosbie at bay.

He had also been a regular contact for Connor Presley and April Lavender over the years. He was one of the few commanders that police press officers had trusted to give journalists off-the-record briefings and gentle steers. But all that changed with the Leveson Inquiry, set up in the wake of the *News Of The World* phone-hacking scandal, to look into the culture, practices and ethics of the British press, yet strangely ignoring the even wider institutionalised hacking by law and insurance firms. Several journalists later ended up in court accused of corrupting police officers with bribes—in other words, paying them for stories, a practice as old as Fleet Street itself. The law had rarely been enforced in over a hundred years. Afterwards, all contact between serving police officers and members of the press was strictly off limits.

But Crosbie didn't care to follow the dicta from high command.

'Whaddsup, motherfucker?' Crosbie asked, while sitting in his three-sided, open-plan office cubicle, still wearing his phone headset as he made the call on his mobile.

'DCI Crosbie. It's been a while,' Connor said.

'Sure has, bro. How's it hanging?'

'You been on an African-American awareness course, or watching Ali G again?'

'Nah, just bored out of my tits in this cunting call centre.'

'Bloody hell, I knew you'd been bumped sideways, but I didn't know it was that far sideways.'

'Ha, I know. Me, doing customer shitting service. I know they are just waiting for me to cock it up. Everything's recorded.'

'I'd be very careful what you say then, Bing.'

'Easier said than dicking done. I hate it. I mean, *fucking* hate it. "Ma man is trying tae stab me again",' Crosbie said, mimicking one of his callers. 'I'm so tempted to shout, "What do you want us to fucking do? You married the psycho prick!"'

'That probably wouldn't be seen as sympathetic,' Connor said sarcastically.

'Aye, exactly. That's what the cunts want me to say. Blow off at some of these common cunts and be out the cunting door.'

'A few too many "cunts" to follow there, but I get the drift. Apart from that, anything I can do you for, Bing?'

'Nah, not really. Just thought I'd let you know I'm not dead and haven't been fired yet. And, who knows, I might even still be of some use to you. Is the Big Yin there?' The 'Big Yin' was one of the kinder terms Crosbie used for April Lavender.

'Nah, she's off home. And I'm going to the gym. Catch you later, Bing.'

'Twatty bye,' Bing replied.

'Twatty bye, indeed,' Connor responded, doubting that his once prime contact would ever be of any use again.

6

Beast Shamer

April received a message from Luigi, owner of her favourite restaurant in Glasgow. He texted exactly how he spoke: with a thick half-Glaswegian/half-Italian-stereotype accent.

Hey April. Why I no see you? Why you no come in for my meatballs? Your fiancé misses you. Xxx

The word 'fiancé' leapt off the screen. What had she done? Luigi had proposed so often to her since becoming widowed that it had become something of a running joke. Then last year, out of the blue, he had produced a diamond ring and, inexplicably, April said yes. She had regretted her decision ever since.

April loved his restaurant and his food. She loved how he made her laugh. She even loved being the object of his desire. But April did not love Luigi. And that was really the crux of the problem. Recently she had been avoiding him, which neither helped nor solved anything. But she was too much a creature of habit to let anyone else into her life. She just wished she'd thought of that before accepting his proposal.

Soon Luigi. I'll come and see you soon. Just been so busy at work. Xx. She hoped that would placate her Italian Lothario a while longer.

Just a two kisses? You used to send me three. Xxx.

April sighed. She just wasn't feeling in the mood anymore. *I'll see you later this week Luigi. Promise.* She then added the three kisses, to appease him more than anything.

The exchange had been no more than a distraction from what April had really planned for her evening. She excitedly messaged her colleague: *What is website called? Beastie Boys something?*

Connor loved the directness and absurdity of April's messages—they made him smile, even if that wasn't her intention. He had also just finished his workout and was in the mood for a wind-up, with the endorphins having well and truly kicked in.

Beastie Boys? What the hell would you know about the finest rap trio that ever walked the earth?

The three dots appeared on his iPhone to let him know April was typing a reply. He could just imagine her peering at the tiny screen with her half-moon spectacles, her sausage fingers pressing several unwanted keys at the same time. Eventually the reply came: *Not Beastie Boys. Beastie something. The one with all the dirty old lords.*

Oh that one. Just Google 'bestiality', and 'secret' and 'cam'. That'll take you straight to it.

There were no three dots this time. He knew April would be typing the words into her search engine. Minutes later he got the reply he expected: *That's not it, you dirty boy. Why would anyone want to do that with animals? Now I have a huge horse's willy on my screen I can't get rid of.*

So it's not all bad. Here's the real link: www.beastshamer.com.

April tapped the link on Connor's message and was immediately greeted by a warning:

The material on this website has been stolen from the British Government. You may be prosecuted in your home territory for viewing or sharing it. Most of the content is of an adult nature with many distressing images. Users enter at their own risk.

The message made April think for only a fraction of a second before she decided to click *Enter*. If caught, she could always claim it was for journalistic purposes rather than just being nosy. 'What the hell?' she said aloud as she was met with another message:

I used to work for the Government's secret services but I became disillusioned with all the cover-ups. That's why I have launched this website, which the UK Government has so desperately tried to shut down.

I believe my life is in danger for sharing some of the state's most shocking secrets. But I shall continue to drip feed classified documents every evening at 7 p.m. BST until the UK Government agrees to prosecute the high-ranking members of the establishment who have been—and many still are—involved in the systematic abuse of vulnerable minors.

April checked her watch, it had just gone 7 p.m. The statement continued:

Today's classified information contains a photograph taken on June 10th, 1983, and shows a student of a top public school taking part in an initiation ceremony where he had to insert his penis into the mouth of a roasted goat's head. This practice has gone on for decades and some of the most powerful men in Britain—from future bankers to politicians and high court judges—have taken part in it. There have always been unequivocal denials that these secret practices even existed. But as you can see, here it is in black and white. It shows that such sordid behaviour is par for the course at the very top echelons of our society. And also how easily the establishment spout their lies and denials. But a picture speaks a thousand words.

April looked at the young, privileged man in top hat and tails, with a huge grin on his face. It was the unmistakable image of a well-known television personality. One of that breed of journalist/presenter/host/entertainer who would make his name for holding politicians to account and making celebrities squirm. For daring to push the boundaries. Someone who had started to believe himself a cut above the stars, MPs and public figures he was paid so handsomely to question. A man who revelled in his influence and status. With his penis in the mouth of a dead goat.

April was already looking forward to tomorrow evening's revelation.

Two hours later a press release from the television host's agent stated that he would be stepping down from his presenting duties with immediate effect.

7

The heist

Monahan was enjoying a morphine-induced dream again. They seemed so much more vivid than normal dreams. Although this was more of a memory: he could recall in minute detail his audacious raid on a bank vault in Zurich.

The Swiss were undoubtedly the best security experts in the world, having kept billions of pounds for despot dictators, stolen Nazi gold and artworks safe from prying eyes, no matter what international pressure was exerted on their institutions.

But their security systems hadn't been tested by the likes of Monahan.

He and his team had been ensconced in a rented apartment in Zurich's Niederdorf district for almost four weeks. That had given them enough time both to plan their raid and carry out several dry runs too.

The banks were virtually impossible to break into. Just one innocuous-sounding codeword from a kidnapped member of staff would set off a chain reaction of shut-downs and police responses. But the banks had a weakness in that they always presumed the bad guys were after the contents of their vaults. However, Monahan was only after a single piece of information: a code held on this particular bank's database. He didn't even know what the code was and he didn't care. He was given an order and he would carry out his mission as usual.

The bank made a point of not having its computer network connected to the web and the outside world. That way it couldn't be hacked. So Monahan had to get his hacker inside the bank and give him long enough to retrieve the code from the system. Their target was the security office based beside the bank's rear entrance. All they needed was the guard's computer, which Monahan had discovered on a reconnaissance mission posing as a delivery man. Monahan always insisted on gathering his own intel. He felt he had more chance of staying alive that way.

Monahan had passed the security office enough to know that when the fat guard was on duty by himself he kept his door open a fraction while having a fly cigarette. Detailed observations correctly predicted that the smoker would be working when Monahan and his team advanced. They struck with the element of surprise, using stealth and under the cover of dark.

The large security guard had just taken a long draw on his illicit cigarette when he was disabled by a brutal blow to his windpipe. As usual Monahan's timing had been perfect. The guard fell to the ground gasping for air and choking on his smoke-filled lungs. Monahan flipped the man onto his front with ease, and secured his hands behind his back with plastic security ties, before wrapping thick gaffer tape around the unfortunate low-paid employee's mouth. Smoke billowed from the guard's nostrils as he desperately tried to expel the cigarette fumes and replace them with fresh air.

One of Monahan's team entered the guard's room and plugged a laptop into his computer. A little under three minutes later, the hooded men left, having got what they came for.

The guard knew he would be sacked for smoking on the job. How else could he explain the unlocked door? He strained and fumbled to get the remote alarm switch out of his pocket. Maybe if he activated it and they caught the bad guys he'd get to keep his job? He huffed and puffed as he moved into position and pressed the button with the tip of his nose. In what seemed like seconds the frantic wail of sirens could be heard descending on the bank from multiple directions. A police control centre was already studying CCTV footage, instantly picking up two men in crash helmets escaping on a powerful motorbike. What they didn't see was the back-up team slowly dispersing in various directions into the night and anonymity.

The police controllers flicked from screen to screen as the bike passed the thousands of cameras in Zurich city centre. A helicopter was scrambled and police roadblocks set up to cover all escape routes. The motorbike seemed to be heading for a trap as it entered the Uetilberg tunnel, overtaking a white Iveco van as it did so. The CCTV controllers flicked to a camera inside the tunnel, but the screen came up blank.

'Must be a malfunction on that camera,' one of the controllers said.

They switched to another camera at the exit of the four-and-a-half kilometer stretch of roadway and waited for the superbike to come roaring into view. It never came.

A senior police officer immediately radioed a command to his men on the ground: 'They're in the tunnel. Close it off. Close it off!'

Police cars screeched to a halt at both ends of the tunnel, and twitchy cops took cover as they pointed their guns towards the dimly lit interior. But there would be nothing to aim at, never mind shoot.

The Iveco van had barely changed speed when its rear doors were thrown open and a metal ramp lowered to the ground. Monahan needed only a little more throttle to take him up the elevation into the back of the van. Seconds later the ramp raised and the doors closed once more. Keeping ten kilometers under the speed limit at all times, the van trundled off into the night.

A smile stretched over Monahan's face as he slept in the hospital bed of his flat, dreaming of happier times.

8

A familiar face

Kelly groaned when she looked at the schedule and saw her patient for the night. The day staff had updated Monahan's notes with more detail than they had previously, after obtaining 'limited information' from his previous healthcare provider. Solid tumours were in about 30 percent of his bone mass. He was dying a slow and painful death. Kelly scanned for any information on the primary source. None given. Often the patient was too far gone to work out what had caused the cancer in the first place.

A nurse had also written that the patient seemed agitated about having enough morphine left and asked for an extra syringe driver to be left onsite. This request was denied by the day doctor who suspected the patient 'may endear to practice euthanasia'. *Seven years at medical school for a fancy way to write 'top himself'*, Kelly thought.

She believed that the doctor was wrong on that front. She'd had plenty of patients looking to end their lives, and they were usually so bleak and depressed they could barely speak. They also rarely got the chance to top themselves as nature soon took its course.

But Monahan was nothing like them. He wanted to be in control and she figured he simply didn't wish to be left without any painkiller again. He was a military man through and through, who planned ahead. She grabbed his case notes and headed off into the night.

9

The Ripper

April had ignored another needy text from Luigi as she added a dash of tonic to her glass of gin, which contained the thinnest slice of lemon known to cocktailology. Over the years the spirit level had gone up and up and up, to now, where there was no room for the ice cubes anymore. She plonked the glass on the table by her armchair, where her ageing cat, Cheeka, joined her, settling down on her owner's lap. It had just gone 7 p.m. and now April was ready for her next scandal from Beast Shamer:

By now I'd like to think you've got to know me a little bit, even if you cannot know my true identity. Nevertheless I have always believed the proof is in the pudding. Yesterday I showed you a picture of a TV personality with his private parts in a goat's mouth. But that was mere tittle-tattle compared to what I have in store for you now. It's one of the first, and biggest, cover-ups in British history: Jack the Ripper.

Now, before you think I'm just another crazy Ripper-ologist who came up with yet another mental theory, these are not the conclusions of years of research. In actual fact I wasn't even looking for anything to do with the case. But when you come across a file marked 'The Whitechapel Murders', it does prick your interest somewhat. So I will shortly reveal the man who carried out the murders of five victims—Mary Ann Nichols, Annie Chapman, Elizabeth Stride, Catherine Eddowes and Mary Jane Kelly. They became known as the 'canonical five' and were murdered between August 31st and November 9th, 1888.

This is not who I think carried out their murders and mutilations, but the actual person who was arrested and confessed . . . and I'll then reveal how the establishment simply made him, and the case, disappear.

I imagine a lot of you will be asking why this sort of archive material hasn't been made available under the UK's declassification acts or even through a freedom of information request. To do that the Government would have to know that these files are in existence in the first place. Quite simply, the Government doesn't know about them.

No, this information is in the hands of a select few, the people who really run our country—the secret services. And, as their name suggests, they like to keep everything secret.

April was getting a tad fed up with the blogger's ramblings. All she wanted to know was the identity of Jack the Ripper.

Anyway, time for the big reveal: the murderer was James Maybrick. 'Who?' I hear you collectively ask. He was a wealthy cotton trader from Liverpool. But why would the establishment want to protect him? Well, that's because he was a Freemason and his brother, Michael, was on the Supreme Grand Council of Freemasons.

An old black and white police mugshot appeared of a good-looking man, with receding hair, a sharp nose and moustache. He was still wearing the stained leather apron he had been arrested in when he was found at the crime scene of the fourth victim, Catherine Eddowes.

Another much grander portrait appeared of Maybrick in all his Freemason finery at some Masonic meeting.

James Maybrick was literally caught red-handed. He had also carved a pair of compasses into the face of his victim. I'm sure I don't need to explain that compasses are symbols associated with Freemasonry. Freemason signs were found at all his crime scenes. He also had a town house right in the middle of Whitechapel. A search discovered an assortment of meat cleavers and surgical instruments, still covered in God knows what.

Of course what is most alarming is that Maybrick was released, and even allowed to keep his bloodied apron and butchery tools, and went on to carry out his most horrendous murder of the lot, with the dissection of the poor prostitute Mary Jane Kelly. Even the establishment had to act after this: rank and file officers complained bitterly, knowing they had let a guilty man go free to kill again. One even put his disgust in a memo to his superiors, and it's still on file.

But they were all warned, to a man, that their careers would be over, and their pensions withdrawn, if they didn't fall into line. They were finally placated by a solemn promise from a Chief Constable that the 'alleged perpetrator would be banished from the City of London, never to return'. A footnote records that this Chief Constable reminded his men to think of the reputational damage that would be done to the Freemason movement over 'the inconsequential lives of a handful of prostitutes'.

Maybrick's brother, Michael, arranged for James to see a doctor, a fellow Freemason, who put him on strong medication just two weeks after his final killing. It seemed to do the trick for a while, but the following year James told the doctor that his murderous urges were returning with a vengeance. His brother was informed and the masons decided there was nothing left to do but have James poisoned. His wife was hastily sentenced to death, for a murder she didn't commit, by a judge who was also . . . you guessed it . . . a member of the Lodge.

You don't have to take my word for it, it's all in these files. This yet again proves the immense influence the people who *really run the country have—not the puppet politicians we elect. These establishment figures not only have the power to make sure that one of their own never stands trial for the most appalling murders committed in the modern history of these isles, but they can also keep his name secret for decades after his death.*

But information is the key, people. With every drip, drip, drip of truth we will expose their lies and cover-ups.

10

Fishy

Kelly was buzzed into Monahan's flat. She asked how her patient was feeling and whether he'd like anything.

'I wouldn't mind another ham sandwich. The last one you made was delicious.'

'It was just a plain ham sandwich. I guess anything would taste delicious after those protein shakes,' Kelly replied, trying to adopt a professionally courteous manner. She made her patient a snack and freshened the bottle of water by his bed. Monahan didn't seem in the mood for talking, so after taking his vital signs, she settled down in the armchair opposite the bed. Satisfied her patient was sleeping, Kelly pulled a biscuit from her bag, along with the newspaper she had bought yesterday. She read the front page, with yet another outlandish theory on the death of Princess Diana, and turned inside for the full report, which even she could see was full of dubious insider quotes and speculation.

'What do you think happened?' Monahan asked, surprising her.

'To who?'

'Diana. What do you think happened to her?'

'Well, I'm not into conspiracy theories. But really it's pretty hard to see how it wasn't fishy.'

'Fishy how?'

'Witnesses reporting a bright white light in the tunnel. CCTV cameras with no recordings. The ambulance stopping to treat her on the way to the hospital—not a chance. I've worked in A&E, they just get there. End of. Then there's the embalming of the body, plus the fact they couldn't find the white Uno . . . the biggest car hunt in French history and they couldn't find it! Yeah, it's fishy. Like I said though, I'm not a conspiracist, these are just facts.'

'*Some* of the facts. What about the driver being a drunk?' Monahan asked.

'His blood results were well dodgy. If the levels they said they found were correct he wouldn't have been able to speak, never mind drive. I just don't buy it.'

'So you are a wee bit of a conspiracist, then?' Monahan teased.

'I didn't think I was, but maybe I am. It is fascinating.'

'It is and it isn't. A surprising amount of information is actually out there. Officially. It's the public who have read too much into it all,' Monahan said dismissively.

'Are you trying to tell me you don't think she was murdered? That it was all just a coincidence?' Kelly asked incredulously.

'No, I'm saying it's as plain as the nose on my face that it was a hit. What's more . . . I know who did it.'

• • •

Kelly thought about what Monahan had said as she drove home. She hadn't asked him to elaborate any further after he'd lobbed his Diana hand grenade into the room.

'Know who killed Diana, indeed. I'd love to see the girls' faces if I told them that one,' Kelly said to herself.

She thought no more about it as she arrived home to the melee of a typical morning with the kids in various states of dress and her mum trying to coax them to get ready.

Kelly had too much going on in her life to worry about the death of a rich and famous person she'd never met. Precisely six minutes after the children had been shuffled out the door in the direction of school, Kelly was in bed drifting off to sleep. She didn't dream once of the late Princess.

11

Full moon

Connor pulled up beside April's battered purple Daewoo Estate, which was swaying gently from side to side as a hefty shape inside moved towards the rear of the vehicle. Connor got out of his Audi TT and stared, perplexed, into his colleague's car. It was hard to work out what was going on through the grime on the windows, which had accumulated over who knows how many months. Maybe the old girl was having an illicit morning liaison? Connor shuddered involuntarily—that was a sight he was sure he'd never recover from.

There was an audible click and the Daewoo's hatchback began its slow ascent towards the multi-story parking lot's roof. A large, perfectly rotund backside began to emerge from the car, crack first. Connor would recognise those buttocks anywhere. Kim Kardashian had nothing on April's ample arse.

'It's a full moon tonight,' Connor remarked.

'Oh, you gave me a fright,' April said, standing upright.

'Pray tell?'

'I had another little accident.'

'Pissed yourself again?'

'That too,' April said, taking the insult in her stride. 'I hit something.'

'Cyclist? Pedestrian?'

'Maybe, but whatever it was I can't get my passenger door to open. I've got to climb out the back now.'

'So . . . wait a minute. For days, perhaps weeks, you had been climbing out of the passenger door?'

'I adapted well. Could nip in and out, quite the thing,' April said proudly.

'Then you hit "something" and had to use the back door?' Connor said, desperately trying not to make any sexual references.

'I think it's time to see a mechanic,' April conceded.

'I think it's time to see a salesman. This is no way for one half of the special investigations desk to be getting around.'

'I'll only dink a new one.'

'And what if you "dink" your rear entrance?' Connor said, still managing to resist any *double entendres*. 'You'll either have to go through the windows like Starsky and Hutch, or you'll be stuck, living in your car like a mental person. Throw in a half-dozen cats and you'll look and smell like an old bag lady.'

'But I hate car salesmen. They always sell me something I don't want.'

'Like cars with doors that open and close?'

They began their morning walk to the Peccadillo with April's stomach already grumbling in anticipation.

'What did you make of the Beast Shamer stuff last night and this Maybrick fella? Do you think it's true?' April asked.

'I have no idea. I Googled him and he certainly seems to have been a contender. Then again so was his brother Michael and a dozen other folk, according to the Internet. Basically if you wore a cape and had facial hair, you can now be considered a Ripper suspect.'

'But it all looked so convincing. The police photos. The memo sent by the Chief Constable. The Freemasonry stuff.'

'I know. It does. There's enough from that last night for another Ripper book. Several, actually.'

'I wonder if it's been picked up by any of the papers.'

'Probably. I guess you're pretty safe to name whoever you want when everyone's dead.'

The pair arrived at the café and took their usual seat. Martel gave April a smile as she took her order—a full fry-up—but spared no pleasantries when Connor ordered a bowl of porridge with a banana.

'Service with a scowl,' April giggled under her breath. 'I'm guessing you've switched back to an "off" phase?'

'And I'm guessing I should have called her. I hope she doesn't spit in my porridge.'

'She wouldn't do that. But I can guess where she'd love to shove that banana,' April smiled.

12

The fantasist

Kelly made the evening journey to work all too quickly for her liking: it felt like she'd only just finished last night's shift. She hoped she didn't have Monahan tonight.

'Hi Kelly, how's you?' Jean the auxiliary nurse asked in her usual cheery manner.

Jean had worked nightshift before Kelly had even been born. She'd be retiring soon and Kelly dreaded the thought, as she'd miss her company and, most of all, her support.

'Uch, the usual, Jean. Tired. Always tired. I could sleep for Scotland. In fact, given the choice I'd take sleep over anything. A lottery win. Chocolate. Sex. Sleep wins out every time.'

'I agree with everything apart from the lottery win. That's my dream.'

Kelly wished she hadn't mentioned the lottery, for now she'd get Jean's jackpot fantasy again. How much she'd like to win. Who would get what in her family. How she'd take all her grandchildren to Disney World in Florida. But Jean managed to stop herself as she had news.

'This came in today. It's more of Mr. Monahan's case notes. Some sort of psychiatric report. Funny how we're getting his stuff in dribs and drabs, isn't it? He's definitely military. We had a similar case years ago. Some old navy captain who had signed the Official Secrets Act and was suffering from dementia. He kept telling us state secrets, not that we understood a bloody word. It was all codes and fleet commands. The MOD wanted to make all his nurses sign the Official Secrets Act too, but our union told them to bugger off.'

Kelly opened the report. It was full of the usual psychiatrist 'arse covering', as the nurses called it, about what the patient *may* or *may not* do. There was nothing definite in psychiatry, therefore its practitioners were never wrong.

But one section leapt out as it had been typed in bold:

Patient Monahan is a delusional fantasist, with an intrinsic belief in almost everything he recalls. This makes him prone to grand claims about his work and exaggerating the importance of his position within the organisation.

Kelly stared at the two sentences: it was almost as if they had been written for her benefit.

'I guess I've got Mr. Monahan again, then?' she sighed.

'You sure have, hon,' Jean said, adding, 'And don't worry, in another thirty years you'll finally have got used to the nightshift.'

'Thanks, Jean. Just when I thought I couldn't be any more depressed.'

• • •

Kelly kept it formal with Monahan as her shift started. She checked his vital signs, washed him, prepared a sandwich and his protein shakes. He said nothing except 'thank you', sensing she didn't want to talk.

She settled down in the armchair beside his bed. Monahan had his eyes closed and was breathing normally. She thought he was going to remain like that until he asked a very softly spoken but clearly audible question: 'Anything strange happen at work tonight?'

Kelly was a little startled. Did he know about the psychiatric reports? 'Define "strange",' she replied coolly.

'Out of the ordinary,' Monahan said with equal composure.

Kelly decided she wasn't in the mood to play games. 'There was something, actually. Some more of your medical notes arrived. Apparently you're a total fantasist who makes the most outlandish claims.'

Monahan pushed his head back as far as it would go into his pillow, as if he was reclining in a sun lounger, and let out a laugh. 'I wondered when they'd start calling me a nutter.'

'And are you a "nutter"?' Kelly asked, hating the use of the term that for so long demonised those with mental health issues.

'Suppose so. But, then again, aren't we all a bit crazy?'

'Are you a fantasist?'

'Again, aren't we all? Don't you dream of being rich? Not having to do this?'

'I prefer realistic dreams, goals I can achieve. And I happen to like my job.' Monahan's question had struck a chord. Without her work, what was Kelly? A divorcee? A mum? She needed to be more than that. She realised her job defined her life.

'But "no" is the answer to your question. I am not a fantasist. I just so happen to have seen many fantastical things in my line of work.'

'What was your line of work?' Kelly asked, her nosiness getting the better of her.

'The military, at first. Then private stuff afterwards.'

'Sounds dubious.'

'You're right. It was,' Monahan said in a nonchalant manner.

'And this was when you killed Diana?' Kelly said sarcastically.

'I didn't actually say I killed her, did I? But yes, she was one of the operations I was involved in.'

'Bullshit!' Kelly said, surprising herself.

Monahan laughed again. 'Now that's the sort of service I expect from the NHS.'

'Sorry. I shouldn't have said that. It was inappropriate.'

'I'd have said the same thing in your shoes. But I can prove it to you,' he insisted.

'Prove it how?'

Monahan put his fingers to his lips, indicating she should be quiet. He then took a notepad and pen and jotted down an address with a code. 'You'll see what the numbers are for.'

Kelly took the paper and peered at it momentarily, before folding it and putting it in her top breast pocket, which also contained her scissors and pen light.

'Indulge me,' Monahan said, smiling.

'I don't have time to indulge myself,' Kelly replied.

She settled back in the armchair. They didn't say another word for the rest of the night. But Monahan slept with a smile on his face.

13

The lottery

'You owe me £2,' Connor said without preamble as he arrived after lunch.

'I think that's going to be your epitaph,' April said, rooting around her bulging purse, before she began counting out several pieces of silver.

Connor sighed loudly. 'Why do we bother with the stupid lottery anyway? We never win. I've got to chase you round the houses for payment and you always, ALWAYS, pay me in pennies.'

'I don't have anything bigger,' April replied, counting out the shrapnel. 'And what's the harm in having a wee flutter, anyway?'

'Because, between us, we put our numbers on four times a week. That's £16 a week, right? Times that by fifty-two and that's £832 a year. Over a decade that'd be £8,320 from our wages, and what do we get back? Nothing.'

'You've got to be in it to win it,' April said cheerily.

'Ah, the mantra of a loser. Why don't I put our lottery money in a jar and at the end of the year we'll divide the kitty?'

'And just where would be the fun in that? Someone has got to win the jackpot, so why not us? We hardly do anything else. You're always away for your boring runs and my biggest spend is on food.'

'Really, I'd have never known,' Connor smirked as April reached for the 'emergency' packet of biscuits in her drawer, which she used to stave off hunger between meals.

'So I say let's plough on. We'll have the last laugh when we win. And win big, we shall. Wait and see.'

'Oh, crap,' Connor said, logging onto his PC. 'We've got a training session in fifteen minutes.'

April's sunny disposition was replaced by a look of abject horror.

14

You've got to be kidding me?

Kelly arrived home that morning having gone to the supermarket beforehand for the weekend shop. Amazingly her mother had offered to take the children to the zoo tomorrow, which meant she would have a whole Saturday of wonderful, uninterrupted sleep. Then perhaps she could do something with them too, like go and see a movie; she was determined to do more than just recuperate before another week of back-to-back nightshifts.

The kids were dressed, fed, and ready for school, with Beth already babbling excitedly about her pending trip to see the pandas with Nana when Kelly walked through the door with the shopping bags. She gave the kids some extra treats for school and kissed them both before they departed.

Kelly put away the shopping and then, with her bed beckoning, stripped to shower. She towelled herself dry, studying her naked body in her wardrobe's sliding door mirror. She turned side-on to inspect her tummy and, with her back to the mirror, looked over her shoulder at her bottom. Finally she cupped and examined her breasts, before affording herself a rare compliment: 'Not bad, Kelly. Not bad at all for nearly forty.'

She began throwing her dirty clothes into the laundry basket and inspected the contents of the breast pocket of her nurse's uniform. On a piece of paper was the address Monahan had written down for her. She Googled it on her smartphone: it was just four miles away.

'You must be mad,' Kelly said, speaking to herself again, as she pulled on a top and pair of jeans that complemented her shape. 'Maybe we're all nutters?' she added, grabbing her pen light before she did something she hadn't done in a long time—denied herself some much-needed sleep.

Kelly placed her smartphone in the holder by her windscreen to follow its directions to the mysterious Monahan location. She recognised various points along the journey as there was always somewhere nearby Kelly had sat with a dying patient or consoled a family. The directions eventually took her down a dead-end street full of lock-ups in various stages of disrepair.

The phone informed Kelly she had reached her destination. She checked Monahan's handwritten note again: *Count four doors from the left. You'll see where to use the code.* Kelly now understood what he meant. There was an old key safe bolted to the narrow wall between the two neighbouring garage doors. She got out of the car and looked around to check the street was empty before entering Monahan's five-digit code. The mechanical key safe seemed to accept the numbers but the moment of truth would come when Kelly turned the handle to open it. It was stiff and clearly hadn't been used in some time, but with a little persuasion it gave up its contents of three keys. She tried them all in the lock on the garage door handle until she found the right one. The others opened two bolt-and-pin systems that had been burrowed deep into the concrete. Someone did not want this garage broken into.

Kelly prised open the door, which swung out towards her, then up high on a pulley system. The light outside did nothing to illuminate the darkness within. She felt the inside of the concrete pillar for a light switch, but got cobwebs instead.

'Yuk, should have worn my gloves,' she complained.

She wiped the webs from her hand and took the light out of her pocket. Its weak beam also struggled to penetrate the dark, but at least she could use it to find the light switch. A fluorescent strip flickered slowly into life, giving off a hum like a hive of bees. Satisfied she could now see, Kelly closed the door behind her to inspect the depths of the garage, which was surprisingly big. It was full of the usual fare, including scattered tools and old, dented paint cans. There were also lots of cardboard boxes. She decided to move one stack to the side so she could gain access to the rear of the garage. The boxes were empty. She pushed the stack out of the way, and then another. It was as if they had been placed on top of each other as a makeshift wall, perhaps as a barrier against prying eyes.

Behind them was the very clear and distinct outline of a car underneath a heavy black and dusty tarpaulin. Kelly took hold of an edge of the cover and heaved it off. She stared in total disbelief at the car.

'You've got to be kidding me!'

It had seen better days, but, even through the accumulated dust and grime, Kelly could clearly make out the familiar shape of a white Fiat Uno, with French number plates. She ran her fingers along the car towards a large dent at the rear end.

'You've got to be kidding me,' Kelly repeated. 'Just what the fuck are you doing here?' Kelly asked as if she expected an answer. She stood still for some time, looking at what she had uncovered, occasionally shaking her head and swearing softly under her breath. Eventually she forced herself to peer in the windows with her pen light, but its weak light failed to illuminate beyond the tinted glass. Kelly tried the handles but the doors wouldn't budge. She then stood as far back from the vehicle as the garage walls would allow and took some pictures of the car on her phone. But she really wanted to get into the vehicle. She tried the passenger door again and felt it move slightly. She now knew it wasn't locked, more likely it had seized from lack of use.

'Come on, Kel, you can do this,' she said, geeing herself up. She pulled on the passenger handle with everything she had, straining to lift the door at the same time. It suddenly gave way with the ripping sound of its rubber seal, which had long since perished and had been wedging the door stuck.

'Gotcha,' she said, pleased with herself. There must have still been some juice in the battery as the car's interior light came on. On the passenger seat she could see a black motorbike helmet and remembered reading one eyewitness account that claimed men wearing them had been seen leaving the crash scene at the Pont de l'Alma tunnel before the paparazzi arrived.

The toppling of a bin directly outside the lock-up startled Kelly. It was followed by the unmistakeable scuff of a shoe on the gravel by the entrance. She looked at the Fiat Uno and suddenly felt very vulnerable. If someone was to enter now she would be trapped. Kelly slipped into the back seat of the car and gently closed the door behind her, which extinguished the interior light. She lay huddled, panicking inside, but trying to slow her rapid breathing lest she be heard. She stayed completely still for several minutes, straining her ears to listen for any more noises outside. There were none. It was time to go. If the police found her here, she could imagine their looks as she tried to explain she was checking out if a patient's Diana conspiracy theory was true.

Kelly crawled out of the car to leave, but at that exact moment the fluorescent light went out, throwing the entire lock-up into darkness. Panic returned. She needed to get out now and bolted for the exit, but something caught her foot, sending Kelly crashing, her body spilling into the daylight outside. She reached down to see what had tripped her, to find the tarpaulin that had been covering the Uno was wrapped like an octopus's tentacle around her left foot. Kelly kicked herself free, stood up and scanned the area. There was nothing of note apart from the overturned bin. Kelly didn't plan to hang around to find out who or what had tipped it over. She jumped in her car and raced off, forgetting to fasten her seatbelt, just as the absent-minded Princess had done back in 1997.

15

Crystal meth

April sat in the training session for the *Daily Chronicle*'s new operating system, Crystal MPS, or Multi-Platform Systems. Her face wore a fixed grin that barely masked her terror. She had hoped to have retired by the time the company brought in a new computer system, telling Connor, 'I had only just mastered the last one, but now they've gone and replaced it.'

Connor had given her his usual quizzical expression. 'I think "mastered" is stretching things a little, don't you?'

He now sat opposite April with a smirk on his face, clearly enjoying her discomfort as the over-enthusiastic trainer, called Rob, continued his lecture.

'The beauty about this system is it really gives you the tools to become a multi-platform operator,' he beamed. April's plastered-on smile grew a fraction wider. It was as if Rob was speaking Swahili. 'So, say you're sitting there with a cracking exclusive. But you just know it won't hold until tomorrow's print edition, right? Well, in the digital age, exclusives are only exclusive for a matter of minutes. That means speed is king, so you just click this button here . . .' Rob said with his actions being displayed on the projection screen above him, '. . . and *voila*, a drop-down menu asks how you'd like to publish your content.'

'Bet you're going to "drop down" any minute,' Connor whispered out the corner of his mouth to April.

'You can even set the time you want to publish, from here,' Rob said, clicking on another drop-down menu. 'So, if a story is embargoed, you don't go jumping the gun. As you can see, once you start playing around with it, it's really pretty easy. Now, any questions?'

April was terrified of asking anything. Afterwards she was close to tears as she confided in Connor in the safety of their broom cupboard.

'I can't do this again. I can't learn another system.'

Connor was truly amazed at the state April would work herself into when it came to technology. 'Calm yourself down, grandma. You don't want to have a stroke.'

'But what if I can't do it? They'll have to get rid of me. Nothing Ron said stuck in my head.'

'It's Rob. And not all of it has to stick in your head. You can still type on a keyboard, right? Well, you'll type your words as normal, and then someone else will send it to all the multi-platforms, or the moon, or wherever.'

Connor's assurances did nothing to placate her. 'But they want us all to be . . . what did Ron say? "Autonomous". Writing straight onto the page. On this stupid Crystal Meth system.'

Connor couldn't be bothered correcting her this time. But the prospect of every journalist writing straight onto the page actually worried him too. There were more than a few of his colleagues whose copy needed a thorough rewrite by the banks of sub-editors just for it to make sense, never mind fit for print. He had never bought into the 'them and us' mentality that existed between the reporters and the subs. Over the years he had been grateful for the way they caught spelling and grammatical errors when he was writing in a hurry for a deadline—and they'd once even averted a horrendous libel he'd included by accident. As one now-retired chief sub had eloquently put it, a decent sub can make a poor writer look good, a good writer look great and a great writer look exceptional.

As far as Connor was concerned, anyone who made him appear better and smarter was alright by him. And he knew he was one of the half-decent journalists. To think that some of the cretins he'd worked with over the years were going to have their copy published by themselves, with no filters, was utterly alarming. He had witnessed reporters who couldn't even spell the name of Scotland's most famous sons. Like the colleague who had once been bollocked for writing 'Billy Connelly' instead of 'Billy Connolly'. Another had gone one better by writing about some famous movie actor called 'Sir Sean Connelly', which was so wrong Connor had almost wept when he read the raw copy.

But at least when he started out there was always some grisly old news editor around to rip the hapless young hacks a new one. That's how Connor had learned, through fear and humiliation. He hated the new touchy-feely world that had turned the cut and thrust of a newsroom into something more like a Human Resources convention.

'Look, I don't care much for this multi-platform nonsense either, but we've just got to play along with it. It'll be alright,' he said, trying to reassure April.

'No, it won't,' she said, shaking her head. 'It bloody well won't. This will be the end of me.'

Connor was tired of arguing. A part of him also believed that April could well be right.

16

The long arm of the law

Kelly didn't enjoy her usual dead sleep. Things kept waking her that would never normally rouse her from her slumber, like the post arriving or the cat meowing for food. But after her visit to the lock-up, her mind was unsettled. The car couldn't possibly be what she thought it was, could it? And even if it was, then what? What was a nurse from Glasgow to do with such information? As for Monahan, she didn't know what to think. What the hell was he caught up in? What had he done? She was scared and she had never felt that way about a patient before.

The doorbell rang. Kelly rolled over and put a pillow over her head. But whoever the caller was, they weren't going away. Normally, if the postman had a delivery too big for the letterbox, he'd just put the package behind one of the wheelie bins. But still the bell rang. Maybe it was a new, persistent postie. But Kelly knew she would never get back to sleep unless she answered the door.

She put on her dressing gown and pulled the cord tight, not wanting to give the mysterious visitor an eyeful. She opened the door and, to her surprise, was confronted with two policemen. The older one was a sergeant with one of those battle-hardened faces that had seen it all. The younger one was a very tall constable.

'Miss Kelly Carter? May we come in?'

'Of course,' she said, a touch nervously and making sure she wasn't exposing too much flesh. She showed them to her living room where the officers took a seat directly opposite Kelly.

The older one spoke first. 'Were you in Laidlaw street this morning?' he asked, already knowing the answer.

'Yes, yes, I was,' she stuttered.

'So you know about the fire?' the younger one asked, expressionless.

Kelly felt as though a fire had engulfed *her*. She blushed and suddenly felt overheated and vulnerable. Both officers stared at her, studying her reaction, waiting to see any sign of a false response.

'I didn't see any fire.' The words even sounded hollow to Kelly. But how could she be sure she hadn't started it in the first place? Maybe the wiring had short-circuited after she left. The place was packed with those empty cardboard boxes, never mind the car. It would have gone up like a tinderbox.

'Can we see the clothes you were wearing to Laidlaw Street?' It was a command more than a question from the older one, who then referred to a description written down in his notepad: 'Red top, blue jeans and a faded green skip hat.'

Kelly led the police officers in silence to her bedroom, where the items of clothing they were interested in were folded over an armchair that acted more as a clothes horse than somewhere to sit. The older one picked up the red top and sniffed it. The younger one did the same with the skip hat. Kelly realised the ridiculousness of the situation of having two policemen in her bedroom smelling her clothes. The officers placed the clothing back on the chair, with the older one asking to speak with Kelly again in the living room. They were keeping this formal and playing it by the book.

'Can I ask why you were in Laidlaw street this morning?' the sergeant asked.

'A patient asked me to check something in their lock-up,' she replied, deciding to keep her answers short and sweet, lest she nervously rambled on and said something she shouldn't.

'What's the patient's name?' It was the younger one's turn.

'Sorry, I don't know if I can tell you that. I mean, I'm sure it'll be fine, but I'll have to check with my boss first or possibly my union. Patient confidentiality and all that.'

'No need to be so formal,' the older one assured her.

'Listen, it doesn't get more formal than this, does it? Two policemen interviewing me about a fire I didn't see or know about. I am not trying to be difficult. But what I can tell you is what I've said already. A patient asked me to check out his lock-up.'

'Were they after something?' the younger one asked.

'No, I don't think so. They just wanted me to make sure everything was alright.' It was the first lie Kelly had told. And she knew the cops weren't buying it by their silence. She decided to match them at their game.

Eventually the older one spoke. 'Did he give you keys?'

'No, there was a key safe by the garage door. I was given the code. And who said it was a "he"?'

'What was inside?' the young one asked, bluntly ignoring Kelly's question.

'Boxes. Paint cans. The usual garage stuff.'

'A car?' the younger one continued.

For the second time that morning Kelly lied. 'I think I would have noticed a car.' She didn't know why she said it, but she did and now it was being dutifully written down in a police notepad.

'Did you set fire to the lock-up?' It was the older one's turn again.

'You sniffed my clothes, what do you think? This is getting silly. I'm a nurse, not an arsonist.'

'We'll be in touch,' the sergeant promised as they made their way to the front door and left.

'Great,' Kelly said after closing it behind them. 'I've been implicated in an arson attack and lied to the police. What the hell are you playing at, girl?'

She slipped into bed without taking her dressing gown off as she felt the need to be cosy and wrapped up warm. About the only thing she truly missed about her ex-husband was when they would cuddle as she drifted off to sleep.

17

Photo evidence

Kelly meant business when she arrived at Monahan's flat for her next shift. She wasn't smiling when she marched into his bedroom and threw her bag onto the armchair by the bed.

'What the hell have you dragged me into?' she demanded.

'Problems, were there?'

'You could say that. Your lock-up burnt down after I'd been there. Then the cops arrive at my door after someone phoned in my car registration and a full description of what I was wearing.'

'All sounds a bit professional, doesn't it, for a member of the public?' Monahan replied, his nonchalant replies getting right up Kelly's nose.

'I'll ask again. What have you got me into?'

Monahan fumbled for the pad by his bed, pressing a button to raise him from his prostrate position to something more upright. He was also buying time as he decided what to tell her. 'I didn't know I was still being watched, but clearly I am.'

'So I was what, then? A sitting duck? Used to see whatever nutjob is after you?'

Her description made him smile. 'You could call them nut-jobs, I guess. But they are a little more hardcore than that.'

'So who are they?'

'Trust me, you don't want to know.'

'Oh, I do.'

'Oh no you don't. Listen, this is getting a bit panto. I apologise. I genuinely wouldn't have put you in danger had I known I was still being watched. I honestly thought I was of little interest now that I'm bedbound.'

'Well, you clearly are and now I'm involved.'

'They're not interested in you.'

'They were interested enough to send the police my way.'

'Only to rattle you. To make you go back into your shell.'

'I would say that's mission accomplished on their part.'

'Good. Again, I'm sorry. So did you find anything of interest in the lock-up?' Monahan smiled mischievously.

'This is just a game to you, isn't it? You know exactly what I found and frankly I don't believe any of it.'

'Good. That means you're not easily led. Not that it matters now anyway as the car has been destroyed. More's the pity. I liked that car.'

'Well, you can have a picture. I took plenty,' Kelly said.

Monahan's eyes widened slightly at the news. 'Why?'

'Because I thought it was so ridiculous. You tell me about Diana and, lo and behold, what do I find? The missing Fiat Uno right here in Scotland. It's all nonsense and you're up to no good.'

'What if I was telling the truth? What if that is the car the French authorities tried to trace for years?'

'And what if it is? What was I supposed to do about it? Why did you send me there?'

'To see if it was still there. And to prove to you I'm no phoney.'

'I don't know what you are. But I do know this will be the last time we meet. I'm telling my boss I'm not sitting for you anymore.'

'Pity. You've helped me a lot, Kelly.'

'It's Nurse Carter, Mr. Monahan.'

The fiery exchange had taken its toll on Monahan, who closed his eyes to rest. But he didn't sleep well. The photos Kelly had taken of the car bothered him.

18

Regrets

'Another day at the coalface done,' Connor said as he packed up his man-bag and powered down his PC. 'All I did was rewrite a bloody press release and some agency copy. Bugger all else on the go.'

'At least you did that. I did nothing. I couldn't get hold of anyone I called either,' April sighed.

'There used to be a time that, when you were quiet, the news-desk would give you something to work on,' Connor moaned. 'Now all they do is get you to rewrite copy some other journalist has already filed. Which is a waste of time as the subs then rewrite your rewrite.'

'At least we still get paid,' April said, putting on her coat and heading for the door.

'I know, but the day doesn't half drag. Much prefer it when I have something to get my teeth into, but there's been nothing happening.'

The pair walked to the staff parking lot, with Connor heading for the gym to work off the day's frustrations. April wanted to go and slump into her favourite armchair at home for the next Beast Shamer instalment, but she was not in the mood to cook for herself this evening. She also knew she should pay a visit to Luigi.

'I better go and see the Octopus.'

'Good luck,' Connor said, rolling his eyes.

April's restaurateur fiancé was a curious mix: half charmer, half sex pest. So much so she had nicknamed him the Octopus because he was always hugging her just so he could feel her up. But April had had enough of his wandering hands and enough of being engaged. Tonight she needed to tell him the truth. It would be better for both of them. Or so she hoped.

19

Normals

Kelly was furious when Sister McIntosh told her she would be sitting for Monahan again. She had confessed all—except the discovery of the Fiat Uno—to her line manager, who had listened sympathetically and promised she would try to get her another patient. But tonight there was no choice.

'I'm sorry, Kelly. There's no one else. I even tried to get an emergency bank nurse to do it, but nothing doing. You are literally the only person available.' Sister McIntosh placed her hand on Kelly's arm as she added, 'Just remember, Kelly, there is only so much we can do for a patient.'

Her words resonated with Kelly. She felt stupid for getting so involved. She still couldn't fathom why she had gone to the lock-up in the first place. Was it just curiosity, or a misplaced desire for adventure to break the monotony of her life? Perhaps it was even some sort of response to the failure of her marriage. But she couldn't deny it; she had enjoyed the thrill of finding the car. She had been both frightened and exhilarated at the same time.

'You're right. I need to get a grip,' Kelly replied.

'If you feel the patient is threatening, or that you're in any personal danger, then we'll just cancel the visit,' her boss assured her.

'No, it's fine. Thanks,' Kelly said and restocked her nurse's bag from the office supplies and made her way to her car.

She sat in the driver's seat, gathering her thoughts. She unlocked her smartphone to browse through the photos from the lock-up, skimming through the 'Camera Roll' album and then 'My Photo Stream'. The hairs on her neck and arms began to bristle as she realised the pictures of the Fiat Uno were gone. For the first time Kelly felt very afraid.

• • •

Kelly tossed her phone stroppily onto Monahan's bed when she arrived at his flat.

'Want a look at my photos?'

Monahan picked up her phone and swiped the screen to scroll through Kelly's picture albums.

'Nice kids,' he remarked.

'Yeah, nice kids. No car. Please tell me, what is going on?'

'Your phone has been hacked. Fairly easy to do these days with some basic technology. But you still need a degree of competence and to know what you're after, of course.'

'So whoever hacked my phone to delete the car pictures also has photos of my kids, right?'

'Possibly. They may use your kids as leverage. I would.'

'What sort of fucked-up world do you live in, Mr. Monahan?'

'A very real one. One that normals like yourself don't have any dealings with.'

'Until now. Thanks to you. I want this to stop.'

'You are of no interest to them. But I am.'

'Don't tell me, because you know too much? This isn't some movie. It's my life.'

'No, not because I know too much. But because I have something.'

'What the hell does that mean?'

'I hope you never find out.'

The rest of Kelly's shift sitting with Monahan passed in near total silence. She kept wondering what Monahan had that was so important. Then she would berate herself for letting her curiosity get the better of her again.

There was real danger here, yet she was attracted to it like a moth to a flame.

20

Meltdown

'Hey-a, why so glum? Have-a you been missing your Luigi?' the Italian said, giving April a customary bear hug as she arrived at his restaurant in Glasgow's Shawlands district, his hand just lingering on her ample backside a shade too long.

'Hello, Luigi. I'm fine, thanks,' April said, trying to keep things cordial.

'Oh-a no. I hate-a when a woman-a says "fine". That means-a she's got the right hump.'

April couldn't help but smile at the way Luigi could suddenly break into broad Glaswegian, and his insistence on speaking about himself in the third person. 'No, I haven't got the hump, Luigi. I'm just tired and hungry.'

'Well, you have-a come to the right place. I have-a special seafood linguine tonight-a. You've got-a mussels, shrimp and squid. It's beautiful, like-a you,' he said, giving April another hug, his meaty arms 'accidentally' brushing over her boobs.

'I think there's more than enough sealife around at the moment. Just the spaghetti meatballs for me, please.'

'A-ha. April Lavender can't get enough of Luigi's juicy meatballs,' he said, announcing her menu choice to the rest of the customers.

April was not in the mood. She wished to dine in silence and unmolested. She berated herself for coming in the first place. Luigi poured her a generous glass of red wine. She looked at his ageing, jowly face, and the over-sized moustache spread across his face; his eyebrows were arched in anticipation for

April to approve of his wine selection, and she hated herself for what she was about to do.

'Luigi, I want you to take this back,' she said, removing the large diamond ring he had given her a year previously. 'I should never have taken it in the first place. I'm sorry. Sorry to have got your hopes up. Sorry for everything.'

Luigi's beaming smile slowly disintegrated into a look of utter despair. Tears filled his eyes and rolled down his puffy cheeks. He stood in silence, looking absolutely crestfallen. Then his rotund shape, clothed in his chef whites, began to jiggle ever so slightly, before he launched into huge, body-shaking sobs.

'Ahhhh-a,' Luigi wailed, and the whole restaurant turned round to see the commotion. The attention did not stop him. 'April Lavender has-a broken-a ma heart. Ahhhh-a.'

April already wanted to die from embarrassment when one of the younger waiters shot her a dirty look.

'That-a devil woman,' Luigi said, pointing a thick, stubby index finger directly at her, to make sure there was no doubt in anyone's mind as to who he was referring to. 'She want-a Luigi never to be-a happy again.' He collapsed onto April's table, sending the cutlery flying and spilling half her wine over the pristine table cloth. He then started thumping the table with his arm. 'Why-a? Why-a? You bitch-a! You BITCH-A!'

April could feel every set of eyes in the packed restaurant boring into her. She decided she needed to leave. April stood up to find the young waiter who had looked at her so disapprovingly already standing next to her, coat in hand. He threw it roughly over her shoulders and pressed his hand firmly into the small of her back, guiding her in the direction of the door.

April heard an almighty crash as she reached the exit. She looked round to see Luigi's weight had overturned her table and he was now lying on the floor, thumping the ground and wailing like an injured animal. 'BITCH-A! BITCH-A!'

She stepped out into the mild May evening, with the door closing on the chaos behind her. April stole a quick glance as she passed the restaurant's large plate glass window to see Luigi slowly being helped to his feet by a crowd of concerned staff and customers.

'That went well,' she said out loud as she began the short walk home, her stomach grumbling from the adrenaline and the lack of food. She stopped at a chip shop, with its hot glass counter full of the saltiest, greasiest foods known to mankind. The young girl behind the counter stared at April expressionlessly, waiting for her to speak. Customer service obviously wasn't high on the agenda in this chippy.

'A bag of chips, please. Large. With a battered fish too.'

The girl stared at April momentarily before replying, 'You want a large fish supper, then?'

'Yes, dear,' April said, smiling. 'With lots of salt and vinegar. And a roll. With butter.'

'Anything else?' the girl asked sarcastically.

'Just Irn-Bru. A bottle, not a can.'

April waddled up the road to her half-a-million pound Victorian townhouse, carrying a white plastic bag wafting the glorious smell of fish and chips.

'Aw, April, what a night,' she said, speaking to herself as was her custom. 'You broke a man's heart, created chaos and now look like a down-and-out with a fish supper and a bottle of ginger. Wonder what I'll do for my encore?'

She sat for the next forty minutes in her kitchen sharing her fish supper with her cat, Cheeka, an animal that truly took after her owner's own heart.

21

Doctor who?

There had been no further visits from the police and no more cryptic clues from Monahan. It was just back to normal. And Kelly was bored by it all.

She arrived at Monahan's at 9 p.m. as usual only to find he had visitors. A doctor and a nurse.

'Oh, hello,' Kelly said, curious. She recognised neither.

'I'm Doctor Davies and this is Nurse Mackay.'

'Veronica,' the strange nurse said, introducing herself less formally.

'I'm Kelly Carter. I'm Mr. Monahan's usual nurse. Is there a problem? Who sent you?'

Kelly was direct but she was used to walking into patients' crowded rooms and restoring order with relatives. Now she was being confronted by two unknown medical professionals and she wanted to know why they were here and who had called them.

'We were part of Malky's old medical team when he was working. We had a call from a Doctor . . . Abassi, is it?'

'Doctor Shabazi,' Kelly corrected him, wondering how he'd got his peer's name so hopelessly wrong.

'Anyway, your doctor fellow was asking a few questions about Mad Malky's treatment. We thought we'd pop by to see how the old dog was getting on,' Doctor Davies explained with a smooth smile.

Kelly hated doctors being overly friendly. She once had a GP who wanted her to call him Andy, which she refused point-blank to do. As far as Kelly was concerned, medical professionals needed to be just that. Not just out of formality but because there will come a point when they may need to deliver bad news and you'd rather hear it from a doctor than 'Andy'.

'I see, and how do you think he's doing?' Kelly asked, looking at Monahan, who was sat with a fixed, blank expression. She wondered why he hadn't spoken.

'As well as can be expected. He's nearing the endgame and he knows it. I've told him to get all his affairs in order and not to do anything rash,' Doctor Davies replied flippantly.

His words hung in the air. Who the hell would say 'endgame' in front of a dying man, and talk about being 'rash'? Was this doctor openly warning Monahan?

Before Kelly could open her mouth, Doctor Davies said, 'Can I have a word, please?' He led Kelly gently by the arm to the hallway. 'I'm afraid Malky has brain mets, so he's going to be saying a lot of crazy stuff before he passes away. Remember he won't think he's ill in the head. But he's a very sick bunny.'

Sick bunny. Kelly had never heard a doctor use such terms.

• • •

'Who were they?' Kelly asked Monahan, after the doctor and nurse left the flat.

He seemed strangely subdued. 'From my old job, as they said,' he replied, dead-eyed.

'Did they give you anything? You seem a bit zonked.'

'Yeah, a shot of something. Don't know what. Has made me very sleepy.'

'Were you in pain?'

'No more than usual.'

'Hmm. I've got to make a phone call.'

Kelly had called out Doctor Shabazi on many occasions during the night. He eventually had given her his mobile number so she didn't need to go through the GEMS central control if she just had a quick query.

He answered at the second ring. 'Nurse Carter. How are you tonight?'

Kelly loved the doctor's impeccable manners. 'I'm fine, Doctor. I just have a quick question for you.'

'I'm all ears.'

'Remember my patient, Monahan?'

'Monahan? Yes. Our Special Forces friend.'

'Yes, exactly. Did you call his previous doctor for assistance?'

'What previous doctor?'

'You know. From the military or wherever?'

'I wouldn't even know how to get in touch with that lot.'

'Oh, that's weird,' Kelly said, feeling a chill course through her body.

'Weird how?'

'Because some military doctor type and a nurse were here when I arrived. Said you had sent for them. Gave him a shot of something they haven't written up on his chart. Warned me not to believe a word he says because he has brain mets. And then they left.'

'Now you listen to me, Nurse Carter. Danger surrounds that man. Grave danger. Do not get involved in any aspect of his life whatsoever. Just do your job and no more. I'm busy at the moment, but I'll pop over later.'

Kelly thanked the doctor for his time and hung up. She appreciated his concern but his words of warning had come too late. She was already up to her neck in Monahan's private life and she knew it.

22

The casual racist

It had just gone 9 p.m. when April's mobile rang. It was Connor. The only reason he'd usually call at this time was for a story, but for once he'd just called to gossip.

'How did it go with the Italian stallion? Set a date for the wedding yet? That'll be another register for him to sign.'

'I keep telling you he's not on the Sex Offenders' Register,' April sniffed.

'Yet,' Connor snorted.

'The truth is, it's kinda all off.'

'Kinda? Or all off?'

'All off.'

'You sure it's not a lover's tiff? You know how passionate these Italian perverts are.'

'I'm pretty sure.'

'Are you? I bet if you call the old letch right now he'll welcome you back into his wandering arms.'

'I doubt it. Not after screaming that I'm a "bitch-a, bitch-a," in front of the entire restaurant.'

'Oops.'

'Oops, indeed. I left him sobbing by our upturned table. It was quite a scene.'

'I bet,' Connor conceded, before he started laughing.

'Didn't think I'd get much sympathy. Know what the worst part was? I didn't even get my dinner.'

'That bastard knows how to hit you where it hurts. I guess it really must be over.'

'Maybe it's for the best. He wasn't really my type.'

'You don't normally go for fat, Italian sex pests?'

'No, I prefer a dusky gentleman.'

Connor nearly sprayed his mouthful of coffee over his phone. 'You can't say "dusky". What century are you living in?'

'Swarthy, then.'

'That's possibly worse.'

'I get confused by all this race stuff. Coloured. Black. Yellow.'

'Yellow? Stop. Please stop.'

'Well, how am I supposed to know? I was raised in Glasgow, not the Bronx. Not exactly the model of diversity. I don't mean any offence but I don't know what I'm allowed to say and what I'm not. Old dogs, new tricks and all that.'

'Okay, let's get this dating profile right. You like a gentleman with darker looks who won't mind your overeating or casual racism?'

'Yup, that pretty much sums me up.'

'April Lavender, I think you might die a lonely old woman who is eaten by your cat. Don't worry, there's enough to keep your moggy going for months, even years.'

'And you'll die a cheeky old bastard.'

'Touché, tubby. Touché.'

23

The 'S' word

A few hours later Doctor Shabazi arrived at Monahan's door. Kelly let him in.

'Thought I'd better pop in see how he is,' the doctor said, lightly touching Kelly's arm. She liked how gentle he was.

'He's heavily sedated. Whatever they gave him has knocked him out cold.'

Doctor Shabazi went into the bedroom and checked Monahan's pulse and blood saturation levels before listening to his chest with a stethoscope. He lifted open Monahan's right eyelid and shone his penlight into it and watched as the pupil lazily dilated.

Suddenly Monahan grabbed the doctor's wrist, powerfully bending it back to breaking point, his face red with fury. 'Leave the fucking hard drive alone!'

'I'm a doctor. I'm not after any hard drive,' Shabazi shouted in protest.

'Malky, leave him. Leave him. Look, you're safe. You're at home,' Kelly said, trying to force his vice-like grip from the doctor's wrist.

Monahan turned slowly towards Kelly, barely able to peel his eyes away from the doctor. A flicker of recognition replaced his anger. He looked at her then back at the doctor, now slumped on his knees by his bed, his face contorted in agony. He let go of his wrist.

'Sorry, but at least it's not broken,' Monahan said. 'I didn't hear a snap. I'm obviously not as strong as I used to be.' That cocksure smile was returning to his face.

'Still strong enough, I'd say,' the doctor replied, rubbing his wrist. 'What did the other doctor give you, do you know?'

'Something to make me sleep, I guess. Listen, sorry about the wrist. I was just having a bad dream and you walked right into it.'

'It's fine. Seriously.'

Doctor Shabazi wrote up Monahan's chart, stopping to shake the pain from his wrist every so often, before walking Kelly to the front door. Once they were out of earshot he said, 'He has not got brain metastasis. Well, not yet. There are sinister forces afoot. Please take care of yourself, Kelly.' He gently rubbed her arm. 'You've been through a lot lately. You don't need any more woes.'

'Thanks, Doctor Shabazi.'

'Please, call me Mohammed.'

Kelly preferred Doctor Shabazi.

Walking back into Monahan's room, Kelly found the patient fast asleep again in his hospital bed. She stood by his bay window and gazed at the Glasgow skyline, then glanced down to watch Doctor Shabazi come out of the building into the street below. Even from this height she could see his bald patch glinting in the fading light. His tall, lean frame took purposeful strides towards his Mercedes Benz and, for a brief moment, Kelly wondered what life living with the doctor would be like. In her twenties she wouldn't have been interested in his type at all. Now approaching her forties, she appreciated someone with his stoical personality and impeccable manners. Heck, she even found him sexy.

She smiled to herself. She hadn't thought about the 'S' word for as long as she could remember. Kelly couldn't actually recall the last time she'd had sex. She'd stopped doing it with her ex-husband long before they'd split up, and they'd been divorced for a year. *Wow, two years without sex.* She looked down at the doctor opening his car door, and smiled naughtily to herself: she imagined him being a caring and compassionate lover.

The explosion was blinding, rattling Monahan's windows despite the flat being on the third floor. The apartments below had not been as fortunate, with their ragged curtains and blinds now flapping in the wind, cut to shreds by the flying glass. Several cars were on fire. But the blast-point had come from the car Kelly had been staring at. Doctor Shabazi's Mercedes Benz had been completely destroyed, and flames rose into the sky out of every shattered window.

Kelly was frozen with fear, unable to peel her eyes away from the surreal scenes in the street below.

There was another mini explosion as the Mercedes' fuel tank ignited. Its force expelled a small, fiery, football-sized object out of the windscreen. It bounced down the road between the carnage of the flaming vehicles before coming to rest in the gutter.

Kelly stared at it in morbid fascination for a moment and then let out a shrill scream. She would never have another romantic notion of Doctor Shabazi again. Instead, she would be forever haunted by the image of his head rolling down the street as a bright orange fireball.

24

The rival

'Get your skinny rentboy arse to Pollokshaws Road, Elvis—
pronto,' DCI Crosbie barked down the phone to Connor, who
just had the time to hear the chaos of the police call-handling
centre in the background in the middle of a major incident
before Bing hung up. Connor pulled on his black jeans and
Berghaus jacket, and called the photographer, Jack Barr, whilst
heading for his car. Most snappers hated to be bothered when
off duty, but not Jack, who had once told a young Connor
Presley he could ring him for a job any time of the day or night.

Connor had only reported on one explosion before in his
life: the Stockline Plastics factory tragedy on May 11th, 2004.
Nine people died in the blast and thirty-three others were seriously injured. It was later discovered that a build-up of leaking
gas from corroded underground pipes was to blame for the
disaster, which led to a countrywide pipe replacement programme. So at least something positive had come from the
misery he had witnessed as one by one the poor families had
come to see the rubble where their loved ones had perished. It
had had a profound effect on him that those nine people had
got up and gone to their work one morning, never to return.

He arrived at the scene of this blast on Glasgow's Southside
while a protective screen was being erected by the forensic
teams. Jack Barr had managed to fire off several frames before
the area was closed off by the men in protective suits.

Connor couldn't be sure, but this didn't look anything like
Stockline. This was more like a bomb blast. He could still smell
the smoke in the air, mixed with the aroma of an overdone
barbecue—before he realised that it was probably the smell of

burning flesh from the occupant, or occupants, of the vehicle. The cops would take an age to confirm the identity of any victims, preventing journalists from hitting their families' doorsteps until all their next of kin had been identified, although he knew his one friendly cop, Crosbie, would help if he could. With the pictures of the crime scene in the bag, his next job would be to hoover up any eyewitnesses he could get hold of. The problem was the street was now cordoned off, but he was determined to get hold of someone who had seen, or at least heard, what was going on.

Then trouble turned up in the shape of Amy Jones. She couldn't have been any taller than 5'1", but you'd never know it as, no matter the occasion, Amy always wore the tallest heels that gravity allowed and the tightest blouse her breasts permitted. Petite, good-looking and about the most flirtatious person Connor had ever met, Amy used what she had, and more, to get the story. Rumour had it several of her cop contacts were rewarded with sexual favours. Connor had no idea if it was true or not, but while rival reporters were all too willing to spread the malicious gossip out of fear or loathing, he couldn't help but admire her. If the roles were reversed and he could get a story from a female, high-ranking cop, then he sure as hell wouldn't think twice about doing the same.

'Hello, Elvis. Did I miss much, honey?'

Connor thought Amy always sounded like she was talking on a seedy sex chatline. 'No, not much,' he replied, keeping his cards close to his chest.

Amy sniffed the air. 'Do you know who was barbecued?'

'Not a clue.'

'Tried speaking to the uniforms?' she asked, nodding in the direction of the constables manning the police line.

'Nah, they'll be as much in the dark as us.'

'We'll see. I always liked a man in uniform.'

'Or out of uniform?' he ventured.

'Now, where's the fun in that? Always prefer them to keep it on, Elvis,' Amy said, casting Connor a look over her shoulder as she headed in the direction of a young PC.

Connor took a good look at his rival. Technically she was attractive, but she just never did it for him, even though she drove his younger colleagues crazy with desire. It was all the overtly sexual stuff. It was a turn-off and frankly a bit tedious, like a bar bore dishing out nudges and winks in a pub. He could see Amy twirling with her hair teasingly as she chatted to a fresh-faced cop, who was trying his level best to stay the consummate professional and not give in to her many charms. Connor was sure he saw him blush, which probably meant mission accomplished as far as Amy was concerned.

'Cat get the cream?' Connor asked, teeing Amy up for more sex talk.

'Oh yes. I love getting the cream,' she replied, licking her lips like a porn star. Connor doubted she got very much from the cop. Maybe the make and model of the car if she was really fortunate, but he and the snapper had the pictures of the burning wreck, and, as the old adage states, a picture is better than a thousand words. But still, with Amy you never could tell.

'Well, I'm going to hit some doors,' Connor said, as he never liked hanging around with the press pack anyway.

'Hey, maybe we could meet up later. You can even keep your blue suede shoes on.'

'Does that pass as a uniform?'

'Buy me a drink and you'll find out.' Amy smiled in her usual seductive style.

Connor walked away smirking at her blatant offer. There's no way he would take it up. Or would he?

He immediately lost interest when he received a text from DCI Bing Crosbie: *Vic = Dr Mohammed Shabazi.*

Connor texted back. *Terrorism related?*

DCI Crosbie took several moments before he replied, *Didn't have you as a racist, Elvis? Just because he's foreign. Tut tut. As far as we know he was on a house call—not Jihad.*

Connor knew he already had more information than Amy Jones, and he started filing his copy. A quick search of Facebook later and he was also able to obtain a photo of a Dr. Mohammed Shabazi without even knocking on a door. He apparently lived in Glasgow, as the chances of their being two doctors of the same name in the city were extremely slim. Connor wondered if people ever really thought about how much personal information they shared about themselves online. He was glad most didn't as it made his professional life so much easier.

In the morning he would suggest his colleague hit the deceased doctor's front door. If anyone could get the recently widowed wife to talk, it was April Lavender.

25

Numb

Kelly sat in her living room with two police officers again. This time they were from Criminal Investigation Department. She thought how, in her four decades on this planet, she'd never had reason to speak to a policeman. Not for a speeding ticket, nor even when one of her patients died in their own homes, because Kelly was qualified to certify death certificates prepared in advance by the doctor.

She had been asked the same questions several times since the explosion and she'd always answered them almost in a monotone.

Why had she called Doctor Shabazi?

Why had the doctor come to Monahan's flat?

Did she know the doctor hadn't told his base he was doing a house call? Why did she think that was?

Was Kelly in a relationship with the doctor?

Each time she heard Doctor Shabazi's name she saw his head, on fire, bouncing along the road.

Kelly kept her answers succinct as she knew they would be looking to see if her answers deviated. But she could only say what she knew. Although with one important omission: when they asked why she'd called Doctor Shabazi in the first place, Kelly deliberately did not reveal that it was because she had suspicions about Monahan's military doctor. Instead she said she had concerns that her patient was 'very flat' and she had wanted to know if his medication had been changed but not written up on his notes yet.

It was yet another lie, but a necessary one, as far as Kelly was concerned. She just wasn't ready to delve into a tale of sinister doctors, possible international assassins and the death of Diana.

In her crash course of dealing with the police, Kelly discovered that whenever there was something they didn't believe, the officers would leave an uncomfortable silence, waiting for you to fill it, perhaps with an admission of guilt. Kelly was guilty of lying to the police, but she hadn't committed any crime. She was helping with their enquiries, although she didn't know how helpful she was really being.

'Why do you think that the doctor came to see you in the middle of a busy shift, breaking all known protocol? As far as we're aware, Doctor Shabazi always played it by the rules.'

It was a question that genuinely stumped Kelly. Did the doctor actually just want to see her? Or was that just some romantic nonsense in her head? And what about all his warnings about Monahan and Special Forces? The doctor sounded like he was talking from experience.

One of the police officers asked for a second time if there was anything else she had talked to the doctor about. It was almost as if they knew there was more.

'No, I've told you all I can remember,' she insisted. Kelly felt exhausted and brought the interview to an end: 'If there's nothing else, officers, I'd like to go to sleep, thanks.'

They both glanced at each other, then snapped their notepads shut almost simultaneously.

'Thank you for your time, Mrs. Carter.'

'It's Miss Carter, and you're welcome.'

Kelly showed the officers the door. After they'd gone, she looked at herself in the hall mirror and stared hard at the woman standing there.

'I guess it's just you and me, babe. Sure as hell no one else is going to believe us.'

26

A healthy breakfast

April ate a double-helping of Crunchy Nut Flakes, chopping up two bananas to plop into the sugary milk. She had also toasted two slices of Mother's Pride white bread and smeared them with full-fat butter and golden syrup. After adding three sugars to her mug of steaming coffee she settled down to gorge. But not before she congratulated herself on being able to forego a full fry-up at Peccadillos. 'Oh what a healthy girl I am this morning,' she said with absolutely no hint of irony.

It had just gone half seven in the morning and April was already showered and dressed, ready to hit the door of Dr. Shabazi's house. But she point-blank refused to go anywhere on an empty stomach. As she once said to Connor, 'A hungry April is no good to man nor beast,' before her colleague had berated her for speaking about herself in third person, like a 'tacky footballer'.

She read Connor's report on the *Daily Chronicle*'s subscription website on her iPad, which for some reason never retained her username and password. She usually needed two goes at her log-in as it was either her email or just 'alavender'. But the password was relentlessly unchanged: 'Cheeka' would do her no matter how many websites informed her that the code was 'weak'.

April was genuinely shocked as it dawned on her that a bomb had gone off only a few miles from where she lived. She then looked at the picture of the doctor, who was ageing gracefully but, April imagined, had been a real looker in his day. She thought of him leaving Iran to build a new life in Scotland only for it to end in the most horrific manner.

April finished her toast, wiping the crumbs from her chin and putting the dishes in the sink for later. She gave the cat a pet goodbye, slung on her fur jacket, then applied a liberal coating of bright pink, glossy lipstick before stepping out of the door, finally ready to tackle the world. The newsdesk had given her the doctor's address, taken from the electoral register, which any person or company can buy. There is a surprising amount of information contained on the register, far more than in the old days, when you just got an address and how long the person had lived there, but little else. Now there were often telephone numbers, email addresses and credit ratings. The *Daily Chronicle*'s newsdesk had passed on the Shabazi's home telephone number too, but April believed there was nothing more effective than presenting yourself in person.

Her old car may have looked out of place in the Shabazi's street, but April definitely wasn't, as their house was only marginally bigger than hers. Four cars were crammed into the driveway, two of which were very sporty-looking. April rightly guessed they belonged to the doctor's two grown-up sons. The photographer, Jack Barr, flashed his headlamps from across the street to let her know he was in position and ready with his long lens, with a clear view of the Shabazi's front door to 'snatch' a picture of the widow, if required.

Now it was April's time to shine. She walked up the gravel driveway, precariously in her high heels, stepping onto the white, non-slip tiles at their front door. Before she even had time to ring the brass doorbell a young man threw the door open.

'What do you want?'

April could see both grief and anger in his eyes. 'I'm sorry for intruding. I'm a reporter from the *Daily Chronicle*. Will you speak to me about your dad?'

'No, I will not. Go away. Leave us alone.'

'I understand. I shan't bother you and your family again. I just wanted to give you the opportunity to tell me about him. I understand some people don't want to talk, but others seem to welcome the chance to speak about what type of person their loved one was. Once again, I'm sorry to intrude at this awful, awful time.'

April turned to go when she heard a voice from deep within the home. 'Let her in, Hussain.'

'Mother, she's a reporter . . .' her son protested.

'Let me speak to her,' the voice said, echoing along the hall.

'You better come in,' he sighed, as he stepped aside for April.

27

The thin blue line

Monahan's street was still cordoned off by police tape, with just one bored-looking constable on duty. He didn't even check Kelly's ID, taking her blue nurse's uniform and bag as proof enough. He held the police tape up for Kelly to crouch under and offered some comradeship: 'You in for a long night?'

'Right through to 7 a.m. You?' Kelly asked in reply.

'Change shift at midnight. Been here since four o'clock. No toilet breaks or nothing. It's pathetic. Forensics finished up yesterday so I've no idea why we've still got to be here.'

The policeman must have been almost half Kelly's age. She thought how quickly disaffected the youth of today seemed to become. It was as if they all wanted to start at the top, and didn't think they needed to work their way up from the bottom. Kelly thought back to her nurse training in the mid-nineties, when she was treated like slave labour. She went on to gain her nursing degree, but today's newly qualified nurses now arrive with all the letters after their name, thinking they know it all. But how can you learn to be a hands-on, autonomous medical practitioner without getting your hands dirty in the real world? And she did mean dirty, with everything a human body had to offer.

At least the exchange had been a welcome distraction until she finally set eyes on the street once more, with its grim memories. The controlled entry to Monahan's building was a right state, with the main door completely blown off its hinges, while all the windows on the ground and first floors of the street were boarded up. She hadn't known whether she'd have it in her to even get this far, but she wanted to return to the scene, to see where the poor doctor had died and to confront Monahan.

As she trudged up the stairs to his top-floor flat, she could hear faint voices from above. She was on the landing below Monahan's door when she stopped in her tracks to listen to a heated conversation. It was coming from the flat directly opposite Monahan's. The one that looked like student accommodation, with the multiple faded names on Post-its stuck to the door. She had never seen anyone come or go from the flat, nor heard any sounds from within, during all her time night-sitting for Monahan. But now she could definitely hear two people. One was an older-sounding man, not the type of voice she expected to come from that sort of flat, and the other was a woman's voice. They were both muffled, and try as she may, Kelly could not make out any individual words. But there was something familiar about the man's tone. It was in its delivery. She knew that voice, but just couldn't figure out where from.

Kelly walked to the top of the stairs and pressed the button on Monahan's expensive security system. The voices opposite immediately stopped talking.

Once inside, Kelly asked Monahan, 'Have you ever met your neighbours?'

'Which ones?'

'Directly opposite.'

'Nope, why?'

'Dunno. It's just that I've never heard a peep from that flat. Not even the front door opening or closing during all my time here. Then, tonight, I hear voices. Sort of arguing. I think I know the man's voice. Can't be sure. But I'm sure I've heard him before.'

'Has the door downstairs been replaced?'

'The entry door? No, it's still hanging off its hinges.'

'There was no need for you to buzz the intercom outside— you just walked straight in?'

Kelly nodded in agreement.

'So perhaps they were talking because they hadn't heard you come in.' As ever, Monahan gave a sly little smile as he dropped his latest bombshell.

'You're saying they're listening out for me?'

'Not just for you. For anyone visiting me, I guess.'

'Why?'

'Why not? Maybe they want to be sure of something. Maybe they want to know something.'

'Diana?'

Monahan's smile was replaced by a laugh that juddered his whole body, before he forced himself to stop, from the pain. 'There's far more important things in life than the death of one woman.'

'But people should know. You should tell them.'

'Tell them what? That the missing Fiat Uno was in my garage? But, oh no, wait a minute, my garage has been destroyed, hasn't it? Along with the evidence. And I have bone cancer that's apparently spread to my brain, so I'm talking crazy at the best of times. And even if I didn't have cancer and the car was still there, what would it prove anyway? I'd be instantly discredited.'

'So why tell me?'

'I don't know. I saw you reading the newspaper about Diana and couldn't help myself.'

'Sorry, I don't buy it. Your whole life is about control. Everything you do is planned and thought through. You've said so yourself. Then suddenly you just blurt something out. Pull the other one.'

Monahan sat in silence, his face almost completely expressionless. It was at least a minute before he spoke again.

'Okay, the truth is, I need something done for me as obviously I'm not quite as able-bodied as I used to be,' he said, sweeping a hand over the bed. 'But I didn't know I was still being watched until my garage was burnt down. That was unexpected.'

'So you used me to test the water? To see if you were being watched?'

'Not deliberately, no. Although, as with anything in life, it's all about percentages. I knew there was a small chance I was being watched.'

'Listen, you fucker. I'm a divorced mother of two children. And you're risking MY life. I don't want your shit. Understand?'

Kelly shocked herself with the ferocity of her outburst. She had never spoken to anyone like this, never mind a patient. Then again, she'd never had a patient like Monahan.

His eyes were fixed as he stared unblinking at a random spot on the floor.

'Why? Why did you get me involved?' Kelly asked, demanding answers.

'Because lives could depend on it.'

'Whose lives?' Kelly raged.

'Many, many lives. To tell you more would be to endanger you more.'

'Listen. Since I started sitting for you, I've become a suspect in an arson attack, been dragged into an international conspiracy, witnessed a car bomb, watched my friend and colleague's head bounce down a street, and been interviewed twice by the police. And now you're worried about endangering me more? It would seem a little late for that.'

Monahan reached over for his notepad and pen and began to write with an unsteady hand. It read:

I am being bugged. All my emails and texts are compromised. You must consider that yours are too. Use a public pay box far from here and call the number below. Repeat the following message twice then hang up.

'Triple M. Code Brown. Comms down. Request assistance.'
Set fire to the note immediately after.

Kelly read the instructions before staring in total disbelief at Monahan. He then handed her a heavy, hardback book, with a handwritten Post-it on the cover, which read, *This is a present for you—keep it with you at all times.* Kelly took off the Post-it to read the book's title: *Lady Diana's Last Days.*

She didn't know whether to laugh or cry.

28

Providing a service

April instantly hit it off with Mrs. Shabazi. She may have been still grieving and in shock from the horrible death of her husband, but she wanted as many people as possible to know what a good father, husband, and doctor he had been. The journalist spent over two hours at home with Mrs. Shabazi, who even posed for pictures for Jack Barr and provided family photos of happier times. Afterwards April called her from the office to read the article she had written about her husband before it was published. When she finished, Mrs. Shabazi had thanked her for the 'beautiful words' before breaking down. She told April that speaking about her husband had been a great help.

It's those moments that April felt journalists never got the credit for. They're always portrayed as lowlife, gutter crawlers that would do anything to get a story. Not as writers who provided a service, for that's exactly how April viewed what she did for families of the bereaved. She was as much of a service as the police officer or the undertaker. And she would never harass anyone for a story they did not want to tell. It wasn't in her nature, even though in the old days she had been told to pile on the pressure by various news editors who didn't have to look into the whites of victims' eyes.

Working together, Connor and April had covered Doctor Shabazi's death in exemplary fashion. Connor had used a contact to find out about the incident and get the victim's name, without corrupting any public official by paying them along the way, even though DCI Crosbie probably broke half a dozen rules police rules by providing the information in the first place. April had followed it up by adding the voice of a real person to the horrific events. It was simple, old-fashioned journalism at its best.

As far as April was concerned, good words and pictures would always win over the multi-media mumbo jumbo they kept trying to teach her.

29

The phone box

Kelly slipped out of Monahan's flat as quietly as she could, dead on 7 a.m. She glanced nervously at the door opposite, with the definite feeling she was being watched. Maybe she was being paranoid. Monahan had a way of bringing out the worst in her. She walked down the first flight of steps then stopped and placed her nursing bag gently on the floor, before removing her black trainers. In just her socks she crept stealthily back up the stairs towards the 'student' door, keeping low down, out of sight of the peephole. Where there had been silence there were now voices, a man and a woman again, talking in an unfriendly tone, not quite an argument, but definitely not the sort of conversation most people have at 7 a.m. She also recognised the voices now. It was unmistakably Doctor Davies and Nurse Veronica. If, indeed, they were even medical professionals.

It all seemed to confirm both her and Monahan's suspicions. His flat was being watched. That's when it dawned on Kelly why Davies had had trouble saying Doctor Shabazi's name: he had only heard it through their listening devices.

Kelly walked back down the stairs, retrieving her shoes and bag. She stayed in her socks until near the bottom of the stairwell, before slipping her trainers back on. The voices coming from the flat had convinced her of one thing: she would make that cryptic call as Monahan had instructed.

• • •

Kelly was always dead-beat after finishing her shift, but this morning she felt she was on red alert. A man in a suit she'd never seen before got into a light blue saloon at the same time as Kelly got into her car. She couldn't be certain, but she believed he'd come from the block of flats directly opposite Monahan's. Maybe he was being watched from all angles?

Kelly pretended to flick through the pages of her diary as she waited for the blue car to pull out and drive off. She hesitated before turning the key in the ignition, wondering if this would be her last time. Maybe it would be her head bouncing down the road like a fireball. She gave a sigh of relief as the car sprung into life then decided she would deviate from her normal route home and start looking for a phone box when she was a good distance from Monahan's flat.

She hadn't been in a phone box for years and wondered who, in this smartphone era, still used them. Kelly often did as a teenager in order to call her pals—as she was banned from using the house phone by her mum except in emergencies—and she recalled them always smelling of pee after drinkers, leaving the pubs, used them as urinals.

Kelly parked her car on the double yellow lines directly outside one phone box. She quickly checked that no one was in the vicinity then stepped inside. The familiar sting of urine hit her in the face. Funny how she found the smell so repugnant in her youth and now clearing up pee and faeces was just part of her everyday life. Kelly inserted a pound coin, which was the only change she had, then dialled the number Monahan had given her. It rang for a brief moment before going to voicemail. Kelly felt like a fool as she read out the words on the sheet of paper, like a bad actress in an amateur production.

'Triple M. Code Brown. Comms down. Request assistance.'

As instructed, she read it twice: 'Triple M. Code Brown. Comms down. Req . . .'

Someone suddenly picked up the phone, abruptly ending the voicemail recording. 'Who is this?' a gruff Scots voice demanded.

'I am just passing on a message.'

'Okay, you can pass one back. Tell that daft cunt I'm locked, cocked, and ready to rock.' He hung up.

Kelly looked at the hand receiver momentarily before replacing it. She shook her head. 'I am stuck in a bloody John Le Carré novel.' She sniffed the air inside the telephone box once more. 'But with the smell of pee.'

30

Headlines get you hung

April had arrived half an hour earlier than usual at the Peccadillo Café. She had slept well, she always did. Connor had once said he envied her, as the merest creak around his flat would wake him up. He would then lie for hours unable to drift off back to sleep. April felt sorry for people who couldn't get a good night's sleep, or a 'dead slumber' as husband number two had described it, shortly before she ordered him to leave the marital home.

But this morning she was hungry, even more so than usual, for some reason. Martel had only needed to ask, 'The usual?' for April to nod enthusiastically, even before she was sitting down at her familiar table, with the *Daily Chronicle* spread out in front of her. At one point the *Chronicle* had been a broadsheet paper, which April felt was always cumbersome, before moving to a more convenient tabloid format. It was marketed as making the paper easier to read, but of course it was really all about reducing print costs as circulation continued to fall.

The front page had the dubious strapline, *World Exclusive*, which April always felt was overdoing it. Was this poor doctor's death really news in New York? She doubted it, but the main headline read: *Bomb Terror Doctor's Widow Speaks Out*.

This left April feeling uncomfortable. Yes, the man's widow had spoken only to April, but 'bomb terror' gave the story a terrorism edge, which so far the police had failed to establish. His widow had also been at pains to point out her husband had never had any interest in radicalised groups of terrorists, which April's editor had demanded she ask about. Someone, most probably the editor himself, had inserted into the third

paragraph on page one that the police had not ruled out a terrorism connection—without pointing out that they had also
not ruled in one either.

The colour drained from April's face. She was desperate to
keep Mrs. Shabazi happy. She had read out her interview over
the phone to the widow, a practice frowned upon by editors,
and now all her good work was undone by a clumsy paragraph
she never wrote.

Right at that moment, April received a text message from
Mrs. Shabazi: *I hate the sensationalism of the front page, but
your tribute to my husband inside is beautiful. Thank you, April.*

April hadn't even got that far yet. She flicked the paper open
to pages four and five, to be greeted with a sanguine-looking
image of Mrs. Shabazi, clutching her wedding photo. April's
interview had been left virtually untouched, charting the life
of the boy from Iran who left his troubled country to start a
better life and who had only ever wanted to care for people.
She was so glad it had hit the mark with his family.

'It's always the bloody headlines that get you into trouble,'
April said as Martel served her fry-up.

'Is that right?' the waitress had replied, not having the faint-
est idea what her eccentric customer was talking about, as
usual.

'But as long as they're alright with the words, then I'm happy,'
April said with a flash of her gold tooth.

'Well, then I'm glad you're happy,' Martel replied, leaving
April to feast, which was always when the journalist was truly
at her happiest.

31

Luncheon

'Where's Mummy?' Beth asked her nana.

'She must be caught up in traffic, or with a patient. She'll be home soon,' Kelly's mum, Caroline, said, glancing at her watch.

It wasn't unknown for Kelly to be late, but she always called from the car to say she was on her way. Caroline wanted to get away sharp this morning as she was meeting one of her friends in town for lunch and needed time to get herself ready. Now she would be in a rush as she had to get the kids off to school.

'Not even the courtesy of a phone call and then she moans at me for not taking them at the weekend too,' Caroline muttered to herself as she got their packed lunches together. She saw the kids out the door, with brother and sister walking together to school.

'Don't dilly dally now.'

'Yes, Nana,' the kids said in unison, well used to hearing the same instruction every morning.

Kelly pulled into the street, giving a toot of the horn to the kids and a frantic wave. She stopped the car and hugged them both through the window. 'Sorry I was late this morning. I ran into traffic.'

'Just the usual then, Mum?' William said.

'Just the usual, son,' she said, ruffling his hair.

'Don't, Mum, you'll crack my gel,' he protested.

'Well, maybe that'll make you crack a smile now and then. Right, off you go. I'm away to my bed.'

Kelly's mum already had her coat on and was standing at the door by the time she pulled into the drive. 'Of all the mornings to be late, Kelly dear.'

Wicked Leaks | 97

'Pleased to see you too, Mother,' she said as they exchanged glancing kisses to each cheek.

'You know I'm meeting Jackie for lunch. And I would like to look immaculate. She always does,' Caroline continued to moan.

'I know, Mum. Say hello to the immaculate Jackie for me,' she said as she closed the front door behind her, too tired to argue.

The grandmother with the perpetually busy social life got into her car and turned the key in the ignition. The force of the blast blew Kelly's front door off its hinges and knocked William and Beth off their feet, a full fifty yards away.

32

Personal record

'There's been another fucking one.'

'Another fucking what, Bing?' Connor asked while midway through his daily five-mile morning run.

'A big bastarding bomb,' Detective Crosbie replied.

'Where?'

'Cunting Kilsyth. Looks like one fatality in a car. Windows and doors blown away in all the whoring houses. Somewhere off Arden Grove. Just follow the fucking smoke.'

'How do you know it's a bomb?' Connor asked, still trying to catch his breath from his morning exertions and hear Crosbie over his running app, which was impatiently telling him his pace had dropped.

'A cunting car explodes, knocking out the whoring windows in the whole shitty street, and you ask if it's a bastarding bomb? Does it sound in any way fucking familiar?'

'All too familiar,' Connor replied while picking up the pace, retracing his steps back to his flat. 'I better get going, Bing. I need to call the office.'

'Wait a minute, you impatient prick. It was a woman who rang it in. She said she was the daughter of the victim. Gave her name as Kelly Carter. Now does that sound fucking familiar too, arsehole?'

'Yes, it does, Bing,' Connor replied, having discovered the name of the nurse who had been on duty with the deceased Doctor Shabazi the day before. 'Thanks. And well done on breaking your own personal record.'

'What are you cocking on about?'

'For using the most profanities in the shortest time possible.'
'Happy to oblige, Elvis. Happy to fucking oblige.'

• • •

Crosbie had been correct, all Connor had needed to do was follow the smoke. He could see it from a couple of miles away when he drove down the Airdrie Road into Kilsyth, passing Auchinstarry marina with its rows of canal boats in their berths, before looping round the disused quarry that had been turned into a pretty recreational park.

The town in the Kelvin valley was only fifteen miles from Glasgow, but far enough to be classed as semi-rural. Its backdrop was a ridge over one thousand feet high, that went from being called the Campsies at the Glasgow end to the Kilsyth hills as they eventually petered out towards Stirling. Connor had briefly dated a girl from the town. He remembered how she had told him it had once been part of Scotland's Bible Belt. At one point the town fathers had even imposed prohibition, forcing the inhabitants to walk to the neighbouring settlements of Queenzieburn or Banton for their booze. When prohibition inevitably collapsed, Kilsyth ended up with more pubs than churches.

Connor raced by a wrought iron WELCOME TO KILSYTH sign. Sure enough he could make out a bible on the town's emblem. He wondered if they should update it to also include a frothy pint of beer. A short distance on he took an impossibly steep hill up Kingsway, guessing correctly that this would be a treacherous route in the heavy snows of winter. He turned onto Arden Grove, where he could see a police cordon. He parked up in a side street then sauntered across to the police line. The photographer, Jack Barr, was already there.

'Get much?' Connor asked.

'Not bad,' Jack said, showing Connor the frames on the screen on the back of his camera of yet another raging car fire and the scenes of devastation in the street.

'Two bombs in a week. I've never seen anything like it,' Connor said.

'Me neither,' Jack agreed, 'and I thought I'd seen everything.'

Connor knew Jack wasn't boasting. He had been working in papers so long he really had witnessed it all, including the Lockerbie disaster.

'Do you know who it was this time?' Jack asked.

'Kind of. It's the mother of the nurse who was on duty when the doctor lost his head.'

'Woah. What the hell is going on?' the snapper asked.

'I have no idea, but she's clearly caught up in some bad shit.'

'Miss me, boys?' It was the sultry tones of Amy Jones approaching from behind, causing Connor to immediately clam up.

'I usually hear you coming in your heels,' Connor replied as way of a greeting.

'Oh, you'll know when you hear me coming, Elvis,' Amy said in her best sex chatline voice, causing Jack to smile. Connor could forgive the photographer as he mostly spent several hours alone on stake-outs. Reporters as flirtatious as Amy always raised the spirits.

Connor wasn't so easily swayed, though. 'How'd you get here so fast? This incident isn't even out on the radio yet.'

'You got here first. Typical man, you always arrive before the lady,' she replied.

Connor had to admire Amy's diversion technique of avoiding his question with a compliment then some innuendo. But why had she not wanted to boast about being tipped off by some ace contact? That was usually her style. It was only then that the penny dropped. Amy had expertly changed the subject as she had been told to not mention who her contact was at any cost. That's because they were obviously sharing the same source: DCI Bing Crosbie.

Connor left the scene of the blast behind as he went to chap doors in the neighbouring street. It would be an easy task finding people to speak with as everyone was keen for any new information. On the way he took a grab from his iPhone of Kelly Carter's Facebook profile picture, which conveniently not only contained a picture of her in a nurse's uniform, but also had her children and an older lady, which Connor reckoned must be the recently deceased. This was why Connor would never upload any private information about himself— all his own social media accounts were used for purely professional purposes and for tracing people like Kelly Carter for stories.

He wondered when people would ever learn.

33

Disappeared

Kelly clutched her mug of tea as she stared absently into the middle distance. Her kids were asleep, which was more than she had been able to do over the last forty-eight hours. Her bloodshot eyes felt sore and heavy, but every time she closed them she saw the explosion and her mum burning to death in the car. It was an image forever scorched into her memory.

The surroundings were unfamiliar. Kelly and her family had been taken to a safe house somewhere near Stirling. She could see the castle from the lounge window and wondered why they had renovated the ancient landmark using blonde sandstone, which stuck out on the old grey ramparts like a tacky double-glazed conservatory. One of her protection officers had explained that they had used the same stone so that over time it would darken to match the rest of the castle. But right now it looked silly to Kelly. At least the mundane conversation had kept her mind off more important matters and the one question that went unanswered: who was trying to kill her?

Kelly felt like she had been quizzed a hundred times by now. She had told them everything this time, from Monahan's cryptic note to the Fiat Uno and her suspicions that the people in the flat opposite her mysterious patient were spying on them. She knew it sounded crazy and like the rantings of a delusional fantasist, but she was too tired to try to leave anything out, figuring it would be a lot easier on her shattered mind just to say what she knew.

A succession of various men had arrived. Some in plain suits. Others in uniforms. She couldn't remember any of their names. But every time she asked them who was after her, they would share awkward sideways glances, then flannel her with some non-committal answer. Finally she had snapped with some senior officer bedecked in brass.

'Ask Monahan what's happening. He'll know. He knows everything. The bastard just isn't letting on. And try breaking down the door of his neighbour's flat, see what they have to say for themselves.'

The officer had left a long pause, and Kelly couldn't decide whether it was to let her calm down or if he was considering what he could tell her. 'First of all, we did force entry into the flat opposite Mr. Monahan's. It looks like it's been empty for a long time. But the flat below confirmed that they too had heard movement and voices, so your suspicions were probably correct. We have a forensic team investigating right now.'

The officer had taken his time again before continuing, his voice softer and lower than before. 'And we have tried questioning your patient, Mr. Monahan,' he added, shifting uneasily. 'But it seems he has disappeared.'

'Wait a minute. You've lost a bedridden terminal patient?' Kelly said in disbelief.

'There's been no sign of him since . . . since the . . . He's vanished.'

Now, Kelly sat alone again, staring at the rain running down the windowpanes. She thought back to how her life had been destroyed in such a short period of time. She wanted to cry and cry and never stop as she thought about her poor mum. Caroline Carter had been someone who put her family first, before herself. But Kelly had been robbed of her mother and her children had lost their loving nana. And not to illness, but in the most violent, horrible, cowardly way imaginable: murdered in her own car. Blown up by a bomb that had clearly been used to warn off Kelly. As if she needed warning after seeing what had happened to Doctor Shabazi. Now, amongst everything else, she also had survivors' guilt. Her mum had been dragged into a lethal scenario through no fault of her own.

Then again, the same could be said about Kelly. But she knew she could have stopped it. She should have refused to sit for Monahan. She should have never gone to that lock-up. She should have taken Doctor Shabazi's advice. But curiosity had got the better of her and she hated herself for it.

It might not have been the appropriate time for it, but Kelly's practical side had plenty of questions too. That was her job gone, for starters. How could she return to work after all that'd happened? And what about the kids' schooling? She needed to inform the head teacher of the family crisis, but then again how much could she say?

Kelly looked at the clock on the wall. It had just gone 8 a.m. and she realised she had been sitting in the same spot for hours after yet another night of no sleep. She knew she wouldn't be able to continue like this for much longer, but her brain just wouldn't shut down.

She prised herself out of the armchair, stiff from being immobile for so long, then headed to the kitchen to make a cup of tea. She might even try something light to eat too. She gave a cursory nod to the armed policeman in the hallway, who had his Glock machine gun slung over his shoulder, one hand grasping the handle, the other placed on the barrel ready for action, despite the early hour. It was a stark reminder of just how serious her situation was.

Kelly put on the kettle then opened the door of the fully stocked fridge. She wondered how many other people needing protection had stood on the same spot as she was now, with an armed policeman by the door while contemplating what to have for breakfast. She closed the fridge, not ready to eat quite yet, and sat down by the breakfast bar with a mug of black tea. She didn't let the bag stew too long, then took it out of the mug and popped it in the swingbin. It landed on top of a newspaper, which had probably been discarded by one of the duty cops.

Kelly retrieved the paper, removed her teabag, which had left an ugly brown stain, and spread it out in front of her.

The entire front page was taken up by a photo of her mum's burning car and firefighters battling the blaze. Kelly pushed her mug to the side and threw the lid off the bin, as she vomited. Only bile came up from her empty stomach, which stung at her throat. When the retching finally stopped she looked back at the newspaper and read the article:

A car bomb blew up a grandmother yesterday in a terrifying attack on a Scots street.

Caroline Carter was killed instantly in the blast, which rocked a quiet residential area of Kilsyth near Glasgow.

The sixty-five-year-old was believed to have been leaving her daughter's house when the device went off.

Last night a Police Scotland spokesperson said: "We are treating this us a major incident."

The rest of the report was continued inside, but Kelly's eye returned to the top of the article, to the name Connor Presley, the by-line of the journalist who wrote it. Kelly thought she recognised the name, not from newspaper reports, but from a colleague who had once dated Connor for nearly a year. She recalled his nickname had been Elvis and he was the flash type, whisking her workmate off on exotic holidays before he'd disappear for weeks on end. It was a casual relationship that had suited them both.

Kelly took note of Connor's email address printed under his by-line, which had become standard in the digital age. She doubted what she was about to do was the right course of action, but she felt she had no choice. The men with machine guns couldn't protect her and the kids forever. She had to think of her own family's safety and security, and the only way to do that was to let whoever was after her know that she was just an innocent bystander in all of this, that she didn't really know anything. Kelly had been warned not to communicate with the outside world. One of the security team had even wanted to remove her smartphone, but she had argued successfully that she required it in case of emergency: if the safe house was attacked, she'd at least be able to call for help. The security team had eventually relented. It meant Elvis was about to receive a message like no other:

This is Kelly Carter. You wrote about my mother. What if I told you the car bomb was directly linked to the bombing on the Southside of Glasgow and the death of Diana, Princess of Wales?

And no, I am not a nutter and this is not a hoax. I wish it was.

34

An email

Connor was walking from the staff parking lot to the Peccadillo for breakfast when he felt his iPhone vibrate. He fished it out of his pocket to see he had a message. What he read stopped him in his tracks, before he punched the air and mouthed, 'Yes!' He now had a perfect follow-up to the story.

He decided to skip breakfast and headed straight into the office instead. All he wanted was Kelly's story about the car bomb and her mum. Frankly she could keep the Diana stuff: that was nutter territory. He felt that his best ploy would be to string her along. Pretend he wanted the Princess conspiracy theory stuff but leave with what he was really after. It was how he had treated people all his life and why, at the age of forty, he only had passing acquaintances instead of friends. Not that he really cared.

Connor wrote back to Kelly as he typed and walked. *This is mind-blowing.* He wanted to hint that he was buying into her conspiracy: *We must tread carefully. How do you propose we proceed?*

By the time Connor had reached the office's front doors, Kelly had replied: *Carefully. Very carefully. I've seen what these people are capable of.*

Connor had learned a long time ago to get the story there and then, and not to let people sleep on it, in case someone talked them out of bearing their soul to a newspaper journalist.

First of all I need to prove you're the real deal to my editor, let me give him what he wants. Please tell me what happened the morning your mother died and the night of Doctor Shabazi's death.

• • •

CAR BOMB VICTIM'S DAUGHTER HORROR
World Exclusive

NURSE Kelly Carter has revealed how she has been caught up in the double terror explosions that rocked Glasgow.

The thirty-nine-year-old mum of two was on duty on Tuesday night when a huge car bomb killed her colleague Doctor Mohammed Shabazi on the city's Southside.

Then two days later her own mother, Caroline Carter, 65, was murdered when her car was blown-up outside the family home in Kilsyth on the outskirts of Glasgow.

Last night Kelly told the Daily Chronicle: "In the space of a week my whole life has been changed.

"I've found myself at the centre of sinister goings-on, having no idea who has decided to attack me, my family and my colleague in such a cowardly fashion."

Kelly and her children, William, twelve, and nine-year-old Beth are being held by the authorities at a rural safe house not far from their Kilsyth home.

The report ran to a full page inside, which was basically full of speculation and rehashed information of what was already known.

But although the information about the safe house had been just a throwaway line in the article, repeated parrot-fashion by Connor from one of Kelly's emails, it proved to be a vital clue for her pursuers. With an intricate knowledge of all the safe houses in Scotland, it was all they needed to know where she was being kept.

And, like the Battle Of Bannockburn in 1314, another fight to the death was about to take place in the shadow of Stirling Castle.

35

The book

Kelly had been on the receiving end of a stern ticking off from a senior policeman for the best part of half an hour. Now she'd had enough.

'Finished?' she snapped.

'I just want you to understand the danger of speaking to the press—to you, your family, and my officers. We're going to have to relocate you tonight,' Superintendent Donohoe repeated yet again.

'I asked if you were finished.' This time it wasn't a question. 'This . . .' she said, sweeping her hands around the room, '. . . won't last forever. We will need to return to the real world away from men with machine guns. Whoever is behind all this knows what they are doing—and I presume it is "they" as no one individual could have planned and carried out these attacks. They obviously think I know something, which I don't. Hiding forever isn't an option. Not for my kids. My only hope is to let them know I'm fighting back. That I have a voice and I'm not afraid to use it. So I'm *not* sorry for going to the newspaper and I'm *not* sorry that it's proved a real pain in the arse for you. My one and only priority is my kids and everything else can go to hell.'

Kelly turned around without saying another word and headed to her room.

The children slept as she packed the meagre belongings they had fled with a couple of days before. It didn't take her long. The last item was the book Monahan had given her, *Lady Diana's Last Days*. She had no idea why she had packed it in her rush to leave her own house, but something Monahan had said about keeping it with her at all times must have registered deep within. Kelly sat down on her bed and opened it for the first time. Her gasp caused the children to turn in their sleep. When they had stopped moving she turned the book upside down and patted the back cover. Into her lap fell a black box. Written on the side was, *Samsung portable hard drive. M3 4 Terabyte.*

Kelly didn't know what a terabyte was, but she knew it would be big. She also knew now why their lives were in imminent danger. Whatever was on this hard drive, people were prepared to kill for. She had no time to explain her find to the officers below. Kelly needed to get herself and her kids out of the house now.

She woke the children and wrapped them in their warm jackets over their pajamas. She had just replaced the hard drive in the book and locked it in her suitcase when the first gunshot made her jump.

'What's that, Mummy?' asked Beth.

'Just a firework,' Kelly said unconvincingly.

William wasn't buying it. 'That sounded like a gunshot.'

The unique rat-a-tat sound of machine gun fire filled the air. It was followed by panicked shouting from downstairs as the police officers came under attack. Kelly remembered her late dad saying how war strategies went out the window as soon as the first shot was fired. She wondered how often the officers below had come under real live fire: by the sounds of things, this was the first time. In contrast to their muffled shouts, the machine gun fire seemed controlled and disciplined. It came in short bursts and in multiple directions.

It was also getting louder as they closed in on their target: Kelly. She turned to the kids and hugged them tightly. 'Now listen. I want you to do exactly as your mum says. No questions. We're going to get in our car and drive away from here as fast as possible. I want you to lie down on the seats and don't look up whatever happens. Understand?'

Both children nodded immediately. Kelly grabbed her bag and slung it over her shoulder then took each of the children's hands.

'Let's go.'

Kelly tiptoed with the children swiftly downstairs. A cold wind hit her full in the face from the front door, which was open. A trail of shiny red blood led inside. But Kelly was committed and heading for that door.

'Stop!' screamed Superintendent Donohoe. 'We're surrounded.'

The man who had looked so purposeful and commanding in his uniform was now dishevelled with a haunted look across his face. 'Don't go outside. You'll die.'

Kelly's eyes were drawn down to the cuff of his shirt, dripping with blood. 'And if I stay here I'll die anyway,' she replied.

There was more machine-gun fire, and this time it seemed to be directly outside the door. The sharp, single, repetitive shots of a police Heckler Koch MP5 returned fire, followed by the unmistakable thump of a body hitting the ground. Kelly and Donohoe both knew this was her moment to flee.

'Here, take my car,' he said, throwing a set of keys in her direction from his uninjured arm, 'It's the silver Volvo right outside.'

Kelly caught them in mid-flight, turned, and headed to the front door with her kids in tow. Her feet slipped on the trail of blood, reminding her of her days when she worked briefly in the operating theatre. Outside it was cold and dark, with a body illuminated by the light from the house. It was of a man dressed entirely in black, wearing some sort of night vision goggles and clutching a machine gun in his dead arms. Kelly did not know if he was a police officer or one of the attackers. She unlocked the Volvo with the key fob, making the indicator lights flash, drawing unwanted attention. She flung open a rear passenger door and hurled the children into the back seat. But just as she opened the driver's door, rapid machine gun fire opened up in her direction, shattering the Volvo's windows.

Kelly hollered into the night air, 'Don't shoot—there are children in the car.'

Her pleas were met with more shots and the sound of metal hitting metal as bullets ripped into the vehicle. William and Beth screamed in terror as their mum crouched helplessly on the ground. She heard the shooter's footsteps running in her direction, and from underneath the car she could see a pair of black boots closing in on her. The boots came skidding to a halt less than six feet from Kelly and she couldn't help but look up at her would-be executioner. The man in black pointed his gun directly at Kelly's head.

Like a rabbit staring at a predator, she couldn't draw her eyes away.

The man in black was then lifted clean off his feet and sent flying through in the air, finishing in a crumpled heap at least ten feet away from where he had stood. A deafening boom shook Kelly, the car, and everything else in the vicinity. A second boom went off, and this time a figure to Kelly's left was sent crashing backwards into one of the safe house's windows, his body lying limp and lifeless amongst the shattered glass.

It was a blood bath, but someone was fighting back. Suddenly a Land Rover roared up beside Kelly and the shredded Volvo. A voice ordered, 'Get in,' and Kelly didn't hesitate, pulling her terrified children into the waiting vehicle. The wheels spun on the dirt as the Land Rover lurched forward, gaining speed. Kelly cuddled her children tightly in the back seat, refusing to let them go or look at her saviours. She vowed she wouldn't let go of them until they were far away from this place.

They bumped along the rough track for what seemed an age until the thick tread tires hit smooth tarmac. Kelly could sense the passing motorway lights through her eyelids. She opened them to take in her surroundings: there were two men in the car, dressed in similar attire to the ones who had attacked the house.

'Thank you,' Kelly croaked, unheard over the noise of the engine and the various rattles of the well-used Land Rover. She repeated herself, louder this time: 'THANK YOU.'

'You're welcome, Nurse Carter,' replied a familiar voice from the driver's seat.

The man's face was completely blacked up, but there was no mistaking the cocky smile of Mad Malky Monahan.

'I hope you've still got my book.'

36

Safe house

Connor came to a roadblock and decided to ditch the car and hike as far as he could on foot instead. Jack Barr was on his way and, for once, Connor had arrived at a scene before him. He had wanted to get as close to the action as possible before day broke. Connor checked his watch. It had just gone 6 a.m. He kept a spare pair of boots in the car, as every good reporter always comes prepared for every scenario. He slipped them on, grabbed a waterproof jacket, slung his man-bag over his shoulder then leaped a farmer's fence. It wouldn't be too hard to find where he was going as all he had to do was follow the flashing blue lights.

He walked for more than two miles, which, on the rough and uneven ground of a ploughed field, took nearly forty minutes. He stuck as close as possible to the hedge and tree lines as helicopters kept buzzing overhead, no doubt ferrying the injured and dead away from the scene. The farmhouse where all the activity was taking place was still about half a mile away when Connor spied a nearby cottage and made a beeline for it. Judging by the immaculate garden and abundant flowers, he guessed this would be the home of a retiree. He knocked on the door, and heard a voice ask, 'Who's there?'

Connor introduced himself, and got the reply, 'Do you know what's going on?'

'Not really, I was hoping you could tell me,' he said truthfully.

The door opened to reveal a frightened-looking elderly lady still in her nightgown. Her rheumy eyes struggled to focus.

'I just need to know if you saw or heard anything,' Connor said.

'My eyesight is not so good, son, but I heard everything. It sounded like a fireworks display. Explosions everywhere.'

Connor knew already that quote would be the headline. 'And it came from that farm over there?' he asked, pointing in the direction of the neighbouring farmstead.

'It used to be the Finalyson's. But they moved out around five years ago. Never did meet the new owners. Just saw lots of cars coming and going. Someone once told me it was a "safe house", but I've no idea for who or what. I think the person who told me had been watching too many television shows.'

The words 'safe house' went off like a firecracker in Connor's head. He now knew exactly who had been staying here. This had been the safe house Kelly had mentioned to him and the one he had wrote about in his copy. A dreadful feeling gripped his stomach tightly. He thought he had kept her whereabouts vague in his report, but he obviously hadn't been ambiguous enough. Someone knew where to look and Connor had dutifully supplied them the clue. He retched and choked back the urge to be violently sick on the old lady's porch.

37

The North

The Land Rover trundled on for over two hours, heading north. Monahan kept to the sixty miles per hour limit imposed by the average speed cameras on the A9. The only thing that would arouse suspicion, Kelly figured, was his blacked-up face. But she reckoned these weren't the type of men to stop for any traffic cops, anyway.

Kelly recognised some of the passing place names as towns and villages she had visited in her youth: Pitlochry, Killiekrankie. She loved how they rolled off the tongue and reminded her of day trips with her mum and dad. Kelly missed her dad. She hadn't even started to mourn properly for her mum.

'Are you still in touch with the children's father?' Monahan asked over the noisy sound of the Land Rover.

'Yes.'

'Call him. Tell him to pick them up at the House Of Bruar. Duggie here will stay with them until he arrives. We need to keep going north.'

'I'm not leaving my kids anywhere,' Kelly insisted.

'The café will be opening soon. They'll be in a safe public place.'

'Every time I'm told somewhere is safe it turns out to be anything but.'

'They'll be safe with Duggie. They are not after your kids. So let's take them out of the equation.'

Kelly looked at the well-built man in the passenger seat. Despite his bulk Duggie had kind eyes. He smiled at William and Beth and said, 'Fancy some bacon and eggs, kids? My treat.'

The children remained silent, holding their mother tightly as they stared at him. Kelly could see the logic in letting them go. She didn't want to, but people had been shooting at her over that damn hard drive. She rummaged in her pockets for her iPhone, then called their dad. Everyone in the vehicle listened to the one-sided conversation.

'Brian. I need your help. Can you pick up the kids from the House of Bruar as soon as you can? . . . Yes, I'm alright, but I need to go away for a while. . . . Yes, it's to do with Mum. . . . No, I can't say anything else. It's for the best. House Of Bruar, as soon as. They'll be with a man called Duggie. . . . Yes, Duggie. You don't know him. Text me when you have them. Bye.'

Kelly hung up. No one else spoke. There was nothing to say. She hugged her children, who whimpered and cried. They understandably did not want to leave their mum, but she assured them she would be alright and was amazed how convincing she sounded.

• • •

After another round of hugs in the parking lot, Kelly returned to the Land Rover and waved goodbye. A few cars were arriving, probably staff preparing to open up the famous tourist spot. Kelly knew it wouldn't be long until they were in the safety and warmth inside, tucking into the bacon and eggs Duggie had promised. Their father wouldn't be far behind. For all his faults, he was a loving dad, when he was there. Weird, she thought, how men can just open a new chapter in their lives and barely blink at the past.

The past. What a peculiar notion that was turning out to be. When she was happily married with a young family and still had both her parents. Now? She almost laughed at her predicament as she drove north with an armed and terminally ill man having just narrowly survived a shoot-out that claimed the lives of God knows how many. Now she had left William and Beth in the care of a complete stranger.

Kelly must have drifted off. She was woken by a text message on her phone. It was Brian: *Got the kids. They're fine. They told me what happened. Please take care. And text me where you're staying. Xxx.*

Brian never put kisses after his texts. He must really be concerned for her. Kelly straightened up as she re-read the message, a slight frown on her face. She wrote back: *Thanks, Brian. I knew I could rely on you. How's your mum doing? Sorry I forgot to ask.*

There was a long pause before she received another text back: *She's fine. Thanks for asking.* Kelly stared at the words, her hand beginning to tremble.

'Stop the car. STOP THE CAR!'

'What is it?' Monahan asked.

'They've got Brian. They've got the kids. His mother has been dead for years,' Kelly shrieked as she surged forward, waving the phone under Monahan's nose. He grabbed her wrist to steady her hand so he could read the text.

'Shit,' was all he could say as Kelly began to scream hysterically.

Monahan pulled Kelly's face into his chest as he continued to drive north, her screams soon subsided into body-wrenching sobs, until she eventually fell silent, comforted to sleep like a baby.

38

A–Z

'Elvis, did you know you name is Ejaculate, Labia, Vag, Intercourse, Shag in the phonetic alphabet?' DCI Crosbie said to Connor, having just called him on his mobile.

'Actually, I think you'll find it isn't,' the reporter replied. Connor had just filed his copy from near the farmhouse in Bannockburn. The place was now swarming with TV crews, photographers, and reporters, including the perpetually flirtatious Amy Jones, who was working her charms with some hapless young journalist who had suddenly discovered he was God's gift to women.

'You're right. But I thought I would work out my own phonetic alphabet. Make it official.'

'Bing, do we have to do this now? I'm up to my tits, as usual.'

'Hear me out, Elvis. I have news for you afterwards. So, let's see. For "A" we have *Arsehole*.'

'Inspired,' Connor scoffed.

'Look, if you're going to be all sarky, it will just take me longer to get to my news.'

'Right, fire away. Neither of us is getting any younger.'

'Okay, "B" will be *Bastard*, "C" is *Cunt*, naturally. "D" is *Dick*, "E" is for *Ejaculate*, as we've already said. "F" is for *Fuck*.'

'Not *Fanny*?' Connor asked.

'I know, I was torn between *Fuck* and *Fanny*, but in the end settled on good old dependable *Fuck*. We then have "G", which will be *Gobble*; "H" is *Hard-on*. "I" would be *Intercourse*, again as we've already established. "J" is *Jobby*. That's a personal favourite of mine. "K" is for *Knickers*.

'Hang on. That doesn't work. It's got to sound the same, not spell the same,' Connor protested.

'*Knockers*, then?'

'Same problem.'

'So that'd also rule out *Knob*?'

'Sure would.'

'How about *KY*, as in *KY Jelly*?'

'Much better.'

'"L" is for *Labia*, as stated earlier. "M" is for *Motherfucker*.'

'Too long,' Connor complained. 'How about *Muff*?'

'Brilliant, Elvis. Much better. You're getting into the spirit of this. Could I have *Knob* for "N", do you think?'

'Why not? It's your alphabet and I can't really see Police Scotland adopting it, however hard you may try.'

'"O" is an easy one, of course: *Orgasm*. "P" would be *Pish*.'

'I'm interested in what you've come up with for "Q",' Connor said genuinely.

'Well, I'm not going to lie to you, that was a tricky one. I thought about *Quarter-pounder*, as in, "My cock's a quarter-pounder".'

'A bit convoluted, but I see what you're trying to do there,' Connor smiled. He was almost starting to enjoy himself.

'Then I came up with *Cucumber*.'

'Well, technically it doesn't work, but then again neither did *Knob*. And also it's a bit lame, Bing, especially for you.'

'There's nothing lame about a cucumber when your girlfriend uses it to ram it up her fanny.'

'I asked for that one, didn't I?'

'But, in the end, the answer was staring me in the face. "Q" has to be *Quickie*. I mean, who doesn't like a quickie, Elvis?'

'Exactly.'

'Exactly. "R" would be *Rimming*. I was actually spoilt for choice with "S". There's *Shitter, Semen, Scrotum, Slippy, Sodomy . . .*'

'But you settled on *Shag*,' Connor interrupted, trying to speed up proceedings.

'Yes, because everyone loves a shag.'

'Well done. Next.'

'With "T" I couldn't really decide between *Tits* and *Twat*. I am more of a tits man, truth be told, but then I do like a twat as well.'

'I see your dilemma. And your final decision?'

'*Turd*. "U" would be *Uterus*, "V" becomes *Vag*, "W" is *Wanker*. "X" is *Ex-Sex*, as in, having sex with your ex. That work, Elvis?'

'Kinda. And "Y"?'

'*Yummy*. As in, "I'd love to fuck a Yummy Mummy." And "Z" is *Zig*.

'Zig?' Connor asked, intrigued.

'Yes, as in, "Zig-a-zig-ah". It's what I imagine the Spice Girls shout out when they com . . .'

'Right. Enough. Well done, Bing. "A" right through to insanity. Now, any chance you can tell me what you're calling for?'

'With information, my friend. No one knows where your Kelly character is. She seems to have vanished.'

'Has she been kidnapped?' Connor whispered into his phone, not wanting to catch the attention of the hungry pack of journalists.

'Looks that way, Elvis. She is definitely not in police custody. I've been listening to the chatter on the airwaves all morning. Which means the attackers must have her.'

'Fantastic,' Connor replied. Like many journalists he was detached from the reality behind a good story.

'Gotta go, Elvis. If I get any more info, you'll be the first to know,' DCI Crosbie promised before hanging up.

Connor stared across at Amy Jones, who flicked her mane of strawberry blonde hair to one side as she took a call on her mobile. Connor then dialled Crosbie back, only for it to go straight through to voicemail.

'I may be the first to know, Bing, but Amy always seems to be the second,' Connor muttered to himself.

39

The chef

When Kelly woke up she was lying in the back seat of the Land Rover with a thick blanket over her. They had come to a stop and she was alone in the vehicle. Kelly lay in silence staring up at the trees outside. She knew she had been sleeping a while, but didn't have a clue where she was. The only sound was the wind blowing through the leaves of the forest, and Kelly couldn't hear any passing vehicles: it seemed to be a very remote location. She looked out of the window to see she was parked up outside a quaint wooden lodge. It looked beautiful, the type of place she'd have loved to have taken the kids.

Pain and anguish gripped at her stomach again as she thought about her children. She began to quiver when the door was opened by Duggie.

'Are my kids alright?' Kelly pleaded with him.

'Of course they are, hen,' he said in a thick Scottish accent. 'I tailed them all the way home. Kilsyth, isn't it? Let's get inside and get ourselves a brew.'

'But the text message?' she asked.

'I'm no' very good with technology. But the gaffer will explain inside.'

Duggie led her up the wooden stairs to the lodge and into the kitchen area, where Monahan was boiling the kettle. Her patient was still wearing his army camouflage clothes while sitting in a wheelchair.

'How you feeling?' she asked instinctively.

'As long as I've got my morphine and my protein shakes I'm tickety-boo,' Monahan managed to beam, despite his hooded eyes and grey pallor.

'Right, I've got work tae dae,' Duggie announced as he picked up rolls of wire and headed outside.

Monahan waited until he was out of earshot before saying, 'He's rough and ready, but great in a firefight. He took out two shooters last night. He's lethal with that shotgun of his. Always has been, mind you. Helped me out of plenty of scraps. He's rigging trip wire around the place, just so we know if anyone wants to pay us a visit.'

'The text. My children?'

'Ah, yes. Don't worry about that. They're fine. We reckon Brian's mobile was cloned. It's actually pretty easy to do if you're near the same phone mast and know the numbers of both phones. You can intercept incoming messages and send outgoing ones as if they were coming from Brian's mobile. Then all whoever cloned his phone had to do was engage you in conversation and find out where you were going. It's the same methods they use in bank scams. SMS smishing they call it, when you hijack a text message thread. You've heard of that, right? Where you manipulate people to get information out of them.'

Kelly silently nodded her head.

'Well, the main thing is the kids are fine.'

'Are they in danger?' Kelly asked.

'No. Someone will be watching them, but they'll only be in danger if you contact them. So we've taken your phone off you.'

'Like a prisoner?'

Monahan smiled that smile of his. 'Just for the time being. You can use it when we're ready for them.'

'You mean, when you use me as bait?'

'Very succinct, Nurse Kelly. I guess we've got to make a stand at some point, don't we?'

Kelly felt strangely empowered. She couldn't confirm it, but she knew in her heart of hearts that her family were safe. She wanted to warn them but couldn't risk it. So now she would face the enemy head on, for the sake of her children. For the sake of her dead mother and Doctor Shabazi. To have any hope of a future, she would stand strong. She was ready.

Duggie's heavy footsteps came through the front door, his large UTS-15 shotgun in one hand and three pheasants dangling dead in the other.

'You didn't use that to kill them, did you Duggie?' Monahan laughed.

'If I'd used Big Bertha, there wouldnae be anything left tae eat, boss.'

'Duggie, you're the only man I've ever known who names his guns.'

'Weapons are my mates, boss. They look after me and I look after them. But noo make way for Duggie the chef. That cunt Gordon Ramsay's got nothing on me.'

Monahan looked over at Kelly. 'For such a rough diamond he is a surprisingly good cook.'

'Aw thanks, boss,' Duggie said as he placed an apron over his squat, muscular frame, which made him look faintly ridiculous.

Kelly did something she hadn't done in a while. She smiled.

40

Bedtime

Monahan had not been exaggerating about Duggie's cooking abilities; he had plucked and prepared the pheasants in no time, flavouring them with herbs he'd collected, along with salt and pepper. Kelly had scoured the cupboards for supplies, finding tins of peas and carrots, along with packets of rice. They weren't ideal accompaniments, but it didn't matter as the game bird tasted sensational.

'This is absolutely delicious,' Kelly enthused as the three of them sat around the thick wooden table.

They made unlikely dinner companions. Kelly was so petite next to Duggie, who had his shotgun slung over the back of his chair, while Monahan sat in his wheelchair, a liquidiser by his plate. He popped pieces of pheasant into the top of his machine, along with some veg, added half a pint of a protein shake then hit the button. The vibrations shook the table for a moment, before Monahan stopped, removed the lid and took a long drink of the multi-coloured goo.

'Ah, magic.'

They all laughed.

'Don't know how you can drink that shit, boss.'

'Uch, it's not so bad, Duggie. Your magnificent cooking added a certain *je ne sais quoi*.'

They laughed again. Kelly felt relaxed. She knew she shouldn't be, but she liked the unusual company.

'How did you two meet, then?'

'Long story, darling,' Duggie replied. 'But, basically, we were flung together for a job. They seemed to like our work and that was that. Twenty-two years later and I'm still saving his skinny arse.'

'I love the way everything you guys say is so cryptic and vague. Mysterious, even.'

'It's a lot more polite than saying how we killed, maimed and blew things up around the world. Especially at the dinner table,' Monahan said.

There was a long pause before Kelly burst out laughing. 'Malcolm, I think I'll rename you Edward Scissorhands. You can cut any conversation dead.'

'What can I say? It's the reality of our lives. And it's now the reality of yours.'

The laughing stopped when Monahan delivered his warning.

'There's a shit-storm coming, Kelly, and you're going to have to be strong. Stronger than you've been before. The bad guys are coming for you and you're going to have to fight for your life. Ever used a gun?'

'Of course not,' Kelly replied, incredulous.

'That's okay, Duggie will teach you the basics.'

'No thanks, I prefer saving lives rather than taking them.'

'It's your funeral. We've got an early start, so it's time for bed. Nurse Kelly can have my room and Duggie takes the spare. I'll do first watch. I hardly sleep at night, anyway.' He wheeled away from the table, taking his plate with him.

'I'm on dishes duty,' Kelly said, clearing the table.

'And I'll just piss off to bed then and get some shut-eye. Chef's privilege since I'm such a fucking great cook,' Duggie said in his usual gruff manner.

Monahan retrieved a gun case from a cupboard before he manoeuvred from his wheelchair onto the couch. Kelly stared in amazement. She had never seen a terminal patient with such high energy levels. She had witnessed big, strong men fade away to nothing. But here was Monahan still putting up the good fight, the very embodiment of Dylan Thomas's exhortation to 'rage against the dying of the light'.

Now that they were alone, Kelly took the chance to ask about his health. 'How are you really doing?'

'Worse than last time we met, but then again I'm not exactly getting a lot of rest at the moment.'

'What's on that hard drive, Malcolm?' She asked the question softly, almost intimately.

'It's complicated. I took some information. Actually, quite a lot of information—from someone who I felt was going to take it east.'

'North Korea?'

'Hell, no,' Monahan scoffed. 'They don't have enough money to pay their electricity bills. The Chinese, on the other hand, would pay a king's ransom. Anyway, when I discovered some fucker from our side was trying to sell it, I took it off him. Unfortunately for me, he is very high up the tree, and told the top brass it was me who was trying to sell the information.'

'And Diana?'

'True, sadly, but in the grand scheme of things it matters little.'

'How can you say that? She was the Queen of Hearts. The nation loved her.'

'She was a middle-aged, mad burd who was threatening to marry an Arab. Heck, she may have even been pregnant already. That'd mean the next king of England would have a half-Arab sibling. The establishment would never allow it. She effectively signed her own death warrant.'

'These are conspiracy theories anyone could get off the Net,' Kelly protested.

'True. And I did,' Monahan replied matter of factly.

'So you are just telling me stuff off the Internet that everyone already knows?'

'Yeah. I don't know why she was killed. But that's what it says on the Net.'

'That sounds as though you're distancing yourself from it. "Oh it's nothing to do with me, guv." I don't understand you.'

'Kelly, you're looking for rhyme or reason, when there's neither. We were instructed to take her out, which we did. It was surprisingly easy as the Arab's security team was total amateur hour stuff. That may sound cold-blooded, but it's not to me. I don't even think about it. It was just another job—a successful hit. I've made my career doing it.'

'Killing people?'

'Some people need killed.'

'A mother who was an embarrassment to the Royal Family *needed* to be killed?'

Monahan shrugged his shoulders. 'Fuck knows. Although I'd suspect it would have been more serious than that. Trading secrets or something.'

'Now you're telling me the Princess was involved in espionage? The most famous woman on the planet—who was followed night and day by the paparazzi—was a spy?'

'Like I said, fuck knows. But she did move in mysterious circles.'

Kelly's eyes began to well up with emotion as she stared at him intently. 'I am sitting here with the man who claims to have killed Princess Diana, but he can't even give me a reason why.'

Monahan held her gaze, unblinking for what seemed an age before he finally replied, 'I'm sorry. Some things just don't have any reason.'

'So all this stuff about getting the real Diana story out there was just a ruse?'

For the first time Monahan looked ashamed. 'I needed to find out if I was still a person of interest. Turns out I am.'

'And now I am too?'

'Yes. Again, I'm sorry.'

'So I really was nothing more than a commodity to you. Something to be used and abused?'

'It's just the way I am. It's how I've been taught to survive.'

'Yet you're not surviving, are you? You're dying, but won't change your ways.'

'I need to survive only a little bit longer then I'll be done. No more morphine or protein shakes. I'll give up the fight and let go.'

Kelly felt nothing but sadness. Her end-of-life-care training had taught her to help people get their minds straight and their affairs in order. But Monahan was a lost cause. 'And what legacy do you leave behind? No wife, I take it? Or kids?'

Monahan shook his head.

'So what do you plan to leave behind?'

Monahan's look of shame was replaced by a steely gaze. 'I don't want the hard drive falling into Chinese hands. They will only use the information as leverage. They won't be interested in getting the information out there. I want to get it on that Beast Shamer website. So everyone knows the truth. Then and only then will you and your family be truly safe. So there you have it, Nurse Kelly. My legacy will be to finally do something right. For the sake of your family, help keep me alive long enough to complete my final mission.'

Kelly could see danger and fury in his eyes mixed with bitter emotion. But she believed she also saw a glimpse of compassion, as she had seen many times before with people when they were reaching the end of their lives.

She moved over to the couch, where she took his pulse, which she felt pumping hard. She placed her fingertips on his temples to take his temperature, which was running high. Suddenly Kelly was overwhelmed by the loneliness of the months since her divorce. Here was a man who understood how it felt to be all by yourself in the world. The stress they had experienced together over the last few days had swept them together, and now an intense emotion gripped her like never before.

Kelly clasped the back of Monahan's neck and pulled his mouth towards hers. They kissed passionately as she straddled him. Everything tingled, from her hardened nipples to the small of her back. Monahan slipped her blouse off effortlessly, while Kelly hurriedly took off her jeans and panties. She manoeuvred on top of him, pulling his face tightly into her as he kissed her breasts. Kelly then arched her behind to let him enter her, and they finally relieved the passion they had both craved and needed.

41

Forgiveness

April Lavender was snoring in her armchair when her cat, Cheeka, woke her up by repeatedly pawing at her face. She took several seconds trying to focus on the clock on her smartphone before realising she needed to put on her reading glasses, which were still perched on her head. It was almost 11 p.m. She berated herself for sleeping so long and forgetting to feed her cat, who was as hungry as she was.

April almost had to pry herself from the armchair as she had been perfectly moulded into the seat. She fed Cheeka and made herself a sandwich as she was feeling peckish too, even though she had eaten earlier. As she headed back to the sitting room to switch the lights out, she noticed an envelope on her doormat. She ripped it open and immediately knew who it was from:

Dear April

I am sorry. I miss you. I should not say things I say. But I am from Italy. I am a passionate man. But I was also wrong to say and do those things.

Please forgive me. Please take me back.

I love you.

Luigi xxx

The engagement ring was taped to the middle of the letter. April ran her finger over the gold and diamond jewellery before re-reading the letter, hearing Luigi's Glaswegian/Italian accent in her mind as she did so. But she was too old to be married to someone so fiery. Maybe thirty years ago she would have thrived on the excitement and the passion, but now just the mere thought of it made her exhausted.

'I'm sorry my old Italian stallion,' she said aloud, 'But I think I've had a lucky escape.'

42

Hardware

'So what's that?' Kelly asked, as Monahan unlocked his long, metal gun case.

'This is your British Army L115A3. Accurate between 600 and 800 meters, but can also be effective at over 1,000 meters, which, for the purposes of my next job, I sincerely hope it will be.'

'You do know most men smoke after sex. They don't play with their guns.

'I'm not most men.'

'Is that from your days in the SAS?'

'Nah, the SAS and SBS will use something different.'

'SBS?' Kelly said quizzically.

'Yes, the Special Boat Service, which everyone seems to forget, although that's just the way they like it. Anyway, depending on the task, the Special Forces have a wider selection of weapons available than the regular forces, but I always preferred the L115AE. You get to keep it after your 100th kill. Officially I have forty-three confirmed kills, but that was before I was taken off the books.'

'So you're like that *American Sniper* guy—what's his name, Chris Kyle? What was he? 160 confirmed kills or something?'

'You know your military history.'

'Nah, I know my movies,' Kelly chuckled.

'The Americans are mental in that they will have a different sniper rifle for the marines, army, SEALS, you name it. They get pretty anal about their weapons—well, they're American, aren't they? Born with a gun in their hand and all that crap.

They have them customised and fitted by a gunsmith to be 'their' rifle. The Brits aren't such loonies.'

'So are their guns better, then?' Kelly asked.

'That's like asking a builder which is the best power drill. He might have a preference, but it's more a case of the skill of the bloke using it, rather than the equipment. I fear the man holding the gun, not the gun itself. If he knows what he's doing, you're fucked. If he doesn't then you've got a good chance of survival.'

'Can you tell me more about your life?' Kelly asked.

'There's not a lot to tell. I was adopted. Didn't know my natural mum or dad. They were from Inverness, I think. I ended up in a children's home by the age of fourteen. My adoptive parents couldn't handle me. Understandable, really. Once I was told I'd been adopted I was a right little shit. So I was sent packing. To be honest, the care home was perfect for me. It was full of little scallywags like myself. It was lawless, but I loved it.'

'Didn't you miss your adopted parents at all?' Kelly asked.

'Not at all. It's weird but I always felt I was adopted. That they weren't part of me. When they finally told me the truth, I went right off the rails. Then I signed up for the army on my 16th birthday and finally I knew I was home. Travelling, drinking, women, and guns. And being paid for it all. I loved it. The beauty was, if you showed any signs of being halfway intelligent—being able to write your own name was a good start—then they promoted you. I soon realised I could go far. Especially since I was a shit-hot sniper. There's a lot of maths that go into shooting from long range, but I just had a knack for it.'

'Sounds very James Bond,' Kelly replied.

'Nah. For the most part it was sitting in the same spot for maybe three days on end doing recon. Then it's all about endurance. The training was to see how you perform when you're fatigued. But I was always a mentally strong bastard. I would never fall asleep, even when I was so knackered every molecule in my body was screaming out for it.'

'Funny, that sounds like me after four straight night shifts in a row,' Kelly chuckled.

'Actually, you're probably right. I'd never thought of nurses like that before. You still have to perform to the best of your abilities regardless of whether it's your fifth night or your first. It's the same with us. I'd say the single biggest battle in my line of work is fatigue. Just never figured it'd be the same for you. You'd make a good soldier.'

They both laughed then Kelly kissed Monahan on the lips before she manoeuvred herself into position on top of him, ready to go again.

43

Busted

Connor watched April waving frantically in the parking lot. It wasn't at him, but at another driver. He grabbed his man-bag from the passenger seat, locked up, then decided to watch what unfolded, just out of morbid curiosity. April was now doing her full semaphore signal routine, like those people with the orange paddles at airports, as she directed the driver into the space beside her car. Remarkably, April had managed to park between the designated lines for once, and not straddling two bays as she usually did.

Connor began his slow approach, intrigued to see who April's mystery driver was. The stranger stepped out of his car and was greeted by a gasp from the ageing reporter. 'I'm so sorry, I thought you were someone else.'

The man chuckled. 'Well, thanks for finding me a space anyway,' he smiled as he walked away.

'Did you think that was me, you daft old bat?' Connor asked.

April turned round, red with embarrassment. 'He has the same car as you. Look, it's even the same colour.'

'*Was* the same colour. I got rid of the silver one a year ago. I've got a red one now. A bit like your face.' Connor switched to baby talk: 'Do you see my big red car over there?'

'A year? I was just so pleased about getting into the parking lot before you.'

'Hell will freeze over before that happens,' he replied as they headed in the direction of the Peccadillo. 'Remember the time I was coming back from Canada and made it into work before you?'

'Oh, you'll never let me live that down, will you?'

'Come on, it was pretty funny. The red-eye from Toronto to Glasgow and, knowing you're always ten minutes late, I could pick up my luggage and still make it in before you. Priceless.'

April started to laugh, so much she had to stop walking. 'That man must've thought I was some sort of mad woman directing him into his parking space.'

'Yip. And he'd be bang on the money. Listen, I'm going to skip breakfast again this morning. I want to see if Kelly has been found yet.'

'And you can't do that from your phone? Don't be daft. Breakfast first—you might not know when you'll get to eat again.'

'Yes, Mum,' Connor replied as he walked and messaged DCI Crosbie at the same time. *Heard anything, Bing?*

The three dots appeared on Connor's screen as the detective messaged Connor back. *Not yet. Although I've been told the bosses are going mad over your use of the word 'kidnapped' in your front-page headline.*

Connor knew why Crosbie was worried about that one. *I don't write the headlines.*

It was in your copy too!!!

He had Connor there. *I got that from a source.*

Well, that source is now regretting using that word.

That's always the case when people see it in black and white. Anyway, give me a shout if you hear anything.

Will do. But I don't start my shift in the call centre 'til 12.

Connor checked his watch then, out of devilment, texted back. *Well, you better boot Amy Jones out of bed as I bet she starts at 10.*

There were no dots this time and Connor imagined Bing showing Amy his text in bed. Eventually the one word response came through—*Busted*—causing the reporter to laugh.

'What's so funny?' April asked as they approached the entrance of the Peccadillo.

'Nothing much,' Connor giggled. 'Question: would you ever sleep with someone for a story?'

'Not again,' April said with a smile, which left her younger colleague wondering if she was kidding or not.

44

A whore's bath

Kelly was woken by a gentle knock at her door.

'Time to get up, hen.'

It was Duggie. Despite the early hour, Kelly smiled to herself; she liked how he called her 'hen', an exclusively Scottish term for a woman.

'I've got you a cuppa,' he added as he pushed open the door to the bedroom, his bulky outline filling the entire frame.

'Here you go. In ten minutes we have to be outside. I'll leave you to it.'

She smiled and thanked him, propping herself up on the pillows to drink her tea. She could feel she was still wet down below. Kelly hadn't had sex for as long as she could remember, but she recalled all too well the aftermath, usually stuffing a pair of knickers between her legs to make sure she wasn't left sleeping on a wet patch. Although, she was now slightly concerned that she hadn't taken any precautions. Kelly hadn't been on the pill since she was in her early twenties. She felt like a naughty teenager who had just done something she shouldn't have. She rather liked the feeling. She felt desirable again. Not a word she would had attributed to herself since her pert and nubile days as a blossoming young adult.

She finished her tea then washed herself at the sink: face, hands, armpits then between her legs. A classic 'whore's bath'. She giggled at the term.

Duggie and Monahan were waiting in the lounge. They were in full camouflage gear. Monahan had even blackened his wheelchair.

'Like it?' he asked, spinning around.

Kelly smiled again. 'You'll certainly have the element of surprise, that's for sure. So, what's the plan? What am I to do?'

Monahan set out in detail what they had arranged. Occasionally Kelly would ask a question, but most of the time she let him talk. Duggie was strangely quiet. She thought that may have been because he was in operation mode: in the zone and ready for action. The big man didn't utter a word. He barely looked in her direction. At the end of the briefing, Kelly made a point of brushing Duggie's arm gently and asking, 'Alright?'

'Aye, hen. Aye.' He looked sad. Kelly wondered why.

All three of them took to the Land Rover, with Monahan behind the wheel. Duggie sat in front, taking the safety catch off his machine gun. Kelly was in the back on the edge of her seat, with her arms resting behind each man's shoulders.

She was excited. She knew she shouldn't be, but she was.

45

Translation

Connor had put a call into Police Scotland's media team, and got the official response that there was no update on the whereabouts of Kelly Carter. But they did tell him that they had launched one of the biggest manhunts in recent memory, with over 100 police officers assigned to the case. That alone was enough to give him a line for the news editor's insatiable daily list.

Connor filed the story, which had about four paragraphs of new information, with the rest padded out with recycled material about the firefight at the farmhouse in Bannockburn. After that Connor had pretty much nothing else to do other than hope and pray DCI Crosbie would come up with a sighting of the missing nurse.

A reminder notification popped up on his email. 'Shit, we've got another bloody address to the masses in five minutes,' Connor moaned.

'What is it this time? Are they shutting us down?' April asked, with dread all over her face.

'Not yet. It's our "digital future", apparently. Not that we have one since they started charging people to read us online. I heard the figures are shocking.

'What does *Mail Online* get every day?' April asked.

'Thirteen million hits. And rising.'

April liked *Mail Online*, mainly for the so-called 'sidebar of shame', which was the paparazzi snaps of celebrities she'd never heard of on a beach she'd never been to. But she was addicted to looking at their honed physiques and six-pack midriffs. 'How does Mail Online make money if they don't charge?' she asked as they made their way to the fourth floor conference room.

'I haven't the foggiest. Adverts, I'd imagine. I don't know about you, but I always shut down any pop-ups immediately.'

'What's a pop-up?'

'For f . . . It's just as the name suggests. A little pop-up advert that appears on the screen of your app. You probably think cookies are for eating.'

'I could murder a cookie right now.'

'You've just had breakfast. You're a bloody bottomless pit.'

They had their pick of the seats in the conference room. They could both remember a time when there were so many staff it was standing-room only at any company announcement. Now it was something of a ghost town.

'Thank you for taking time out from your busy days,' the Chief Executive Officer said, beginning his address via video-link from the *Daily Chronicle*'s London HQ.

'Not that we had much choice,' Connor said under his breath.

'Today we have exciting news about our vision for taking the company forward,' the CEO continued.

'Job cuts,' Connor whispered, causing April to snigger.

'To keep pace with the constantly changing digital world we have to adapt accordingly.'

'Definitely job cuts,' Connor said again, with two of his colleagues from the newsdesk now trying to stifle their laughter at his running commentary.

'To do that, we need to be out there in the wider market. So our stories can be shared the world over. The only way we can do that is to end our online subscription service. We have learnt a lot from this experiment.'

'Lost millions,' Connor whispered.

'And we will take those lessons forward with us. Over the coming months we will begin implementing a restructuring of the company.'

'Oh, you better believe there'll be job cuts.'

'It will start with my decision to step down as CEO of this magnificent company.'

'Given the bump.'

'This will allow new blood to come in with new ideas.'

'Someone younger and cheaper,' Connor continued.

'Who will be able to take the company forward to the next level.'

'Several rungs down from where we are now.'

'I shall give a more precise leaving date once we have informed our shareholders. But until then we shall hopefully have time to have a farewell glass of Chianti,' the CEO concluded.

'Ff-ff-ff-ff,' Connor said, giving his best Hannibal Lecter impression. By now the whole room was chuckling at Connor's quips, safe in the knowledge that it was only a one-way video-link.

46

Boulder

The rough road came to a clearing by a river and Monahan explained that he would need to stay with the Land Rover while Kelly went by foot with Duggie. His plan was to use Kelly as bait, to flush out the man he called a traitor. It was a high-risk operation but with a little bit of luck they would soon be back in the vehicle bumping their way over what passed for a road to safety.

Kelly followed Duggie like an obedient dog for more than an hour. The sun rose up over the Cairngorm peaks, smoothed into giant black humps that looked like a pod of whales in the half-light.

She hadn't gone hiking in years. The last time had been with Brian before they were married. They'd climbed the Cobbler on the brilliantly named Arrochar Alps mountain range, drank themselves stupid in the local inn, then shagged themselves silly in a tent. But Kelly hated camping. You had to be drunk to get any sort of sleep, but drinking made you constantly need to pee. It wasn't long before she insisted on a B&B instead, forcing Brian to go camping on his own. She could never figure out the attraction, but he truly loved the great outdoors, hiking all day then sleeping on a bed as hard as the rock underneath it.

How she hoped the kids would be safe with him. The thought stiffened her resolve, banishing any remaining nerves, readying her for what was to come. They approached the crest of a hill, making sure to stay off the horizon, where they'd be more visible. Duggie silently indicated for her to crouch low. Hugging the terrain he then crawled towards a cliff edge. Kelly followed. Duggie eventually stopped crawling, took a small but powerful pair of binoculars from a pocket somewhere and scanned the gorge below. He then handed them to Kelly and pointed at a spot far below. Kelly peered at a brilliantly green-coloured loch, which had a small stretch of narrow golden beach.

Duggie whispered, 'See that boulder on the beach. It's surprisingly smooth from being sat on by a thousand arse cheeks. Sit on that and wait. I'll be ready.' He slipped his backpack off and placed it in front of him. Within moments he had assembled a powerful rifle with a sophisticated-looking sight. 'I'll leave my backpack on the edge of the cliff. It will look like a rock from down there. As long as you can see the backpack then you know I'm there. If it's gone then so am I. This goes everywhere with me.'

Duggie pointed towards a path and told her to head down to the loch. 'Good luck. Once we've flushed this bastard out we can take it from there.'

Kelly trudged down to the loch, dodging low branches and climbing over tangled tree roots exposed by the elements. Without Duggie's big frame traipsing along in front of her she suddenly felt all alone. She eventually reached the boulder on the beach. He was right: it was surprisingly smooth and comfortable. Kelly looked back to the cliff ridge to see the outline of Duggie's backpack. She felt reassured he was watching over her.

Now the second part of the plan was to swing into operation as Duggie would radio Monahan. He would also email, text and call Monahan, safe in the knowledge that at least one form of their communications was being monitored. They would then sit it out and see who came calling. Monahan was most insistent that it wouldn't be the police. An hour passed. Then another. Kelly was just beginning to wonder what to do when a hand cupped her mouth and she was dragged silently from the boulder out of sight into the undergrowth. She was briefly able to glance towards the ridge, expecting to see a flash of light as Duggie the expert marksman came to her rescue.

But there was nothing. Not even his backpack.

Kelly was flipped onto her front and her hands were quickly fastened behind her back with plastic ties. She was then turned onto her back with ease, as if she was nothing more than a rag doll. She looked up at the faces of half a dozen men in the same black survival clothes worn by Monahan and Duggie. She knew there would be no one rushing to her rescue this time.

She felt used and abused by Monahan, just as she had all those years ago when she lost her virginity to a boy who didn't deserve it.

Kelly felt a jab in her right arm as one of the men roughly administered some sort of fast-acting sedative. Her eyelids suddenly became heavy and she wanted to sleep, but she was still eerily aware of what was going on. It was a bit like being able to hear a party in full swing in a neighbour's house but you can't join in.

At some point, she can't remember when, the men in black handed her over to some other men in a building that looked like a doctor's surgery. One that hadn't opened yet as most of the lights were off or dimmed. A man in a suit led her to a room where he examined her, so she figured he must have been a doctor. He looked everywhere, giving her an internal examination before deciding to swab her vagina. She heard him say, 'This one's been busy—we'll soon find out if it was with Monahan.'

Afterwards she was strong-armed into another vehicle and sandwiched between two men in the back seat. *Psychie nurses*, Kelly thought to herself. She always claimed she was able to spot a psychiatric nurse. 'They are as crazy as their patients,' an old nursing sister once told her.

The car or bus, or whatever she was in, seemed to be in transit for hours. Kelly was quite enjoying the detached feeling. It was as if she was floating. She didn't have a care in the world.

Not of the kids. Brian. Thoughts of her mother. Her late father. Monahan. Doctor Shabazi. Nothing at all stayed in her mind long enough to elicit any sort of emotion. Kelly wondered if this was what junkies experienced. Heroin taking them to a place they never wanted to leave, and where they would do anything—including rob from their own grannies—to stay there. She understood now. It was nice to take a holiday from it all. A brain-break, Kelly decided to name it. She chuckled to herself. The chuckle soon became a hearty laugh. Eventually she couldn't stop.

'Brain-break,' she said, laughing louder and louder. 'I'm off on a brain-break. Wish you were here.'

Kelly felt another prick in her arm and she turned groggily to see one of the psychiatric nurses giving her an injection. Within minutes she fell fast asleep. She would stay that way for the rest of the journey.

47

Loose woman

'Heard anything, Bing?' Connor asked DCI Crosbie after getting no new information through official police channels.

'Only that I am a fucking great lover,' DCI Crosbie replied.

'Sorry to burst your bubble, pal, but I bet Amy Jones says the same to everyone,' Connor replied. He was not in the mood to play his usual game of cat and mouse with the detective for information.

'Are you saying my girl is a loose woman?' DCI Crosbie said with mock hurt.

'If it was the 1950s I might use "loose woman", but frankly I couldn't care what anyone gets up to between the sheets. All I'm telling you, fella, is she uses it.'

'Well, she uses it fucking well, let me tell you.'

'I'd rather you didn't. This isn't behind the bike sheds.'

'Well, funnily enough she dressed up as a slutty schoolgirl the other day, and I was to be a strict cunt of a headmaster. Quick as a fucking flash she whipped off her . . .'

'And she just so happened to have all these role-play costumes handy, did she?' Connor asked suspiciously.

'Come to think of it, she did have quite a few to choose from.'

'I bet. Will it be the naughty nun tonight? The lesbian librarian? The knickerless nurse?'

'Fucking hell, Elvis, are you psychic?'

'No, I'm just pointing out that it's a routine, Bing. To keep getting info out of you. But she will burn you and move on. She always does.'

'Yeah, but until then, what a ride.'

'She's dangerous, Bing.'

'Now you just sound jealous. And let's be honest here, Elvis, it's a lot better than the occasional meal or drink you take me for.'

'Oh, have I not been paying you enough attention, darling? Sorry, I promise to make it up to you.'

'Good. I look forward to it. Until then, if you don't mind, I'll continue pumping away with Miss Jones.'

'I give up. Don't say I didn't warn you. Please tell me if you hear anything about the real nurse before you shag the naughty one,' Connor said, hanging up. Sometimes he genuinely despaired at his fellow man's total absence of rationality when it came to sex.

48

Nurse Drury

Kelly woke in the same daze she'd felt before being forced to sleep. She had no idea how long she'd been out of it, but she felt in no way rested.

'So you're awake, are ye?' a voice said in a broad Ayrshire accent.

Kelly was always amazed that there were so many dialects for such a small country. She wanted to answer but couldn't: the words in her brain wouldn't form in her mouth. She managed to shift her eyes to see the source of the voice. Sitting in the corner was an obese male nurse. He stood up to approach Kelly's bed, his tire rolls of fat wobbling under his blue tunic, which was too small for his bulk, but probably the largest made for the NHS. And in her experience the NHS made some very large uniforms.

He leaned over her and smiled. His front row of teeth, top and bottom, had rotted down to black and brown stubs. His breath emitted a hideous odour, like meat that had gone off, and Kelly felt her stomach turn. She had never seen or smelled such a repulsive member of her profession. Kelly had no idea nurses like this even existed anymore, he was like a throwback to the Victorian asylums.

'Ahm Nurse Drury, but ma pals call me Jim. You can call me Jim if ye want tae as I just know we're gonna be pals. Right lets dae yer vital signs, and see what's what.'

Jim checked Kelly's chart, scanning a page, before flipping over to the next one. 'So you're called Kirsty Adams and ye've been sectioned 'cos ye were threatening folks. Uch, that's no very nice, Kirsty,' he smirked.

Kirsty Adams? Kirsty Adams? You've got the wrong person, Kelly wanted to shout but couldn't.

'Oh aye, what huv we got here? You've been swabbed doon below. Says ye were working as a prostitute. Funny, ye dinny look like a dirty, wee prossie. We get loads in here. Maist are junkies. But ye look awright. Ye must be wan of those high-class prossies,' he said, with glee in his eyes.

He began to slowly roll up the sleeve on Kelly's hospital-issue, starched pajamas, taking his time—too much time, Kelly thought. He was clearly getting some sort of thrill from the experience. 'Nice arm,' he whispered. Kelly had never been complimented on her arm before. 'A little thin, mind you, but we'll soon fatten you up,' Jim continued. But it wasn't just her arms he was interested in. Jim gently pulled her pajamas up to expose her breasts, making some sort of noise of appreciation. Kelly tensed inside but again she was powerless to defend herself.

'I just need to give you a mammary examination, make sure there are no lumps.'

Jim cupped Kelly's left breast with both hands.

'Oh yes,' he groaned, 'what a perfect specimen.' He slowly moved his hands over to the next breast and began to knead and massage it too. 'Oh aye. Oh, that's magic. Fucking magic.' Jim spread his hands over both Kelly's breasts and squeezed them so tightly it hurt. His whole body shuddered as he stood motionless for several moments. He pulled Kelly's pajama top back down.

'We must dae that again sometime. But don't go telling anyone. It'll be oor wee secret.' Jim seemed awful pleased with himself as he returned to his seat, with a visible stain at his crotch.

'Uch, look what you've made me dae. I've goan and made a mess aw masel.'

Jim dabbed at his crotch with some paper towels from the sink, before collapsing in the armchair. Moments later he was snoring loudly.

Kelly tried to force her muscles into action. Even if she could turn her head she would get some orientation. She didn't even know what time of day it was. Using all her willpower and strength to fight against the drugs, she managed to move ever so slightly. The room had a row of small windows along the top of one side. Too narrow for anyone to fit through, and too high to reach. They had either been blacked out or it was night-time.

The place had the feel of a nightshift, as there wasn't the noise and bustle you get on a hospital ward in daytime. Jim had felt comfortable enough to molest her without being caught, which also suggested it was some time in the wee small hours.

Kelly had once spent a month on assignment on a mental health ward during her training. She'd hated every minute of it. But she recalled how a fellow student, Angela McKerney, had been right at home. This had been Angela's calling in life. She had loved working with damaged minds, explaining to Kelly how there was no bigger satisfaction than seeing someone who is so ill they can't walk or talk, return to the community as a functioning human being. Kelly could empathise with that—she knew for herself how fragile people's mental health can be.

She could still hear Angela's words in her ears: 'Sometimes folk just fall off the end of the Earth for a while.' But Kelly knew she just didn't have the patience. Angela had told her what the problem was: 'You're trying to apply your rational thinking to a brain that is broken.'

Now here she was, trapped and overly medicated. Thankfully she could still think clearly, even if she couldn't act on her thoughts. She would need to attempt something. She just had no idea what. Kelly closed her eyes to think. This time she fell into the deep sleep she so desperately needed.

49

The hunt

'I've rung around every hospital in Scotland and not one of them has admitted a Kelly Carter,' April complained as she slammed her pen onto her notepad and took off her reading glasses to rub where they pinched her nose. She had decided to check accident and emergency rooms in case Kelly had been injured in the firefight at Bannockburn. It was a long shot, but desperate times called for desperate measures.

'Maybe she hasn't been registered yet?' Connor suggested helpfully.

'What do you mean?'

'My aunt's a district nurse. Has been for forty-odd years. She had to have patients' doors booted in by the cops several times when she couldn't get anyone to answer. That's despite going through all the procedures by calling the patient's GP to see if the patient was there. Then the hospital. When all that failed, the last resort would be two big polis kicking their way into some old dear's flat. Never once were they lying dead behind the door. She said they usually had been admitted to hospital but hadn't been registered yet. The admission system didn't improve with computerisation. So my aunt's missing patient was usually lying in a hospital bed or still in the back of an ambulance while she was having some unscheduled DIY done to their homes. The old dears probably died of shock when they came back to find the council had fitted a new steel door for them.'

'Interesting. Moving a patient from hospital to hospital might also be a good way of keeping them off the system. Especially if you knew people were looking for them,' April pondered.

'Or, if they were totally out of it, you could give them a false name. Then you'd have no chance,' Connor concluded.

April stared at all the notes and numbers she'd scribbled down in her notepad and knew that if someone had changed her name, as Connor suggested, then her hunt for the missing Kelly Carter was futile.

50

A guardian angel

Kelly had no idea how long she had been on the ward. For all she knew, it could have been days or weeks. But she had got to know the routine. Every morning two members of the auxiliary staff would give her a bed bath. They would talk to her and ask her how she was feeling. When she could barely grunt a reply, they'd look dolefully at each other and mutter sentiments like, 'That's a shame.' Kelly would be spoon-fed while more medicine was then administered through a needle or by mouth. She dreaded the handover to the night staff, fearing that the pervert, Jim, would be on. He would fondle her breasts roughly until he was satisfied, but, fortunately, he did no more than that. Kelly loathed the man. He wasn't just a disgrace to the profession she loved, he was a disgrace to the human race.

But this morning, an auxiliary called Cathy told Kelly that the lawyer was coming onto the ward. Kelly didn't even know lawyers visited mental health wards. But Cathy explained it was part of the procedure for a court-appointed lawyer to interview anyone who had been sectioned to ask if they believed they were wrongly being detained against their will. If the patient said they were, the lawyer would take their case before a Mental Health Tribunal.

Cathy whispered into her ear, 'If the lawyer asks if you want help, try your best to make a noise. I know you're no mental— it's that medication they've got you on.'

Kelly liked Cathy. She was looking out for her, like a good nurse should.

'She's coming now. Try your best, hen,' Cathy said, offering some final words of encouragement.

The lawyer looked like a lawyer, in her pencil skirt suit and briefcase. She was young and pretty but wore a severe look on her face, probably in an effort to be taken seriously. She was all business, like her clothing, requesting that the staff leave the room so she could talk to the patient alone. Cathy offered to stay to help, but the lawyer dismissed her out of hand.

When they were alone, the lawyer tried what could have passed for a smile. 'Hello Kirsty, I'm Fiona McDade. I'm a lawyer. As part of the free advocacy service under the Mental Health Act I am here to make sure patients are not being illegally held against their will. Kirsty Adams, do you feel you are being held against your will?'

There was a long silence as Kelly tried her hardest to respond. Inside, she was screaming, 'YES!' but outwardly she was silent, her movements restricted to a widening of her eyes and flaring of her nostrils.

The lawyer softened her tone slightly. 'Are they over-medicating you? Is it the drugs that have left you like this?'

Kelly's eyes opened even wider, but yet again no noise would come.

'Okay, I am going to leave you my card. You are well within your rights to call me at any time.'

Call? Call? How could she call when she couldn't even speak, never mind move.

The lawyer looked pitifully at the figure in the bed. She instinctively knew the patient needed her help but, without the consent, there was nothing she could do.

The room door opened gently as Cathy the auxiliary nurse let herself in.

'Do you mind?' the lawyer said sternly. 'I am trying to conduct an interview with a potential client here.'

'Aye, aye, don't get your silk knickers in a twist,' Cathy said, approaching the bed. She freed Kelly's left hand, which had been tucked tight under the sheets, and placed it in the law-yer's. 'Now Kirsty, hen, squeeze once for no and twice for yes, understand?'

The lawyer felt a faint but definite squeeze of her hand. And then again.

'Good, lass. Right, now ask your question,' Cathy said to the lawyer.

'Do you feel you are being held against your will?' Fiona McDade repeated.

Again the lawyer felt Kelly squeeze her hand twice.

'Are they over-medicating you?'

Two more squeezes.

'Would you like me to represent you?'

This time there was a slight delay before Kelly squeezed the lawyer's hand. The second one made Fiona McDade wince with pain.

51

The snatch

April looked glum as she put the phone down on another wasted call. 'That's the prison service. I thought I'd see if they had a Kelly Carter in their custody. Yet another blank. I am now officially all out of ideas,' she said, flummoxed.

'I'm going to hit her ex-husband's door today. See if he'll cough,' Connor said.

'Good plan.'

• • •

Connor and Jack Barr pulled up outside Brian Fairburn's flat in Kilsyth. Kelly had ditched her married name the day their divorce was complete.

There was no one more cynical and battle-weary in the business than Barr. Connor and all the other reporters were prepared to put up with JB's mumps and moans as he was probably the best snapper there was at 'snatches'—the age-old art of newspaper photographs capturing someone in the split-second they leave their house, car or place of business. Barr revelled in his reputation as the 'snatch king'.

Their simple plan was to knock on Brian's door to ask if he knew Kelly's whereabouts. If they couldn't get Brian, they would knock on the neighbours' doors to find out what they knew. Judging by the look of the block of flats—all smart windowboxes and well-kept communal grounds—most of the residents were probably elderly. Which would mean nosy neighbours.

But just as Connor was about to open the passenger door, there was a knock at the window. A grey-haired, stocky man in a black suit was blocking Connor from getting out.

'Not today, lads,' he said through the crack in the door, in a no-nonsense tone that immediately had him marked down as a cop in Connor's book. The last time he saw an officer like that they were from the Royal Protection Squad. Or shadowing the Prime or First Minister. They were the type who wore a permanent scowl and didn't do small talk.

'And why not?' was all Connor could think to say, having been unexpectedly confronted.

'Because I said so,' was the menacing reply.

'So much for freedom of the press,' Connor said lamely.

'Boo hoo, take it up with your MP,' came the mocking reply.

Connor looked at the photographer, who shrugged his shoulders.

'Okay, well, you have a nice day, officer,' Connor said in defeat.

'Don't you worry, I will,' the cop replied. 'Now off you fuck.'

Connor was raging with himself as they drove off. He'd come away empty-handed. Not only that, but he had also been bullied by a policeman, which wasn't something that had happened before. It was usually the other way around. Connor loved standing his ground with the flat foots at crime scenes as he knew the law better than they did. But he hadn't even had the chance to go toe to toe with this hard case. He'd been blindsided and he wasn't happy.

'Seen that bastard before?' Barr asked as they drove back to the office.

'Nope, but I'd love to know what unit he's from.'

'Maybe your cop contacts can help. Here, show them this.' Barr handed a tiny Sure Shot camera to Connor. On the back screen was a picture of the man who had blocked them from doing their jobs. It may have been taken from an awkward angle, but it was sharp as a tack.

'You might be a moany bastard, JB, but no one can take a snatch like you.'

Something that passed for a smile broke across Jack Barr's craggy, weathered face.

52

The tribunal

Fiona McDade had submitted an emergency motion to the Mental Health Tribunal. The lawyer had grave and immediate concerns for the wellbeing of a patient called Kirsty Adams. As far as she was concerned, her client was being deliberately over-medicated to keep her sedated and was being held against her will. The papers showed no criminal charges were pending and there was no suggestion that the patient was a danger to anyone other than herself.

Legally, the tribunal had five working days to report their primary assessment, but they only took twenty-four hours before Fiona McDade was summoned before the board.

Fiona was well known to the panel and prided herself on being a constant thorn in their sides as she had made mental health cases her specialty. There were easier ways of making money, but since learning her own grandmother had been sectioned for falling pregnant as an unmarried eighteen-year-old, she had made it her life's work. It was the reason she studied law in the first place. Times had moved on since the days of forced adoptions and teenagers of legal age being wrenched from their family homes. But, as far as Fiona was concerned, our mental health treatment still left a lot to be desired. There were some staff still working who had once administered electro-shock treatment and claimed it had been a travesty when the method of literally frying patients' brains had been abolished.

One such nurse was Jim Drury, who was a dinosaur of the profession if ever there was one. Fiona had raised three gross misconduct cases against the obese male nurse on behalf of three separate clients, only to see them all thrown out. At the end of the day it was the word of damaged minds against that of a cunning and warped one. But Fiona was on Jim's case. She was determined to stop the arrogant son of a bitch. So she had been more than alarmed to see from Kelly's medical notes that Jim Drury was her night nurse. She knew what happened when Drury was left to his own devices.

Fiona was fired up and in full flow when she came face to face with the board. As the meeting was opened with the usual formalities, she butted in: 'Let's cut to the chase: what are you doing about my client, Kirsty Adams?'

'Miss McDade . . .' the chairman of the board, Mr. Russell Richards, began.

'Don't "Miss McDade" me. Just tell me right now what you are doing to stop the over-medication of my client, Kirsty Adams.'

'Miss McDade . . .' Mr. Richards sighed, 'if you would allow me to speak.'

'Well, get to the point then, would you?' Fiona snapped.

Russell Richards was a retired mental health consultant who had crossed swords with Fiona McDade on several occasions. He had once privately told her she was heading for a break-down if she continued to overwork herself and didn't learn to relax. His advice had clearly fallen on deaf ears. Fiona McDade was more manic than ever.

'If you would be quiet for one moment, Miss McDade,' Mr. Richards said sharply, 'then I'll tell you. I went to see your client personally but was unable to help.'

Fiona McDade's face went crimson as she was about to fly off the handle.

'And before you give me an ear-bashing,' Mr. Richards continued, 'the reason I was unable to help is because she is no longer a patient of NHS Glasgow or, indeed, any other trust. Kirsty Adams has been discharged. She's gone, Miss McDade. Case closed.'

53

Hips

Connor was in a filthy mood when he returned to the broom cupboard. But there wasn't anything in the world that couldn't be cured by a cup of tea, as far as April was concerned.

Connor moaned his head off on the way to the 'breakout area', that horrible modern management term for a falling-apart kitchen with a few tables and chairs. 'In the old days, they had a canteen,' he had once remarked. The *Daily Chronicle* had long since moved offices from a rundown Victorian warehouse to a stainless steel and glass city centre building. Connor missed the old dump as at least it had character. They also seemed to have more fun back then. Like the time management had held a competition amongst staff to come up with a new name for the canteen to coincide with its 'refurbishment', a grand title for a lick of paint and the replacement of a few cracked floor tiles. Connor had gleefully sent in his suggestions, including, 'The Slug And Lettuce', 'Burger Ming' and 'Can't Cook, Won't Cook'.

The last had been in reference to the time he'd asked one of the surly school dinnerlady types for a cheese toastie. In tones that could have greatly benefitted from customer service training, she'd replied that there was 'nae cheese'. While Connor was deciding what other delicacy to choose from the array of delights on offer—from bloated, soggy pasta to a sad, burnt slice of pizza—the dinner lady demanded, 'Dae yae no want yer toastie?'

She stood behind the counter wearing an outraged look and no gloves while holding two slices of bread.

Connor was confused. 'But I thought you said there was no cheese?'

'Aye,' was all she replied, as if speaking to an imbecile.

'Then that's just toast.'

Strangely, he missed those days. Back then, editorial shared the building with the vast print works and the smell of ink. Connor had made friends with many of the 'inkies', the print workers who operated the machinery. And, despite their unions having long since been tamed, they still drove flashier cars than most of the reporters.

Now Connor and April worked in the equivalent of a call centre. There was no atmosphere and large-scale redundancies meant there was no buzz either.

'I miss smoking at my desk,' April said fondly.

'You still pretending you've quit?'

'Shhh,' she said, looking over her shoulder as if she was about to be busted. 'My daughter will kill me if she finds out. She made me promise to quit once and for all, and so I have. For good. Kinda.'

'Well, you always were a woman of conviction.'

They got themselves a couple of weak coffees from the free vending machine, a management compromise for ditching the canteen when they relocated premises.

'I'm pissed off allowing myself to get pushed around like that. I should've stood my ground with that cop.'

'Easier said than done after the event. But when he's sprung on you like that . . .' April sympathised.

Connor liked the way that April always backed him up even when he hadn't been at his best. 'Thanks. I'll be better prepared next time. JB got a cracking snatch of the bastard. Going to run it past Bing to see if I can find out who he is.'

'And I've got some lawyer to call back. She's a friend of a friend who says she has a story for me,' April said, rolling her eyes. 'It'll probably be about a client's damp council house. Why do people always think that's a story? I mean when has the *Daily Chronicle* ever done a story on a damp council house?'

164 | Matt Bendoris

'You never know, she may have just found Lord Lucan. If you're Lucan for trouble . . .?' Connor said in his best Elvis voice.

'. . .You came to the right place,' April replied, with a shake of her prominent hips.

54

M74

Kelly was in the back of yet another vehicle and heading once again to a destination unknown. She had been hastily discharged from hospital, for reasons she couldn't fathom, and was then picked up by complete strangers. With the break to her routine it had been a while since her last medication and the veil of her drug-induced existence was starting to lift. But she didn't recognise any of the roads until they hit the M74, heading south to the border with England.

No one spoke in the car, which was fine as Kelly didn't feel like speaking even if she could, but she vowed to pay close attention to the road signs and junction numbers in case she was able to call for help at some point in the future.

The occupants of the car were unaware she was taking anything in as a long line of saliva hung from Kelly's mouth. She felt the strength returning to her hands, but resisted the urge to remove the drool. It was best to keep up the pretence that she was still in a world of her own.

Now her priorities were to get back to the real world. And Kelly was determined to make it.

55

Never judge a book by its cover

'Hello, is that Fiona? This is April Lavender from the *Daily Chronicle*. Sorry I missed your call earlier.'

'Can we meet?' came the terse reply from the lawyer.

'Of course, there's a coffee shop on Royal Exchange Square.'

'I know it. See you there in twenty minutes.'

April didn't even know what this Fiona character looked like. But she reckoned she would know her when she saw her. From the tone and urgency of her voice, April suspected a damp council house was the last thing on the lawyer's mind.

• • •

Fiona was almost exactly as April had expected, although she looked younger than she sounded. She was certainly as highly strung as the reporter had thought she'd be, puffing on a cigarette outside the coffee shop as April arrived.

'April, isn't it? Fiona McDade.'

'How did you know?' April asked, wondering if she looked just as she sounded on the phone.

'I Googled you,' Fiona replied, without any trace of a smile.

'Oh yes, apparently I'm on many Internets,' April said with a flash of her gold incisor tooth.

Fiona frowned slightly. 'That doesn't make any sense. You will be found through most search engines, but there is only one Internet.'

April laughed at her own stupidity. It wasn't the first time she had been told by a total stranger she wasn't making sense. 'Sorry, I'm hopeless with technology. Totally hopeless. Now let me get the coffees and we'll sit outside so I can join you for a smoke.'

Fiona gave her order then eyed up April as she made her way into the chain coffee shop with its perpetually cheery baristas. The lawyer was beginning to think she'd made a terrible mistake. The old dear was clearly past it. April had come highly recommended, but maybe that was from yesteryear, as everything about her screamed of faded glory—from the harsh, peroxide hair to the clothes that were clearly bought a few dress sizes ago. She just didn't seem to have the wherewithal for what needed to be told. Fiona made her mind up, put her cigarettes back in her bag and got up to leave.

'Uch, I'm not that boring, am I?' April said with her usual self-deprecation as she arrived back with the coffees just as her subject was about to scarper.

'Sorry, I've made a mistake. It's my fault. I shouldn't have wasted your time.'

'That's okay, but I've got the coffees now. Sit with me for five minutes. Have another ciggie.'

Fiona looked at the smiling moon face staring back at her then checked her watch and, deciding to go against her better instinct, she sat back down.

'I know I might not be what you were expecting, Fiona, but I was like you once. I was even as skinny as you, as hard as that is to believe now,' April added, patting her hips.

Fiona smiled, something she hadn't done in a while.

'But I'm a good listener. And also if I can't help, I know someone who can.'

Fiona sighed heavily, took a sip of coffee then lit another cigarette as she weighed up April's offer. 'Okay, here goes. But I will tell you this on the cast iron guarantee that you act fast. Believe me, speed is everything. We don't have much time to save a life. I have a client called Kirsty Adams, who's been held on a mental health ward. Although now I realise her name isn't really Kirsty Adams. It's the missing nurse, Kelly Carter.'

'I knew the bastards must have changed her name,' April said a little too loudly, earning glances from the neighbouring tables. 'I checked everywhere. Thank God you've found her.'

'*Had* found her,' Fiona said. 'I'm afraid Kelly Carter has gone missing again.'

56

Smash and grab

The car that Kelly was sitting in had an expensive feel to it—from the black leather seats to the array of buttons including temperature control. The windows were tinted, making the interior dark and gloomy even though it was bright outside.

A stern-looking driver shot her an occasional glance in his rear-view mirror, as if checking his captive was still there. He needn't have worried: Kelly knew there was no hope of escape, especially while the car was hurtling down the M74. Another male sat in the front passenger seat and had one of those child mirrors Kelly used to have when her kids were young, to keep an eye on what was happening in the back. The men up front had a military look to them: square haircuts, wide shoulders, permanent scowls and eyes that constantly scanned for danger.

Sitting next to her was the obese male nurse, Jim Drury, who was barely able to fit in the rear seat, despite it being a large car with generous proportions. His body spilled out in all directions, with the seatbelt emphasising his massive moobs. Kelly thought to herself there would be many women who'd like a pair of breasts like his. Jim's blue nurse's tunic was stained down the front from whatever he had eaten that morning. Although, judging by the general state of his personal hygiene, it could have been yesterday's breakfast. Or the day before's.

A syringe full of some yellow liquid was stuffed into his top pocket, something no self-respecting nurse would ever do. Kelly reckoned the injection would be for her, maybe when they got closer to their destination or if she kicked off. He was angled so he could face her, his fat legs invading her footwell. At least in this situation he wouldn't be able to molest her, but that didn't prevent him running his black training shoe up and down her calf. She wondered who in the world would find it a turn-on to have their lower leg roughly rubbed by the rubber sole of a training shoe. Then again, as far as this pervert nurse was concerned, it was all about power and pleasuring himself. Kelly had never truly despised someone before. Not even Monahan when he had put her and her children at risk. But she truly despised this creature that passed for a man.

Jim could see the loathing etched across his patient's face. He had seen that same look several times before. He smiled, showing off the blackened stumps that remained of his teeth then made a crude gesture: flicking his tongue—which was coated in thick, white oral thrush—through two of his chubby fingers held up in a V-shape.

The driver spotted the nurse's vulgarity in the mirror and sharply reprimanded him: 'Cut it out.'

'Uch, I'm only having a bit aw fun wae the wee lassie,' Jim protested meekly.

'Not on my watch,' the driver replied, looking daggers at the nurse in his mirror.

At least Kelly knew she'd be safe with these soldier types. The driver had an English accent. There seemed to be a kindness behind his intense stare, and she liked the fact he had put the disgusting nurse in his place. It felt strangely satisfying. Kelly closed her eyes and imagined revenge fantasies.

'What the . . . ?' the driver shouted.

Kelly opened her eyes to see flames engulfing the entire windscreen.

'Pull over, pull over,' his colleague in the passenger seat demanded.

Kelly looked at Jim, who was now white as a sheet. The car veered violently over to the hard shoulder, causing other road users to swerve to avoid the blazing vehicle. It had only just come to rest when both the driver's and Kelly's windows were shattered. An arm appeared from outside and a blade flashed before Kelly's eyes. She shut them tight waiting for the feel of the cold steel. Instead the knife tugged briefly at her seatbelt before freeing her. Moments later she was hauled by the armpits through the missing window, banging her head in the process. She wriggled to help free herself from the blazing vehicle, grimacing from the intense heat that seemed to smack her in the face.

She was flung unceremoniously into the back of a Land Rover, which looked familiar. It was Monahan's—with the man himself sat in the driver's seat.

Kelly sat up to look at the carnage outside. Duggie was pointing his huge gun and barking instructions to the blazing car's passengers to get out and lie down on the ground, face first. He then leapt into the Land Rover, and Monahan accelerated away. The whole rescue operation had taken less than thirty seconds.

Kelly looked back out of the rear window to see the limp body of the driver being dragged to safety by his colleague, while the fat nurse tumbled comically down the embankment, gathering momentum as he disappeared out of sight. Kelly saw the tops of some small trees shake as they stopped Jim Drury's immense bulk.

'Here we are again, Nurse Carter. Just like old times, huh?' Monahan said.

'Aye, old times were the best of times, sir,' Duggie said, smiling.

'The fire, how did you do it?' Kelly asked, amazed she was able to speak again. She figured the surge of adrenaline from being rescued had finally purged the drugs from her system.

Both men laughed before Monahan explained. 'That's a crude but rather effective technique. You fill the entire headlamp full of lighter fuel. When the bulbs heat up, POOF. Well, you saw the effect. Quite dramatic, isn't it?'

'But how did you know which car?' Kelly said, her heart still pounding in her chest.

'Uch, that wiz easy,' Duggie said, beaming from ear to ear—he clearly was at his happiest in a combat situation. 'When we found out where the bastards were keeping you, I kept an eye oot for the moment they tried to move you. When I saw Green Slime in a black Lexus, then I knew you were going somewhere.'

'Green Slime?' Kelly asked.

'Intelligence Corps. We call them "Green Slime". Can spot them a mile away. So one wee hole in each headlight and glug, glug, glug with the lighter fuel. Then we only needed to keep on your tail and let the chemicals do the rest. The great thing about these modern motors is they have their lights on whether you want them or no'. So it was always going to kick off. Just had to make sure we were there for the fireworks.'

'I can't thank you enough. They drugged me. And I was molested by that fat bastard.' Kelly began to cry.

'Is that so?' Duggie said, anger burning in his eyes. 'I had ways and means of dealing with his type, didn't I, boss?'

'You certainly did, Duggie. I'm still trying to forget them,' Monahan smirked.

Kelly looked at her two saviours. Her malice towards Monahan had gone. She'd never felt more grateful. But she could also see the toll all this action was taking on her patient. He looked wiped out.

57

Big Fergie

'It was more than a damp council house story,' April told Connor as she hung up her jacket on the back of the door in their broom cupboard office. 'It was Kelly Carter.'

'What?' Connor said as he ceased typing.

'My lawyer. She had a client called Kirsty Adams,' April said, consulting her notes. 'She'd been sectioned, drugged up so much she could barely speak. Then she goes missing. Her lawyer sees a photo of her client with one of your articles about the shoot-out at the farm and Kelly being kidnapped, and puts two and two together.'

'Why didn't she contact me? My email's at the bottom of those stories.'

'Because she didn't know you.'

'She didn't know you either.'

'No, but her aunt knows me. We used to be neighbours. She vouched for me.'

'So what do we have?'

'She appears to have been sectioned less than a week ago. So a couple of days after the farm shoot-out. Then she disappeared again yesterday afternoon. Her lawyer claims even the health board don't know where she is and she's pushed real hard. Having met her, I believe her. She has nowhere left to turn. So she wants us to put out an appeal—"Did you see this girl?" That sort of thing. She believes Kelly's life's at risk.'

'I think she's right. Let's go speak to Big Fergie,' Connor said, heading in the direction of their news editor, named so because he bore an uncanny resemblance to a chubby version of Manchester United's legendary manager, Alex Ferguson.

174 | Matt Bendoris

The pair explained to Big Fergie what new information they had. April wrote it up in her usual quick and succinct manner, while Connor put the official calls into Police Scotland, who reluctantly issued him with a terse statement about enquiries being 'ongoing'.

The splash would have their joint by-line. Newspaper etiquette meant April's name came first, as she had brought the story to the table and all Connor had done was put in the calls to the cops. That wasn't always the case in the cut-throat industry. In previous years Connor had seen his own by-line bumped from a front-page story for a reporter who had gotten nothing more than a 'no comment' from official sources. But April and Connor were different, they worked as a team.

58

Red jacket

Monahan took the turn-off for Briandale services, but instead of hanging a left at the roundabout he took a right, driving under the M74 before reaching a forest track about quarter of a mile later, where a fast-looking sports car was parked up, alongside a far more ordinary-looking Ford Mondeo.

'This is where I bail on you, honey,' Duggie said with a smile that belied his gruff manner.

'Will I see you again?' Kelly didn't know why she'd said that. But she just felt the need for them all to stick together.

'Uch, I'm like a bad penny—I always turn up.'

Duggie transferred his weapons and a heavy hold-all to the sports car. Second later he tore off down the dirt track and was soon obscured by dust.

Monahan unzipped his bag and took out an electric razor. 'We need to change our appearance,' he said above the hum of the spinning blades. 'They'll be looking for some guy with stubble and driving a Land Rover. Not someone who's clean-shaven in a wheelchair.'

'And it's easy as that?' Kelly asked sceptically.

'You'd be surprised. You know how store detectives radio each other on the same network? Say they see some guy stealing stuff who is 5'11", with blond hair and wearing a bright red jacket. They use their radio so all the other store detectives will be on the look-out for someone wearing a bright red jacket. But if in-between stores the guy wearing the bright red jacket switches to a green one, then the store detectives in the next shop don't give him a second look. He almost perfectly fits the description of the thief, but no one looks at him.'

'It can't be that simple, surely,' Kelly said, screwing up her face.

'That's what my new recruits all think, too. It's actually part of their training to go into a store in a bright red jacket and nick stuff. Then they change to green. Not one of them is ever caught. So it's time to set about changing your appearance, Miss Carter. Fancy a trim?' Monahan smiled, producing a pair of scissors. 'I'm quite nifty with the blades. I've had to cut my fair share of hair in the field.'

• • •

Kelly couldn't help but admire her new bob. The last time she'd had this hairstyle it had been in her wedding photos. She was surprised how she still suited the look even after the passage of time. She admired herself in the car mirror, pulling her hair down on either side of her face. Both sides were the same length.

'You weren't kidding when you said you were nifty with a pair of scissors. My own hairdresser would charge me over £60 for that. Just think of the career you could have had.'

'It would have certainly been different. Although scissors can still be extremely lethal.'

'Yeah, but I think you'd find customers would start to fall off if you started stabbing your clients to death.'

'I'd only do the annoying ones,' Monahan joked.

Kelly no longer looked at Monahan just as her patient. She also looked at him as her lover. Her gratitude for being saved made her forgive him for using her. 'If only we were twenty years younger,' she sighed.

'You wouldn't have cared for me much back then. I wasn't a particularly nice person.'

'Who said you were particularly nice now?' she jested.

Silence fell between them as they thought of the possibilities. For a brief moment she had even forgotten she was running for her life. The moment was broken by Monahan.

'We don't have the time to dwell. We have work to do.'

Kelly knew she'd had a glimpse of the man Monahan could be before his shutters came down. Now he was all business again. 'How do you keep going like that when you're so sick?' she asked softly. 'Your motivation is incredible.'

'How do you do it? To keep going like you do?' Monahan asked in return.

'Because I have to. I have to get out of this for my kids' sake,' Kelly shrugged. 'And you?'

'I need to get the contents of this hard drive into safe hands. Someone who won't hand it straight over to the authorities. Do you think your reporter friend would help?'

'He's not my friend. But he is a reporter. Would do anything for a story, I guess.'

'Well, there are enough stories on that drive to last a lifetime. We'll think of a way of contacting him in the morning. Right now I need some sleep,' Monahan said as he wound the driver's seat back and closed his eyes. Kelly lay her head on his chest, listening to her lover's breathing and the strong beat of his heart. In actual fact, it was too strong. Kelly would expect faster, weaker or irregular beats in her terminal patients. She could only imagine his heart's enduring strength was as a result of Monahan's extreme fitness.

59

Chandelier

April had been in from 7 a.m. to man the hotline number that had been printed at the bottom of her front-page splash about Kelly Carter. The article asserted that the nurse had been held in a mental health institution, before going missing yet again. The quotes all came from Fiona McDade, who made the bold claims that her client had been kept against her will and over-medicated to sedate her. The lawyer was gravely concerned for Kelly's safety. She appealed directly to the *Daily Chronicle*'s readers to get in touch if they saw her.

But the early start had completely thrown April's routine, meaning she had missed her hearty breakfast at Peccadillos. Connor's arrival at 10 a.m. had been a welcome distraction from the hunger pangs, especially as he came armed with two bacon rolls for her, along with a paper cup full of sugary tea.

'You're a life-saver,' April said ripping into the grease-soaked bag.

'And you're a greedy pig,' Connor replied as he watched her set about the breakfast as if she hadn't eaten in days. 'Anything from the hotline?'

'Nothing much,' April said, through mouthfuls of food. 'Although one reader asked if I could help with their damp council house.'

'You're kidding? Do councils only build damp houses?'

'Seems that way. The only other thing was a car fire on the M74 yesterday. It's a bit odd as neither the police nor the fire service mentioned it in their routine press briefings. But a reader saw it—and a fat man rolling down an embankment.'

'Interesting. Maybe Bing knows something about it. I'll ask him.'

April was now feeling more like her old self, having satisfied the chasm that was her tummy. 'How'd you like that?' she said while looming over Connor's desk, her half-moon reading glasses perched on the end of her nose, and one cheek of a fleshy buttock sliding onto the corner of his desk, causing it to creak in protest. She pushed the screen of her new smartphone in his direction.

'Who took these for you? Your daughter?' he said, failing to hide his displeasure at her intrusion into his personal workspace.

'No, I did. It's my front room. I've been getting it done up.'

Connor flipped through a series of blurry snaps, several of which had one of April's chubby fingers partially covering the lens. Only every fourth or fifth was in focus. The ones that he could make out showed a room with cream decor and matching couch, along with a lot of gold fittings. There was also a chandelier that was clearly too big for the size of the lounge. 'Don't you bang your head on that?'

'Not with my heels off,' April quipped. 'It's a bit bigger than I thought. I got it from a charity shop and I could hardly return it, could I?'

'You don't half like your bling. It's like a rapper's mansion.'

'Most of my neighbours are Jewish. I love their style. I wish I had been born a Jew. I love Yiddish: *Oy vey*, *Shalom*, *Mazel Tov*.' April threw her spare arm up in the air and began to shuffle half her backside about Connor's desk as she tapped her foot. His whole workstation swayed to her rhythm, forcing him to grab his monitor, which wobbled precariously.

'What the fuck are you doing?'

'The Horah. It's a Jewish dance.'

'Don't do that again. You almost wrecked my desk.'

'I feel like I'm a Jew in a Christian's body.'

'Well, there's plenty of room for both faiths in there. So who did you get to decorate? Not that wee alkie you sent round to my place, was it?'

'No,' April said, suddenly looking shamefaced as she lifted her frame from Connor's desk, causing his screen to wobble yet again. He swore under his breath.

'I haven't used him since you sent him packing,' she said.

'I only sent him packing after I found him sleeping on my couch while my walls remained decidedly unpainted. I then discovered the bastard had helped himself to the beer in my fridge then filled the bottles up with water and put the caps back on. I mean, where did you even get a decorator like that? Was he sleeping rough on the streets?'

'He was cheap,' she protested lamely.

'He was homeless.'

'I got someone my daughter knows. He's started his own business. Lovely chap. Much nicer than you. He doesn't shout at me for starters. You should use him next time.'

'Yeah, yeah,' Connor replied, having already lost interest. He messaged DCI Crosbie: *Any calls yesterday about a car fire on the M74? Apparently someone saw a fat bloke rolling down the embankment.*

Connor stared at his screen. There were no three dots, which meant Bing wasn't typing a reply. He would have to wait for his response.

60

Disabled space

Two police cars were illegally parked in the disabled spaces at the Gretna Green Outlet Park right on the Scotland/England border.

Gretna was famed for its anvil priests, who would wed couples eloping from England so that they could marry under Scots law, without their parents' consent—a sort of eighteenth-century Las Vegas. Over 5,000 couples a year still wed in this rather charmless and tacky town, with their vows concluded on the strike of an anvil. But Kelly liked it as she could remember having lunch with her folks in Gretna as a kid on one of their long journeys south to catch the overnight ferries from Hull to mainland Europe.

Monahan instructed Kelly to pull the Ford Mondeo up beside the patrol cars in the last remaining disabled space. He produced a blue badge from the glove compartment to show he had permission to use the parking bay, unlike the cops.

'My VIP parking pass. A forgery, of course, but I don't think we'll have too many people arguing with a man in a wheelchair.'

They studied the officers, who were stopping and asking people questions. The cops were clearly on the look-out for them. But Monahan was confident they had changed their appearance enough for his store detective theory to work. It also always helped that the police were looking for two dangerous men and a woman. Not a cripple in a wheelchair.

Monahan played the part of the invalid perfectly, lifting and slinging his apparently useless legs out of the passenger side of the car after Kelly had retrieved the wheelchair from the trunk. As she leaned in to help lift him, she whispered, 'What a performance. You should get an Oscar.'

They both giggled, relieving the tension of the moment. Their relaxed demeanour also gave the impression they had nothing to hide.

'Let's get a coffee and something for you to eat. You must be starving,' Monahan said. He was right, but Kelly hadn't even contemplated food up to this point. Now the mere thought made her very hungry.

'Remember cash only—no cards,' he warned as they took refuge in a sandwich bar and Kelly made her way to the till. Whilst the waitress was preparing her order, Kelly was suddenly struck by a feeling of guilt about her children. She hadn't given them a second's thought until now and she felt awful.

She returned to the table with the food and drinks.

'What's up, Kelly?'

'I need to speak to my kids.'

'Not a problem. You can call them after you've made another call for me first. But like everything, this will require a little subterfuge,' Monahan smiled.

61

Fat bastard

April had grabbed herself a chocolate éclair and a large caramel latte from the hospital's 'restaurant'. She thought the title was a little grand for the food they served. However, she appreciated that the hospital's caterers still had plenty of stodge on offer and not everything had been replaced with health food. She definitely liked the look of the pie, beans, and chips and would have ordered them had she not already eaten, not that that had ever stopped her before. Instead she settled for the takeaway treats, then waddled her way in the direction of the psychiatric ward.

April had decided to get on with some old-fashioned legwork. Unfortunately, her short legs didn't like to work too often and she was feeling the strain as she walked the seemingly endless maze of corridors. 'This place is a labyrinth,' she said to a nurse walking briskly past.

The nurse gave a meek smile and stopped. 'Where are you going?'

'The psychiatric ward. It's to see a friend, but I actually don't even know she's there. Thought I'd pop in to check,' April said, telling a half-truth.

'It's not much further. Just to the end of this corridor and turn left. You'll see the ward entrance just on from there,' the nurse replied, before walking off.

'Thank you,' April shouted at her back. 'This place must keep you fit. Any further and I'll need to call an ambulance,' she added, which earned her a backward glance and smile from the nurse.

184 | Matt Bendoris

April followed the instructions and finally found the entrance to Ward 29. There was an intercom system, but the door was open for visiting time. She walked down a corridor lined with private rooms on each side. Each had an occupant. She saw one woman walking around the perimeter of her room in what must have been a well-worn route. In another, a man remonstrated mildly with the ceiling. None of the patients made eye contact as they were too busy in their own little worlds. April also noticed all the door handles were no more than grips—so nothing could be attached to them, like a cord or a rope—to prevent these poor tormented souls from harming themselves.

April wondered why there was still such a stigma attached to mental health when a recent report revealed around a quarter of the entire country would experience some sort of psychiatric issue over the course of a year. One of the most common conditions was depression. April had been through that more than once in her life. A friend once asked how she could possibly be depressed when she was always so cheery. But that's the real problem with mental health, you can't see what's really going on inside.

April made her way along the corridor. She was hoping a kind member of staff might give her a description of who Kelly Carter had left with. It was a long shot, but worth a try. As she approached the nurses' station she saw what could be unkindly described as a blob sitting behind the wooden counter. His badge said his name was Nurse Drury and his uniform was so dirty that he'd either had a hard shift or, more worryingly, had arrived for work in that state. He too was eating a chocolate éclair, even though he needed to lose a lot more weight than April Lavender.

'Snap,' April said, brandishing her own pastry, which was still in its paper bag.

Her friendliness wasn't reciprocated. 'Can ah help you?' Nurse Jim Drury replied, his forehead and cheek still sporting angry grazes from where he had tumbled down the motorway embankment, having escaped the car inferno on the M74 the day before.

'I hope so. I am trying to find a friend.'

'Name?'

'Oh, April Lavender.'

'Nah, we've no patients by that name.'

'Oh, silly me. That's my name. My friend is called Kelly Carter.'

'We've no patients by that name,' Nurse Drury repeated in a bored and robotic fashion.

'Here's the thing. I know she was in here because her lawyer, Fiona McDade, told me.'

'And I'm telling ye, we've no patients by that name.'

'But I'm told she was in here under a different name. Kirsty Adams. All I'm wondering is if you had a woman in her late thirties, thin, pretty, with longish, brunette hair, who was admitted then discharged over the last few days.'

'Even if we had, unless you're a relative, I wouldnae gee you that information anyway. Got it? Now if that's all, ahm busy.'

April stared back at the 'busy' nurse and his half-finished chocolate éclair and knew a liar when she saw one. His raised voice had made April the focus of attention: an auxiliary nurse in her green uniform stared at the reporter, before suddenly remembering she had something else to do.

'Well, thank you for your time, Nurse Drury. I hope you treat your patients with more respect than ward visitors, but I rather doubt you do.'

She was met with a blank stare back from the man, whose rolls of stomach fat were resting on his workstation and even lolloping onto his keyboard. His reply was to finish off the remainder of his chocolate éclair in one bite, chewing open-mouthed like a cow, so April could see it all being mashed up with his saliva before disappearing down his throat.

Defeated, she made her way back through the labyrinth of corridors, wishing she could have said so much more to the repulsive nurse. But causing even more of a commotion wouldn't have done her any good and was also the last thing the patients needed, with their already fragile minds. She got into the lift that would take her down to the exit when a small-ish woman in a green uniform dashed in beside her, just as the doors were closing. They had the lift to themselves.

'I told that fat bastard I was taking my break, so I don't have much time. You were asking about Kelly?'

'I was,' April replied gratefully.

'You're right, they had her registered as Kirsty Adams. Damn shame what's going on with that lassie. There's nothing wrong with her. They're keeping her drugged up. That's why I told her to try to speak to the lawyer. But she was taken away yesterday before lunchtime. Two men came for her. They didn't look like they were from another hospital.'

'Any idea where they were headed?'

'Haven't a clue. At least she's away from him. One day I'll catch him doing what he does to the lassies in the ward and when I do, I'm blowing the whistle.'

'Here . . .' April said, fumbling around in her bottomless bag, before eventually finding what she was after. 'This is my card.'

It stated: *April Lavender, Senior Reporter, The Daily Chronicle.* It also had her mobile number, direct line, email and Twitter handle on it.

'I thought I recognised you from the paper,' Cathy said, staring at the card. 'You did a story on my cousin years back. She was a chef in one of those fancy London restaurants who needed a heart transplant. You did a smashing piece on her.'

April was pretty sure she hadn't interviewed too many chefs in need of a major organ replacement during her career, but, despite that, the story failed to register.

'You don't remember her, do you?' Cathy said, perfectly reading April's blank expression.

'Sorry, please don't be offended. I can hardly remember stories I've written in the last week. My mind is like a sieve. How is your cousin doing, anyway?'

'Dead.'

'Ah, sorry to hear that. I guess she didn't get the transplant in time?'

'No, she did. But she died on the operating table. It was just too late. She kept your article though. Used to show her visitors all the lovely things you wrote about her.'

April felt terrible. Not only could she not remember this poor girl's name, she knew she was just another story out of the thousands she had filed over the years. Like most reporters, she hardly ever stopped to think about the impact, both good and bad, her words had on real people and their lives.

'What was her name?' April asked as the lift reached the ground floor.

'Agnes Anderson.'

A lightbulb was suddenly turned on somewhere in April's head. 'Long, blonde hair. From Drumchapel? I remember now because the headline was something like, "From the Drum to the Dorchester".'

'Aye, that was Agnes,' Cathy beamed, pleased April had finally remembered.

'Please give me a call if you hear anything,' the reporter said as she walked out of the lift.

'I will. And I'll let you know when I catch fatty red-handed too,' Cathy promised.

62

Scotch Corner

'Hello, I'm calling from PPI solutions. We believe you may be eligible for a big cash pay-out,' Kelly said, adopting her best English accent.

'Not interested,' came the curt reply before the line went dead.

There probably wasn't a household in the UK that hadn't been plagued by PPI calls, both automated and human. The PPI—Personal Protection Insurance—compensation industry had grown out of the billions of pounds bankers had been forced to put aside after years of mis-selling policies to millions of their customers. Eventually the Government regulator had enough and ordered the bankers to pay back the money plus compensation.

'Hello, I'm calling from PPI solutions again. We appear to have been cut off. We believe you may be eligible for a big cash . . .'

'Are you thick or something? I said I wasn't interested.'

The line went dead once more. Monahan, sitting in his wheelchair by the pay phone, handed Kelly a scrap of paper and urged her to try again.

'Hello, I'm calling from PPI solutions and no, I'm not thick—you must be the thick one as I'm trying to give you money.'

'Are you absolutely insane? What's the name of your supervisor?'

'Kelly Carter,' Kelly replied to silence down the line. She then asked Connor Presley if he had a notepad handy before giving him a series of coordinates.

'Got that?' she asked.

'Got it,' he replied before hanging up.

'Okay, good girl. We need to move,' Monahan said.

'What about my phone call home?' Kelly demanded.

'We'll drive to Scotch Corner for that. It's about 100 miles south from here. They'll think we're heading to the Hull ferry to make our way to Europe. But we'll then double back and drive north.'

Gretna Green, Scotch Corner, and the Hull ferry: it felt like Kelly was reliving her childhood all over again. She would have never imagined back then that she would now be visiting the same places as an escaped mental patient on the run from the law.

'Think your reporter friend can be trusted?' Monahan said, holding up the hard drive.

'Elvis? I think so. As much as any reporter can be trusted, I guess.'

'I mean, is he likely to hand it over to the police?'

'I doubt it. He's not the type to reveal his sources. All that old-fashioned journalist stuff.'

'Well that old journalist stuff just earned him a 300-mile round trip,' Monahan said with a sneer.

63

What's it like?

Two hours later Monahan and Kelly were nearing Scotch Corner, the traditional watering post for travellers heading north and south. Now it was just a large service station for the junction of the A1 and A66, but Kelly's folks would always stop there for a comfort break and some lunch before the final one hundred-mile dash to the Hull ferry. She smiled to herself, remembering how her mum always made sandwiches for the journey, refusing to 'take out another mortgage to pay motorway services prices'. Kelly used to be annoyed at her mum's apparent meanness. It was only when she became a parent herself she fully understood: the prices were outrageous. And she would rather her kids ate one of her homemade healthy sandwiches than a burger. Mum really did know best.

Kelly's eyes filled with tears, which ran freely down her cheeks as her childhood memories made way to her recalling her mum's horrific last moments. That was no way for a good woman to die.

'What's it like to kill someone?' Kelly asked Monahan.

'What are you, a schoolgirl? That's the sort of question I'd expect from a class of kids.'

'It's a good question, though.'

Monahan eyed Kelly. 'What's it like to have a patient die in front of you?'

'It's fine. I've just got to make sure they are comfortable and pain-free.'

'But there's no emotional attachment, right?'

'Not really. Or I'd go home in bits every night.'

'So it's just a job, right?'

'Yes, just a job,' she conceded.

'Ditto, it's just a job for me too. I started off as a sniper. So if I'm shooting someone from a mile away, I'm concentrating on getting the maths right, considering the wind speed and even the Earth's curvature. And when I get it right, the target goes down, it's job done. Move onto the next one. There is no philosophy to it. I don't sit and mope. As you said, you'd hardly be a great nurse if you went home in bits at the end of every shift.'

Kelly let the silence spread between them before she asked, 'Have you ever felt remorse?'

'No, why should I?' Monahan replied defiantly.

'For killing so many.'

'Nope. And you? Could you have done more for your patients? Given them another day or week or month of life?'

'No. It was their time.'

'Exactly!' Monahan replied, his eyes suddenly burning with fire.

'Who are you to play God?' Kelly said, now thoroughly disgusted.

'I could ask you the same. Aren't you playing God by pumping patients up so full of morphine or prolonging their lives with other drugs?'

'I am helping people, relieving them from their misery.'

'Again, so am I,' Monahan replied.

'Now you're just being flippant.'

'I don't think I am. Sticking a knife in the neck of a brainwashed jihadist is what I consider putting someone out of their misery.'

Kelly changed tack. 'Do you remember the ones you killed in close combat?'

'Every one of them,' Monahan said softly.

'Do you remember the Princess?'

'Of course. She still looked beautiful. Hardly a mark on her. But dead,' he said bluntly. 'You just know it when you see it. That they're gone. But I hardly have to tell *you* that, do I?'

They had arrived at Scotch Corner, and Kelly let herself out of the car to call her ex- husband Brian. But all she got was his voicemail. She left a short message assuring him and the kids that she was alright.

Kelly then sealed the hard drive in a watertight bag Monahan had handed her, along with some duct tape. She knew what she needed to do.

64

Barefooted Bond

Connor had always wondered what it would be like to be a real-life James Bond. But there was nothing exotic about the fifty-odd miles of road from the M6 across the north Pennines to connect with the A1 at Scotch Corner. Much of it was two lanes. The rest was perpetual roadworks converting the single carriageway—the product of the original road planners' stunning lack of vision—into a modern dual carriageway. Connor found himself on one of the long stretches of single-lane road, stuck behind a convoy of articulated trailer trucks, with no chance of overtaking without risking his life.

The route was scenic enough, not that he took much of it in. He needed to retrieve the package Kelly had left for him before anyone else did.

After three hours he finally reached the traffic lights of Scotch Corner, which slowly directed him to make a 360-degree turn and head back the way he had come. He now wished he'd stopped at the services to use their toilets as he desperately needed a pee. He wondered if James Bond ever had the sudden urge to 'go' while on a mission. He pulled into a large layby packed with trailer trucks and managed to find a small space sandwiched between two of the massive transporters. Connor located the café Kelly had told him about and walked behind the building in as casual a stroll as he could muster, lest he was being watched. But he needn't have worried as no one was interested. In his suit, he looked like just another sales rep, stopping off for a break.

Connor walked over the sodden grass towards a picnic bench, which was an island in the middle of its own makeshift pond created by floodwater. He once again checked he wasn't being watched, then tried unsuccessfully not to get his socks wet as he walked into the giant puddle that surrounded the picnic table and slipped his hand under the far end, patting around for the package Kelly said she had stuck to the underside. There was nothing.

He sat down on the damp wooden seat and felt under the bench's top with both arms, covering the sleeves of his suit jacket and cuffs of his shirt in old green and black moss. But all he could feel were hard lumps of chewing gum. There was nothing left for it other than to stick his head under the table and look, which was easier said than done. Connor slithered under like a limbo dancer, knowing full well that if anyone cared to gaze in his direction now they would think he was most definitely acting suspiciously. He checked the underside of the table, but could see no package. There were just two strips of missing moss, as if it had been yanked off by the duct tape that Kelly said she had used. Someone had beaten him to it. Connor stared despondently into the murky puddle directly underneath the missing strips. On a whim he thrust his hand into the brown water. He immediately felt something and pulled it up. It was the hard drive—thankfully it had been placed inside a waterproof bag.

Connor wriggled out from underneath the picnic table, with his entire suit now covered in slimy moss and mud. The bottoms of his trouser legs were wringing wet. He squelched his way back to the car, passing a bemused trailer truck driver having a cigarette at the back of the café. 'If you fancied a swim, there's a pool in Darlington.'

'Thanks,' was all Connor could muster. *Thanks a bunch*, he thought to himself. He started up his car and turned the heating on full before taking off his shoes and pouring the dirty water out of them into the gutter. He would have to drive back to Scotland in his bare feet.

'They never show that in the movies,' he said to himself. 'And I still need a pee.'

65

Simples

'I can't find your number,' April said in a tone approaching blind panic as she called Connor.

He knew the warning signs all too well. His colleague was experiencing some sort of tech difficulties. He spoke to her as he would a child: 'And what number is that?'

'This one. The one I'm calling you on.'

Connor was well used to April's quirks but now even he was confused. '*This* number?'

'Yes,' April snapped impatiently, 'your mobile number.'

'But you called it,' he said as he finally made it past the slow-moving trailer trucks and on to the northbound M6.

'I know that, dummy. I need your number to send to Kelly's lawyer, Fiona. I told her Kelly had been in touch, but she wanted to speak to you directly. But all that comes up on my screen is your name. No number. See?'

'Yeah, I think so. Well, two options, really. There's an "i", for information. It's over to the right of the names.'

'An "i". Okay, I've got it,' April replied, scribbling down Connor's instructions into her notepad as if handling an exclusive revelation.

'Press that and you'll see my number comes up. You can then copy and paste it.'

'And then what?'

'Well, you then text it to the lawyer.'

'Copy. Paste. Send. Okay, got that,' she added, still furiously writing away.

'Or you can just "share contact".'

'With who?'

'The lawyer.'

'Ah right, got that too. Simples.'

'Simples, indeed.'

A moment later Connor got a text from April: *HELLO*. He shook his head and smiled, 'Technology will never be your best friend, will it, Miss Lavender?'

66

Retrieve

'Connor, Fiona McDade here,' the lawyer said, all business as usual. 'You've heard from Kelly?'

'I have, Fiona.'

'Where was she?'

'Let's just say it would be better for all concerned if we didn't go into that.'

'But you actually spoke to her. It wasn't just a text?'

'We chatted. Briefly.'

'Did you feel she was under duress?'

'I would say stress rather than duress,' Connor said.

'What do you mean?'

'Well, she had an explicit set of instructions to give me. But I didn't get the feeling someone was holding a loaded gun to her head.'

'But you can't be sure.'

'No, I can't.'

'What were the instructions?'

'To retrieve something.'

'What?'

'I can't say exactly. But she wanted me to retrieve a package.'

'And did you?'

'Yes.'

'What are you going to do with it?'

Connor didn't like being asked by anyone what he planned to do with anything. He especially didn't appreciate the constant probing by a lawyer. 'Who knows? Look, I've got to go. But your client is alive and well, that's the main thing.'

'Where are you . . . hello? Hello?' But Connor had ended the call.

Fiona looked over to Officer McGill, the archetypal stone-faced 'man in black' who was sitting across from her. He had contacted Fiona asking for—no, demanding—any information she had about Kelly Carter. Fiona was not the type to be bossed around or intimidated by anyone. But Officer McGill seemed to be the only person who had a hope in hell of finding Kelly. Fiona would do anything to help a client, even a pact with the Devil himself, a contract she was sure she had just concluded.

'Happy?' she asked.

'Yes, thank you.'

'And I'll get to see my client as soon as you've rescued her, right? That was the deal,' Fiona demanded.

'Of course,' Officer McGill said as he got up to leave. 'As soon as we've got her back, I'll call you.' But Kelly Carter was the last thing on McGill's mind. He was a lot more interested in what she had left for the reporter to retrieve.

67

Big Foot

Stevie Brett's council flat was a mass of technology. There wasn't a surface that didn't have some sort of electronic device sitting on it with wires spewing in every direction. He rarely left his cluttered home as he was paranoid that someone would break in and steal his equipment. But as Connor once told him, 'No one will steal it as they wouldn't know what to do with it.'

Stevie had been one of the reporter's contacts for years. They'd originally met in court, when Stevie was being tried for hacking into the national crime database. His case had collapsed when computer experts failed to agree on Stevie's hacking methods. When one forensic IT expert finally admitted he couldn't even be sure the defendant had committed a crime as his electronic tracks had been covered so well, the already bamboozled and ageing judge had heard enough and threw the case out. Afterwards, Connor had taken Stevie for a coffee at the Peccadillo, and he got an exclusive on how this reclusive computer geek had been persecuted by the authorities. It wasn't great, but was enough to make a page-lead. When Connor switched off his voice recorder, Stevie had grinned, leaned closer, and then whispered how he had successfully managed to hack into the crime database.

'You wouldn't believe the shit they've got on there. I found a newsreader who has been up on domestic abuse warnings. He's never been charged. But two cautions are sitting right there on his file. The bastard is on TV every night while he likes to slap his wife about.'

It had been clear Stevie was desperate to boast about his achievements to someone—anyone, really. Connor was glad he'd chosen him: he could see the endless possibilities flash before his eyes.

But the political landscape had changed much since then, mainly because of the Leveson Inquiry. Stolen information—such as that obtained by Stevie's dubious methods—was of less use now as every story and source had to be accounted for. But Connor and Stevie still stayed in touch.

'Hi, Stevie, how you doing?' the reporter asked as he arrived at his contact's East Kilbride flat. 'What's your scam this month?' It was an opening gambit Connor had been using for years, referring to Stevie's numerous and inventive excuses given to the Department of Work and Pensions so that he could keep his benefits without actively seeking employment.

'Big Foot,' Stevie replied.

'What?' Connor said, failing to stifle a chuckle.

'You know, the Yeti. Sasquatch. The Ape Man. The missing link.'

'Yeah, I know what it is, but what has Big Foot got to do with your benefits?'

'Connor, Connor, Connor, such lack of imagination. There was a report from up north, in your paper as it happens, of a Big Foot sighting by some local nutter.'

'Uh-huh,' Connor replied, dubious.

'Well, I told them I was going hunting for the beast.'

Connor exploded with laughter.

'I said, "Think about it. If I get footage of a real life Big Foot, I'll make enough money never to be on benefits again." They agreed.'

'At least you give them all a laugh, Stevie.'

'That's what they said. That I always give them a laugh. So that's me for the next month. Instead of actively seeking employment, I'm actively seeking Big Foot. The possibilities are endless. After this I'll go hunting for the Loch Ness Monster. Then there's the UFOs of Bonnybridge.'

'It's amazing that people still buy into all that shit. I mean, here we are in the 21st century, carrying cameras on all our phones, yet no one has snapped a credible picture that proves any of that guff. Yet still they believe,' Connor ranted.

'People are stupid,' Stevie concluded.

'How have you been, anyway?' Connor asked.

'Uch, pretty shit, truth be told. I had another attack last month. Nearly never made it this time.'

Ever since Connor had known him, Stevie had suffered from chronic asthma. The previous year he had fallen into a coma for two weeks. Doctors feared he would be left brain-damaged, if he made it at all. Amazingly he pulled through—unscathed physically, but scarred mentally.

'I get frightened at times. Then morose, knowing that one day I am going to die right here, all alone in this fucking flat, gasping for breath.'

'Might be a good time to quit the fags, then?' Connor suggested.

'And deny myself one of my few pleasures? I might extend my life by a couple of years, but so what. It's not much of a life, is it? No girlfriend. A family who haven't spoken to me in years.'

'You did send them a hell of a lot of abusive emails, mind you. Then there was the Buddha incident,' Connor reminded him.

Stevie laughed at the memory. 'I'd almost forgotten about that. They didn't reply to my emails so I threw their Buddha statue from the garden right through their front window. That's what I call karma.'

'That's what I call three months in jail,' Connor retorted.

'True. But prison wasn't so bad, especially since I became the go-to IT man for all the cons. Even the governor asked me to fix his laptop. He didn't have a firewall so it was rid-dled with viruses. I removed all of them and installed my own. Look, I caught the dirty bastard on his webcam having a wank.'

Stevie spun around his laptop to show a freeze-frame of the governor's 'cum face'.

'For fuck's sake. And last month he was up at a Holyrood Select Committee,' Connor said.

'I know. Funny, huh? I'm still figuring out what to do with them. I'll probably send them to the mobiles of all his prisoners. I'm still in touch with most of them.'

'Well, when you do, please tell me so that I can do the story,' Connor insisted.

Stevie liked that thought. 'So why are you here, Connor? You don't pay many home visits these days.'

'True. That's because my bosses hardly let me out. Seriously. They want it all done over the phone so you don't go racking up expenses out on the road.'

'So how can I help?'

'You can start with this,' Connor said, producing the portable hard drive.

Stevie wasted no time plugging it into his laptop. A couple of clicks later he whistled. 'Holy shit.'

'What?' Connor asked.

'Where the fuck did you get this from? The military?' Stevie said, urgently pulling out the USB cable.

'I don't really know where it's come from, to tell the truth,' Connor admitted.

'Well, don't be bringing that shit to me.'

Connor had never seen Stevie looking so spooked.

'Not only is it encrypted, it will no doubt have a GPS homing signal too. I just hope I unplugged it in time before they come kicking my door down, or worse.'

'What do you mean, "or worse"?'

Stevie turned and stared directly at Connor before shaking his head slowly. 'You haven't got a fucking clue, have you?

You're up to your tits with this one, Elvis, and you don't even know it.'

'How?' Connor asked genuinely.

'The people who share information on hard drives like this aren't the sort to bother with the court system, know what I mean? This is hardcore, Elvis. And frankly it frightens the shit out of me. If I was you, I'd return it to its rightful owner as quickly as possible and pray they're feeling merciful.'

'What the fuck is on it, Stevie?'

'I don't know and I don't want to know. Frankly, I'd prefer if you take it and leave now,' Stevie said, sliding the hard drive across the table to Connor like it was radioactive.

'Seriously?' Connor asked incredulously.

'Seriously. Go, Elvis. Get that thing out of my flat.'

Connor had never seen Stevie genuinely scared like this. He hadn't even looked worried when he was in court being prosecuted. But that hard drive had frightened him. The reporter left Stevie's first floor flat to the sounds of the computer hacker snapping shut the several locks on his door.

68

The truth

April had her whole evening mapped out. She would get home around half six from work, ping one of her dinners in the microwave, pour an extremely generous measure of gin, add a dash of tonic, then plonk herself in her favourite armchair for 7 p.m., with Cheeka on her lap and her iPad at the ready. Then it was just a case of going on to beastshamer.com. She eagerly looked forward to the nightly revelations. Connor had told her that the scandal site was now so popular it would start trending every night on Twitter with each new exposé—not that April could fully get her head around what 'trending' meant, no matter how often Connor had explained it. She had stopped asking and would now just give a knowing nod of the head instead.

April wasn't such a fan of the Beast Shamer blogger's style of delivery. She would rather whoever was behind the website would just post the official classified material, without all the commentary. But, like a tawdry TV talent show judge, they seemed to revel in building the tension.

Tonight, April actually found she was grinning in anticipation as she clicked on the site and waited for it to open. But her grin disappeared when she, and no doubt millions of others, were greeted with the following message:

There will be no release of classified documents on this site tonight. But in the very near future I hope to bring you everything I know. I apologise for the wait, but I promise it will be worth it: in particular, the real truth about what happened to Princess Diana in that Parisian tunnel on August 31st, 1997.

What I shall reveal will truly shock the world. Once again I must stress that this will not be speculation, or the half-baked conclusions of the Diana conspiracists. This will be actually what happened—straight from the official, unpublished UK Government files. And let me tell you they have vastly different conclusions from the 2007/08 inquest, which returned a verdict of unlawful killing. You may remember that her driver, Henri Paul, and the paparazzi were made to share blame for the deaths of Diana and Dodi Fayed. You may also recall that the coroner, Lord Justice Scott Baker, ruled out the possibility that the couple were murdered.

The files that I shall publish here shortly may change his mind. What's more, the file names names.

'Bugger,' April fumed, realising that was all the blogger was prepared to post tonight. She phoned Connor. 'Did you see that?' she asked.

'Yeah, I've just read it,' Connor said as he started up his car outside Stevie Brett's flat.

'Do you think Beast Shamer has something to do with your hard drive?'

'I didn't until it mentioned Diana.'

'What do you think it means?'

'Two things. The blogger is either waiting for someone to pay him off handsomely to shut down his site, or he doesn't actually have the files yet.'

'And if he doesn't have the files?'

'It means I'm probably in danger.'

'Oh my,' April gasped. 'What are you going to do?'

'I honestly don't know. But doing nothing won't be an option. I have a funny feeling trouble is going to find me.'

69

I.D.

The man in the car was relieved to see that Connor Presley had left the computer hacker's apartment with his man-bag, which presumably still contained the hard drive. It meant he wouldn't have to pay the computer hacker a visit right now. That could wait. But he would still need to check they hadn't made a copy of what was on the hard drive.

That would be bad, for all concerned.

• • •

Connor had been trying to text Jack Barr's snatch of the cop they had encountered in Kilsyth to DCI Crosbie, to see if he could help identify him, but the image kept bouncing back. In fact, Connor hadn't heard from Crosbie in a while. He hadn't even replied to his last message asking about a car fire on the M74 and a fat man rolling down an embankment. Connor decided to call Crosbie instead.

'What is it, Elvis?' Crosbie said frostily.

'Just wondering why you hadn't replied to my last text.'

'Busy.'

'Too busy to even swear?'

'Okay, I've been too fucking busy.'

'I thought Amy might be keeping you on a short leash.'

'Nah, not really.'

Ah, the truth, Connor thought to himself. His rival Amy Jones had convinced his best cop contact to keep all his juicy information for her ears only.

'Look, that's fair enough, Bing. I can understand Amy wanting to keep you to herself. But I need you to do me one last favour.'

'I think I've done you plenty of favours, Elvis.'

'You have, but I need you to eyeball someone for me. A cop.'

'Text it to me.'

'It won't text. Are you in work?'

'Yeah, I'm still in the fucking shithole. I get my cunting screen-break in an hour.'

'That's more like the Bing I know. I'll see you then.'

Connor checked the map on his iPhone. It was forty-eight miles from East Kilbride to Bilston Glen police call handling centre in Midlothian. He would just make it on time.

• • •

DCI Crosbie was outside the main gates having a cigarette when Connor pulled up, flashing his lights to catch his attention. Crosbie opened the passenger door and got in while still smoking. Connor coughed in disgust.

'For fuck's sake, Bing. You know I don't smoke.'

'It's my fucking fag break. I'm only allowed three regulation breaks on my shift, so put a fucking window down, Elvis.'

Connor waved the smoke away from his face as he showed the snatch picture of the cop from Kilsyth.

'Ha, Charlie McGill. What a cunt,' DCI Crosbie said, exhaling another plume of cigarette smoke in the reporter's direction. 'He was Royal Protection Squad. Met him briefly when Diana was in Scotland for the opening of the Garden Festival in 1988. Remember that one, Elvis? When she went up in that spinning tower thingy and pretended to be all scared, burying her head into Charles' shoulder and doing her whole coy act?'

'I certainly remember the pictures. Why does everything come back to bloody Diana these days?'

'Everything? What you yakking about?'

'Forget it. It's just her name keeps coming up lately and I've no idea why.'

'Anyway, Charlie McGill is your man. I never forget a cunt.'

'Handy to know.'

'Well, gotta go and log on again. I can't begin to tell you how shit my life is now.'

'At least you've got Amy.'

'Aye, at least there's that, for however long that lasts,' Crosbie said, slamming the door shut and sparking up another cigarette for his short walk to the call handling centre's front door.

Connor was happy as he drove off, happy that his number one police contact had not only given a name to the man in the photo, but that cracks were beginning to show in his relationship with Amy Jones.

The man in the car following behind Connor was far less pleased, though. He had a lot on his mind.

70

The Mad Bat Society

'How'd you get on with your computer geek?' April asked Connor the next day in the confines of their broom cupboard office.

'Not great. He freaked out.'

'Why's that?'

'Something about the hard drive. He asked if I'd got it from the military. Then basically showed me the door,' Connor explained as he took the hard drive from his man-bag and placed it on his desk. Both journalists stared at it in silence.

April was the first to speak. 'Do you think that has the truth about Diana's death on it?'

'What is it about Diana at the moment? She's everywhere I turn. And why does the whole world think her death is a conspiracy theory?'

'Because it *is* a conspiracy. Come on, you must admit it stinks. She starts dating an Arab, could even have been pregnant with an Arab half-brother of the future king of England, then dies in a collision with a car that is never found, in a tunnel with all the cameras turned off.'

'And blah-di-blah.'

'No, it's not blah-di-blah. Why did the ambulance taking her to hospital pull over to treat her?'

'To save her life?'

'No ambulance would delay getting her to an emergency room. They pulled over to let her die.'

'I see. And you know this how?'

'The investigation, stupid. The facts are all there. Even without any conspiracy theorist spin they are pretty startling. A doctor treated Diana at the scene for forty minutes—why?'

'To save her life,' Connor said half-bored, having had these discussions before down the pub with other conspiracy-happy colleagues.

'He orders the ambulance driver to drive slowly. Why?'

'Because she was so gravely injured?' he offered in vain.

'They then pass one hospital to go to another further away,' she continued.

'Maybe the first one didn't have the facilities for such injuries?'

If April heard her younger colleague, she ignored him. 'The doctor then orders the ambulance driver to pull over to work on her some more. My cousin is an ambulance driver and he said you never drive slowly or stop with a critically ill patient. Your one and only priority is to get them to the hospital as fast as you can.'

'I bet your cousin has never had to drive a dying princess.'

'And what about the embalming?'

Connor sighed. Get into a conversation with a Diana conspiracist and they always mention the controversial embalming of the Princess just ten hours after her death. Many believe it was to cover up the fact she was carrying Dodi Fayed's child, or illegal drug use—possibly both. At the 2007/08 inquest into the royal's death, the Frenchman who carried out the procedure admitted he had done so without official authorisation, saying he feared that the Princess's body would deteriorate in the heat of the Parisian summer.

'How much can a body go off between the time she died and being flown home the next day, huh? It's a cover-up. She was bumped off, plain and simple,' April concluded.

'Or she was being driven by a drunk driver, plain and simple,' Connor countered.

'The bar he was in said he only had one drink and a coffee. But his blood levels said he was three times over the limit. What a load of *merde*.'

'I love how animated you get over Diana. But have you ever seen a Frenchman having just one or two drinks?' Connor laughed, infuriating his colleague more.

'That's a stereotype. The same can be said of Scotsmen. Or Welshmen.'

'I know it sounds like a stereotype but I have seen the French having lunch. I once witnessed three guys do seven bottles of wine over an hour. Then they got back on their skis and off they went.'

'Bet you've never seen many Frenchmen falling down drunk in the street, though?' April asked.

'True, but only because they are permanently under the influence and just top themselves up. Why do you think it's the law to have breathalysers in every vehicle now?'

April carried on regardless. 'And the paparazzi photographer found decapitated three years later in a burnt-out car? Locked from the inside and no car keys ever found,' she said, her eyebrows arched towards the heavens.

That, Connor conceded, was suspicious. 'His head is said to have come off in the intense heat.'

'With a hole in the side of his skull?'

'I once read a story about a man who was cremated on a funeral pyre in India. His head exploded with the popping sound of a champagne cork,' Connor recalled.

'And the keys?'

'Melted beyond recognition, I'd imagine,' Connor said feebly, knowing his argument was growing weaker.

'You really are a member of the Flat Earth Society, aren't you?' April said, looking at her younger colleague with nothing short of disdain.

'Better than the Mad Bat Society. Look, even I would have to admit that there are many things about her death that don't add up. But had she been wearing a seat belt she would have survived. The bodyguard is living proof of that. He was the only one in the car with his belt on, hence that's why he's still alive.'

'Probably because all the other seat belts had been sabotaged.'

'I give up with you, April. There is nothing I can say to convince you Diana died because of a drunk driver and her refusal to wear her belt. Let's change the subject.'

'Sure. So I bet you believe JFK was killed by a lone gunman, don't you?' April teased.

'I'm out of here.'

'Aw, I was only having some fun,' she laughed.

There was a knock at their door and the editor's personal assistant, Joan, popped her head into their office. 'The boss wants to see you, Elvis. He's with a man in a suit. Cop, I reckon. Looks serious.'

'Thanks for the heads-up, Joan,' Connor said, returning the hard drive to his man-bag, which he slipped into his top drawer. Turning to April, he said, 'Don't leave the room and don't let anyone take my bag.'

71

Tak-Ma-Doon

Kelly and Monahan were both stiff from all the driving and an uncomfortable night spent sleeping in the hire car in an industrial estate's parking lot off the M6, hidden between the rows of articulated trailer trucks.

Monahan parked the Mondeo at the viewpoint on the uniquely named Tak-Ma-Doon road. Kelly loved this single-lane strip of tarmac, which snaked upwards from Kilsyth over the hills before dropping down into Carron Valley and the town of Stirling beyond. To the left, she could see the iconic, rusty-coloured Forth Bridge and the flames spouting from the chimneys of the Grangemouth Refinery. Straight ahead was the new town of Cumbernauld. To the right, she could see the peak of Goat Fell on the Isle of Arran.

But, unfortunately, this was not a time to sit around taking in the views. Kelly looked at Monahan. His skin was deathly grey, his haggardness accentuated by the white bristles of stubble. He'd lost so much weight that his trousers were now too roomy and flapping around his legs. Her patient was weak and she had enough experience of end-of-life care to know that time was running out. That's why she had decided to bring him home. To her mother's home, to be precise. He needed peace to die.

The plan was to leave the car at the viewpoint and do a sweep past the house to see if anyone was watching it. If the coast was clear, they'd go in.

Kelly took Monahan's hand and they began the trek back down towards Kilsyth. Her parents had bought the old farmhouse on the outskirts of Kilsyth back in the seventies. As a kid growing up, Kelly felt as though they lived in the middle of nowhere: in the winters she would get snowed in while the other kids made it to school. In the summers she could walk for hours over the hills by herself. The house had great views of Kelvin Valley; it was also ideal for spotting any unwanted visitors.

They'd only just got started with their slow trudge when they disturbed a red grouse, which took off noisily by the fence separating the road from the fields. It gave them both a start, but helped relieve the tension and they shared a laugh then a brief kiss. They spotted a pair of soaring buzzards, catching a thermal by the hill locals called Tamtain. It wasn't big enough to be classed as a Munro—which is any mountain over three thousand feet—but it was impressive enough.

'That's what I love about Scotland,' said Kelly. 'We're sandwiched here between one million people in Glasgow and Edinburgh yet it feels like we're in the wilderness of the Highlands.'

'You're such an old romantic, Kelly.'

'Hey, less of the old,' she replied, playfully slapping his arm.

'I'll tell you, there's nothing romantic about the Highlands when you're doing your winter training. Thought I was going to die as a young recruit when I lost the feeling in my hands and feet. Turned out to be mild frostbite. I always thought the people who died on Scottish mountains each year were idiots. You know, climbing Ben Nevis in their flip-flops and shorts, not realising it's so cold at the top that the snow never melts. But as I lay there in a ditch with the best Nordic equipment the British Army had in their locker, thinking I was about to breathe my last, I realised just how deadly our mountains are.'

'They're not even that high, are they?'

'I think that's the problem. Ben Nevis is about 4,500 feet. It's a false sense of security because folk can walk up it in four hours instead of four days, like Mont Blanc.'

Kelly liked talking about the mountains. It was a brief respite from the death and carnage. 'I won't want to leave when I see my kids, you know. I'm tired of running.'

'I know. I'm done in too. But don't drag the kids back into this just yet, okay?' Monahan made her promise.

'Okay,' she reluctantly replied. Kelly had noticed Monahan was becoming seriously short of breath. It's always the breathing that gives the game away with terminal patients. Kelly could instinctively sense when someone was in the final stages, although she wasn't always right. She remembered sitting through the night with one woman, who she was convinced had taken her last, only for her chest to explode into life a minute later. She continued that way for five hours, which had been a blessing as it meant Kelly hadn't needed to wake the woman's family, who were taking a much-needed rest.

At the mere thought of sleep Kelly suddenly felt exhausted. Her legs became heavy and weary as she trudged down the road. 'When will this all end?' she asked Monahan, who marched with a determined look in his eyes even though his body was in a dreadful state.

'Soon, Kelly. Soon I'll be out of your hair forever.'

'I don't want you out of my hair. You desperately need a bed and to be seen by a doctor.'

Just as Monahan went to protest he stumbled and fell to one knee. Kelly instinctively grabbed him and he bounced back onto his feet.

'No arguments. Rest first and we'll figure out everything else later,' Kelly insisted.

72

Stolen goods

Connor was shown into the room, and Joan closed the door behind him, which meant it was 'serious', as she had warned. His acting editor, Fraser Commons, was sitting behind his desk wearing a half-smile, which looked out of place as he wasn't the jolly type.

'Connor, this is Officer McGill from Special Branch.'

He gave a nod of acknowledgment to his editor before staring at Officer McGill. It was the same cop who had pounced on him before he had even got out of the car in Kilsyth. The officer gave him a snide look in return.

'Funny, I could have sworn you were Royal Protection Squad,' Connor said, looking directly at McGill, whose cocky expression seemed to wane just a fraction as he tried to work out how the reporter had known.

'Not for many years now,' McGill replied, apparently trying to keep things light.

'Give up around 1997, did you?' It was Connor's turn to be cocky.

An uncomfortable silence fell between the two men, only to be broken by the editor.

'Connor, this gentleman is looking for a hard drive that is the property of the Ministry of Defence. He believes it may have been passed to you.'

'Any information used from it will be considered stolen data,' McGill intervened.

McGill may have had the element of surprise during their last encounter, but Connor was well prepared for him this time around, and the reporter wasn't up for playing ball. 'So, what's on it? WikiLeaks stuff? What the French ambassador said to the US President and that sort of shit?'

'It's closer to home than that and it's all highly classified,' McGill replied.

'I see. So what has it got to do with Kelly Carter? And why were you outside her estranged husband's flat acting like a cock?'

The exchange surprised the editor, who had no idea of McGill and Connor's prior encounter.

'Again, that's classified information.'

'Oh, right. So this is basically a one-way street. You tell us nothing and want everything in return?'

'Only the hard drive, Mr. Presley, and that's the last you'll hear from us. As we wouldn't want to bother you with a handling stolen goods charge.'

Connor laughed out loud. 'This is priceless. You march into Scotland's biggest selling daily newspaper, claiming to be from Special Branch when who-the-fuck knows where you're really from. Then threaten me with petty crime. Is that honestly the best you can do? What about handling stolen state secrets? Or would that be too heavy and give the game away?'

'The hard drive, Mr. Presley,' McGill demanded.

'Piss off. I don't have your hard drive.'

'Are you sure?' McGill asked, with all pretence of diplomacy gone.

'Yeah, I'm fucking sure,' Connor said, eyeballing McGill, before his editor intervened.

'Now, now, gentlemen, if Connor comes across the hard drive, we will return it to you without delay, isn't that right, Connor?' He said it as an instruction, rather than a request.

'Of course, as is procedure with any stolen items that come my way. Give me your contact details and I'll buzz you if anything comes up,' Connor replied in the friendliest voice he could muster, only to be betrayed by his eyes that were still looking daggers at McGill.

McGill took a plain business card from his pocket and handed it to the reporter. There was no emblem of any police force on it, or design of any kind. All it stated was 'Charlie McGill', alongside a mobile phone number.

'Simplistic,' Connor said sarcastically while examining the card. 'Special Branch cost-cutting, are they? Saves on ink, I guess.'

The journalist excused himself and returned to the broom cupboard, where he crumpled McGill's card and threw it in the bin.

'What was that?' April asked.

'Some twat's business card.'

'Don't you need it?'

'I've got a funny feeling I'll be hearing from him before he hears from me,' he said while retrieving his man-bag with the hard drive and slinging it over his shoulder. 'Gotta go. If anyone asks, just say I wasn't feeling well or something.'

'Take care,' April said, lightly touching her younger colleague's hand.

'Yes, Mum.'

Connor headed for a side entrance—just to make sure—and called his computer expert contact whilst walking to his car.

'Stevie, I need you to tell me what is on that hard drive. It's vitally important.'

'I told you I want fuck-all to do with this, Elvis. It's dangerous and I'm way out of my depth.'

'You're never out of your depth when it comes to IT stuff, Stevie. Come on, help me out,' Connor protested.

'Flattery will get you nowhere this time. The answer is no.'

'Look, I just need a copy so I can return the hard drive and get the authorities off my case.'

'They'll never be off your case with this.'

'Stevie, it's just a copy. For fuck's sake, I need this.'

There was silence down the line before he finally replied. 'Okay, I'll make you a copy and we'll store it in the data storage centre, where no one can get hold of it. After that, we're through, understand? I never want to hear from you again.'

'A bit extreme, Stevie, but have it your way.'

Connor was greeted with an ironic laugh down the line. 'You still don't have a fucking clue, do you, Elvis? Ignorance is bliss, huh? See if that defence helps when they kick down your door.'

'I'll pick you up in twenty-five minutes. Look out for me,' Connor said before hanging up and starting the car.

73

Home

Kelly walked past her mum's house, which sat just off a bend on the road. The drive was empty and there were no signs of life from within. She turned on her heels and gave a small wave to Monahan walking around fifty feet behind her. He was stooped like an old man crippled with pain. She needed to get him a doctor and a shot of morphine—fast.

Kelly walked up to the keysafe attached to the brick stonework at the front door and entered the five digit code, which was 1950—the year her mum was born—followed by seven. Her mum had thoughtfully had it installed for William in case he cycled to her house only to find she was out.

A twist of the lever later and the contraption gave up its contents. Kelly opened the door then conducted a quick search of the rooms to confirm the place was empty, before Monahan stumbled into the hallway. He now barely had the energy to stand as she helped slip off his backpack. It weighed a ton and contained goodness knows what tools of death.

He gave her a weak smile of gratitude then collapsed on the floor, going down in stages as he clung to her before passing out.

• • •

Monahan woke with a start as a stranger leaned over his bed. He grabbed the man's wrist as he had done to Doctor Shabazi, but this time he didn't have the strength to bring it anywhere near breaking point.

'Whoa, it's okay. I'm Doctor Finlay.'

'As in *Doctor Finlay's Casebook*?' Monahan asked.

'Exactly.'

'Who do you work for?' Monahan demanded.

'The NHS.'

'Then I've got to get out of here,' he said, throwing the covers back. But his legs wouldn't move.

'No need, Mr. Monahan. This is off the books. A favour to Kelly. She used to work at the practice many moons ago. We were sad to lose her.'

Monahan wasn't interested in the doctor's sentimentality. 'How long have I got?'

'Ah, the age-old question. I'd say, staying bed-bound with complete rest, ten days maximum. But I don't reckon you're the type to follow doctor's orders. So half of that. If you're lucky.'

Monahan eyes focused on the ceiling as he calculated if he'd have enough time left.

74

Looking for Lucan

The data storage centre in the north of Glasgow looked like it should be housing furniture rather than digital archives. Its giant shipping-container metallic structure would never win any architectural awards, meaning it was right at home with the other faceless buildings on this anonymous industrial park. Stevie Brett was twitchy as hell in the passenger seat of Connor's car. Irritatingly, he tapped his right foot constantly, emphasising his painfully thin legs through his jeans.

'You'll snap those pins of yours if you keep tapping them,' Connor said, half in jest and half in hope it would make him stop.

Stevie halted his annoying habit as he turned his head vaguely in Connor's direction, only to resume the leg-tapping a moment later.

Connor tried a different technique. 'How long have you had an account at this place, then?'

'Around the same time as my court case. This was where I stored things of interest.'

'Hid the evidence, in other words,' Connor chuckled, desperately trying to lighten the mood. 'What about court orders? Can't they just seize what you keep in there?'

'They've got to know you have an account, first,' Stevie said as his leg thump-thump-thumped away at the footwell of the car.

'So it's pretty secure, then?'

'You could say that. Normally you need twenty-four-hour notice to enter, but you can get access in the case of emergencies. Today is an emergency.'

They pulled up outside the main entrance and, as Stevie had phoned ahead, the electronic gates opened automatically due to vehicle registration number recognition. There were cameras everywhere pointing at every square inch of the parking lot and entrance. Stevie pressed an intercom button and stared straight down the lens of the entry systems camera as he gave both his and Connor's name. They were let inside to a small area, which was more like a holding pen—the outside door automatically locked behind them. At another intercom they were asked to display photographic ID. Stevie showed his passport, whilst Connor opted for his driving licence instead of his press pass as he didn't want to attract attention to himself.

They were then buzzed through to a sparse reception area, where a member of staff asked them to sign a visitors' book and state the reason for their visit. Stevie penned, *Emergency upload*. The receptionist asked if Stevie could remember his seven-digit access code. He confirmed two random numbers from it and was given a key fob that would only open the doors leading to his specified rack. The final security measure was a wall-mounted keypad, where Stevie typed in his memorised PIN number. Immediately a KVM keyboard flipped down in front of him, while the clunk and whirr of various mechanisms filled the confined space as Stevie's personal hard drive was retrieved from the seven-foot-tall storage racks.

'It looks like a pizza box,' Connor remarked.

'Well observed,' Stevie replied. 'That's what we geek-types call them.' He plugged Connor's portable hard drive into his own laptop before plugging it into the storage system.

'And there's no way anyone from outside can access what we leave in here?' Connor asked.

'Correct. It's a ring-fenced network. There is no public-facing access. What data we leave in here, stays in here.'

Stevie accessed the contents of Connor's hard drive. Feeling safe and secure this time, he took his time to browse, with Connor looking over his shoulder. There was a massive number of folders on the desktop. He opened one at random to see various scanned police reports, along with a series of black and white photos showing men at some orgy, having sex with young boys. The abusers were all old, with saggy bodies, but were in high spirits, clearly enjoying themselves. Their victims were mostly submissive, dead-eyed, while others were in obvious distress. Connor thought two of the men looked familiar.

'I always suspected politics was full of kiddie fiddlers,' Stevie said. 'That bastard there,' he said, pointing at the screen, 'was always banging on about how single mothers were ruining the country, or some shit. Don't remember him championing the buggering of underage boys, mind you.'

'It's the fucking Westminster paedophile ring.'

'It sure is,' Stevie replied before clicking on another file. 'And look at this cunt. A minor royal. With a minor. How fucking ironic.' He turned to Connor. 'You do realise this is *the* list. I mean, the cops have something like 1,500 cases of historic sex abuse crimes that they've been investigating. Well, this looks like the lot. There's hundreds of them. Oh, here's our friend Cyril Smith. And I thought he looked disgusting enough with his clothes on.'

'Who's compiled all this?' Connor asked.

Stevie shrugged. 'Who's to know? A disgruntled civil servant, perhaps. Or, more likely, the security services. They've probably seen the way the wind is blowing and knew the Government would eventually launch an inquiry, so they could have bunged all of their most incriminating files onto this and taken the rest off the system. And no wonder—if all this came out, it would rock the very fabric of the nation. Folk wouldn't know what to believe. I mean, look at this guy. Recognise him?'

The black and white picture was of yet another naked man in the throes of passion with a poor child. He was good-looking and vaguely familiar. Connor was convinced he knew his face before the penny finally dropped. 'Fuck me.'

'Fuck me, indeed. One of Britain's best-loved actors. A married, devoted dad. Recently got the OBE, I believe. Everyone loves him. Yet he's a fucking nonce. Sickening.'

They both sat in silence, apart from the noise of the computer's cooling fans, as Stevie flicked through the seemingly endless files full of depraved pictures and various police reports that had obviously been filed then shelved.

'It'll take about five minutes to upload all this stuff,' Stevie explained.

'So child abuse really is everywhere, in every walk of life. This will bring them all down. It's right here on this hard drive. It's irrefutable proof. No one will be able to doubt it,' Connor said, almost in awe of the magnitude of what he was looking at.

'And if your paper doesn't have the balls to print it then that's the beauty of the Internet. We can get this stuff out there. Pictures, police reports, the lot.'

'Click that one there,' Connor said excitedly, pointing to a file titled 'Lord Lucan'. 'If you're Lucan for trouble, indeed,' the journalist said recalling April's swinging hips in the breakout area.

'What did he do again?' Stevie asked.

'Murdered the nanny then did a bunk. Was supposed to have fled to Africa, finally declared dead recently . . . but according to this, he'd been hiding in plain sight.'

They both stared at what appeared to be a fairly recent photograph of an old man posing beside a well-known landmark.

'Remind me, where's that?' Stevie asked.

'The Commando Memorial at Lochaber. So he wasn't hiding in a damp council house.'

'Council house?' Stevie asked, bewildered.

'Sorry, it's an in-joke with April.'

'What the hell was he doing at Lochaber?'

'He was an old soldier. Every military man I've known always makes a pilgrimage at some point to that memorial. I went there once with a troop of Gurkhas.'

'But what the fuck was he doing in Scotland?'

'Makes perfect sense. He was a toff, with toff friends who have Highland estates. Many even have their own private airfields.'

'So a murdering old bastard like him could evade justice and live out his life in the Highlands and no one was any the wiser?' Stevie said, shaking his head.

'Not quite. Someone clearly knew where he was,' Connor said as he read on through the file. 'This even has his pseudonym: "Avery Manford". Here's Avery's National Insurance number too. Probably so he could draw his pension.'

'So the establishment protected one of their own. *Quelle surprise.*'

'Yes, but this file was obviously their insurance policy. To make sure Lucky Lord Lucan toed the line.'

'Lucky, indeed.'

'Look, it appears he saw out his last days in some nursing home for ex-servicemen. What a cunt. He only served for a couple of years and that was in peacetime.'

'Wonder if he regaled the old troopers with his war stories?' Stevie said.

'Yeah, like how he bludgeoned an innocent woman to death with a lead pipe. I'm sure the real war vets loved that. That's a point, though: if he lost his marbles, he'd have started telling everyone he was Lord Lucan.'

'Bet he wasn't the first resident to claim that,' Stevie joked.

'True. Amazing, though. How do you hide one of the country's most notorious fugitives? Plonk him in a care home with all the other forgotten members of society.'

'Oh shit, wait a minute,' Stevie said as he studied another file intently, before he began to chuckle.

'What is it?'

'Diana's the joke. I was looking for the failsafe—the bit of security someone would have installed in case this fell into the wrong hands—and I've found it,' Stevie said, tapping the screen for Connor to look. The picture of Diana in the Parisian tunnel was not one that the reporter had ever seen before. There was sheer terror on the illuminated face of the Princess, taken in what must have been milliseconds before the fatal crash.

Stevie laughed again. 'This is what fucks everything up. This will all be dismissed as yet another Diana story. She is the modern equivalent of JFK to conspiracists.'

'Shit, this really does suggest that she was murdered. Just as Kelly told me. That picture could only have been taken by someone riding right beside her car.'

'Oh, Elvis, and therein lies your problem. The establishment will say it was taken by the paparazzi and proves that the good ol' Queen of Hearts really was hounded to death by the scumbag press. Either way, it means Diana will be the main story here yet again and cast doubt on the authenticity of everything else. You'll just be another Diana nutter trying to sell yet another wacky theory.' Stevie stopped and scratched his head. 'That's strange. The rest of the Diana file is encrypted.'

'Why's that strange? It's a Government file.'

'Yeah, but why just that one, Elvis? Why can we read all about Lord Lucan and not Diana.'

'Because someone forgot to encrypt it?' Connor said, more in hope than with confidence.

'The other way around, I'd say. All the encryptions on the other files were deactivated except the Diana one. These people don't do oversights, Elvis.'

'It's weird, alright.'

'Actually it's worrying. I have a feeling that these files aren't what we think they are.'

'You mean they're fake?' Connor asked.

'No, they're bait,' Stevie said, frowning.

'I wonder what fishy they're trying to catch?' Connor pondered.

'Maybe it's not a fish but a mole. These files are juicy enough to encourage even the deepest sleeper agent to break cover. They'll never let this get out,' Stevie said, the anxiety returning to his voice. 'Elvis, we better leave this building.'

75

Phone home

'Kelly Carter's been trying to get you,' April said with her usual lack of telephone manner.

'I haven't got any missed calls,' Connor said, checking his iPhone while driving.

'No, she's been calling your office phone. She hasn't got your mobile. She lost hers or something.'

'Where the hell is she?'

'At her mum's home in Kilsyth. She wants you to interview someone.'

'Shit. I can't right now. You'll have to do it.'

'But it's your story.'

'It's *our* story.'

'Should I tell her lawyer?'

'Probably. But wait 'till after you've seen her. Call the lawyer after you've left. We don't want Miss McDade telling her client not to speak to the press.'

'She wouldn't do that after all we've done for her. Would she?'

'She might. You never know with lawyers. They are not the journalist's friend.'

'Okay. I'm heading out now. Shall call you afterwards.'

'Take care. There's a lot of strange shit surrounding this whole scenario and I still don't know what it is.'

'I will,' April assured him. She would need to trust her own intuition. It had always served her well in the past when it came to stories—though not so well when it came to choosing men.

76

Targeted

Connor drove Stevie back to his flat in virtual silence. The stolen hard drive was in the journalist's man-bag on the rear seat, out of sight but not out of mind.

As soon as they pulled up, Stevie knew there was a problem. 'My bathroom light's on. I've been broken into.'

'Don't get twitchy,' Connor said, trying to calm him. 'You could have just left it on.'

'What, with my obsessive-compulsive behaviour? Not a fucking chance. I switched that light on and off again exactly ten times before leaving.'

The two men sat in the car glaring at the dim glow from Stevie's bathroom as if they expected to see something.

'We may as well get this over with and walk towards the light,' Connor said, getting out of the car.

'Yeah, like moths to the flame,' Stevie said.

The pair tiptoed as quietly as possible up the concrete stairs, but they were surprised just how much noise they made— from their footfall to the rustling of their jackets. When they reached the second-floor landing they could see that Stevie's door looked intact, with no sign of a break-in. Stevie unbolted the various locks and they entered the flat's hall, with Connor jamming the door with a foot in case they had to make a quick exit. Stevie did a quick scan of his small flat, which didn't take long. 'No one's here.'

'Anything missing?' Connor asked as he locked the front door behind him.

'No, but someone's been here.'

'How do you know?'

Stevie pointed at a corner of his ceiling. 'Because when I left here today, I had a CCTV camera up there. Now I don't.'

Connor could just make out the tips of the multi-coloured wires that had been cut. 'I'm calling the cops,' Connor said while tapping '999' into his iPhone. 'We've got to at least have this documented. Anything incriminating you want to hide before they get here?'

'Not as incriminating as what you have in your bag.'

The pair didn't say much else whilst they waited for the police to come. Connor was on a second cup of coffee when he saw an unmarked car pull up and two men in suits approach the flat.

'Looks like we're getting a special visit, Stevie.'

Stevie buzzed the men in, and Connor waited by the flat's door to meet them. One was around 6'2", in his late forties and with fair hair. He was most likely the superior of the pair. The other was squat and definitely the muscle.

'Evening, gents. Warrant cards, if you don't mind,' Connor demanded.

The men in suits shared a quick look before producing their identification. Connor examined each one closely. 'CID. You lot don't normally act this fast.'

'True,' the fair-haired one said without further explanation. He was definitely the man in charge as Connor had predicted. 'May we come in?'

The men filled Stevie's small cramped hall before being shown into the living room, which was like a computer laboratory. They looked at the mass of equipment briefly before turning to face Connor and Stevie.

'Anything missing?' the fair-haired one asked.

'Not that I can find. Although they did nick my camera,' Stevie said, pointing at the stub of wires in the top corner of the room.

'Destroyed rather than stolen, I'd say,' the cop observed.

'I can't see you fellas dusting for prints, so are you going to investigate this break-in or not?' Connor demanded.

The two men in suits shared another furtive glance before the fair-haired one said, 'Follow me.' He led Stevie and Connor to the front door and pointed at the array of locks the paranoid occupant had added over the years. 'There are five locks here, yes? Yet no sign of forced entry.' He then walked into the bathroom, where the light had been left on. He turned his attention to a panel behind the door. 'These screws have been turned recently as the paint has come off them. I'd take a guess that whoever came in here had blueprints of the premises. It saves time when you know where to look for things.' He then marched back through to the sitting room and straight over to the corner where the CCTV camera had been. He moved the couch that was below it, thrust his hand down the back of it and retrieved the mangled remnants of the camera.

'Destroyed, as I suspected. But still here. So it could have just fallen off the ceiling, however implausible that may be.'

'So what are you telling us?' Connor asked.

'You're the reporter, do I have to spell it out to you?'

'I never told you I was a reporter.'

'You didn't have to.'

'What the fuck is going on here?'

'Clearly I do have to spell it out to you. A break-in with no locks or door damage means they had a key. Or several keys in this case. And they had blueprints for the entire apartment, which they obtained in a hurry. Have you ever tried getting blueprints for you own property from the local council? Takes months. And, finally, we have the "fallen" CCTV camera. Your flat wasn't broken into, Mr. Brett. It was targeted. I'm sorry, boys, I have no idea what you two have got yourself into. As far as we're concerned we've investigated a call for a suspected burglary and found there wasn't one as nothing had been stolen. Case closed.'

The men in suits headed for the front door, with Connor and Stevie following in a trance. The fair-haired one ominously wished them both 'good luck' before closing the door firmly behind him.

It took several moments before either could speak. It was Stevie who broke the silence.

'I told you I wanted fuck all to do with this, but you wouldn't take no for an answer. Know what you've done, Elvis? You've killed us. You've killed us both.'

77

Hobnobs

Monahan woke to April Lavender's considerable weight on his bed, causing the mattress to sag. She was sitting with a cup of tea in one hand and a Hobnob biscuit in the other.

'Oh, sorry I woke you, but there was nowhere else to sit. I'm April Lavender. I work with Connor Presley,' she said, sending crumbs pinging from her gums in Monahan's direction.

'Nice to meet you,' Monahan replied, his voice hoarse from lack of lubrication. 'Where's Connor?'

'He's busy. He said I should speak to you.'

Monahan eyed April up and down, just as Kelly's lawyer, Fiona McDade, had done previously. He was obviously disappointed by what he saw.

'Don't worry, looks can be deceiving,' April said, as if reading his mind. But in truth she had seen his disapproving look several times before.

'I need to know if he still has the hard drive,' Monahan said, ignoring her friendliness.

'He does. He hasn't let it out of his sight,' April reassured him.

'Has he made a copy?'

'I honestly don't know. He was taking it to a computer-geek chappy he knows. But making copies and all that stuff is a bit technical for me.'

Monahan remained silent, as if processing the information.

'I didn't expect Kelly to come back to Kilsyth,' April said cheerily, to break the awkwardness.

'Neither did I. But she wanted to see her kids. I've begged her to hold off for now. She's agreed for the moment. Then there was this . . .' Monahan said, sweeping his hand across the bed.

'I imagine you've felt better,' April said sympathetically.

'I am dying, Miss Lavender. My time is short. Can we get on, please?'

'Oh, yes, silly me,' April said, finishing off the last of her Hobnob before rooting around in her bag for her notepad, pen and Dictaphone. 'Won't be a tick,' she assured him.

'I wish your colleague had come instead,' Monahan sighed in frustration.

April did not like this man, but she did well to conceal it. 'Don't worry, I will go over everything you tell me with him.'

'No. There's no point. Have him call me,' he said, changing his mind and turning his head towards the wall with his eyes closed.

April guessed that was the end of her interview before it had even got started. 'Fine. I shall,' she replied. In truth, she was happy to leave this difficult subject behind. She took her cup and saucer through to Kelly in the kitchen. She was the person she really wanted to interview, anyway.

'That was quick,' Kelly said.

'He didn't want to speak to me. He wants to talk to Connor. I'll have him call.'

'More tea?' Kelly asked, putting the kettle on after April had nodded approvingly.

'You look absolutely shattered, dear,' April said, putting her hand on Kelly's forearm. 'Sit down and tell me everything.'

Kelly talked solidly for nearly an hour, charting all that had happened to her—from the pervert nurse Jim Drury, to being rescued on the M74—as April scribbled down copious amounts of notes, and her Dictaphone recorded every word as back-up. It was sensational stuff. April only hoped that the *Daily Chronicle*'s editor had the balls to publish it all.

When she finally left the old farmhouse April remembered to text Fiona McDade as she'd promised: *Kelly's back in Kilsyth. At her mum's place. April x.*

Fiona had never added a kiss to any text or email she had ever sent, so she replied with a simple *Thank you.* The lawyer then fulfilled her own promise to Officer McGill: *She's home— at her mother's house.*

It was the information he had been desperately waiting for.

78

Highest bidder

'Connor Presley here. I was told to call you.'

'I would have preferred to meet you in person,' Monahan croaked down the phone.

'Not possible. How can I help you?' Connor said curtly.

'Have you seen what's on the hard drive?' Monahan asked.

'Yes.'

'What did you think?'

'I think you had the establishment by the nuts until the Diana crap—half of which was encrypted by the way,' Connor replied.

'Encrypted? Fly bastards. They will never let the truth out about her.'

'The truth? What, that Prince Philip conspired with the security services to stop Diana marrying a Muslim? What a load of shit.'

'So you're a non-believer?'

'Yes, you could put me down as a non-believer.'

'But it's true.'

'That Prince Philip had her bumped off?' Connor snorted.

'No, not the old Greek. But she was bumped off. I know, because I was there.'

'Okay, then you are just another nutter who claims they were part of the Diana conspiracy,' Connor said.

'Are you recording this?'

'Yes. Sorry, I should have told you. I always record my phone interviews,' the reporter said unapologetically.

'I'm glad you are.'

'Look, the Diana stuff demeans everything else on that hard drive and yourself too. If we tried to release it they would just paint you as some lone wolf who had been drummed out of the military years ago.'

'Technically, they'd be correct.'

'Great. So you've debunked yourself. Look, Diana is long dead, but some of the people in those files are still active. They're in the House of Lords. They're still on TV. One of them is an elected Member of Parliament. Surely that's more important than your Diana stuff?'

'But I want the truth to finally get out. All the facts. I can tell you the truth. The stuff that's been encrypted as well.'

'There's still no proof. Just your word against theirs. Why did you take the hard drive in the first place?'

Monahan was momentarily silent, before he answered, 'To get the truth out, just like I said.'

'But who gave you it?'

'A friend.'

'Where is he?'

'Dead.'

'Because of this hard drive?'

'Most definitely.'

'Were you going to sell it to a newspaper?'

Monahan laughed down the phone. 'Are you kidding? A newspaper couldn't afford this stuff. These are state secrets. Nations would pay anything for these. Even Beast Shamer could pay more than a newspaper.'

'How would Beast Shamer have that sort of money?' Connor had not expected Monahan to bring up that website.

'The site is run from Moscow. It's state-sponsored,' he explained.

'I see,' Connor said suspiciously, wondering why Monahan had deliberately brought up the name of the website. 'So is that to be your last act on Earth? Sell to the highest bidder?'

'No. To the right bidder. Beast Shamer will bring those pae-dophile bastards down. The establishment would just suppress it if you tried to publish it here: High Court injunctions, hide behind their expensive lawyers, claim they are too ill to stand trial. But Beast Shamer will release it, drip by drip. There will be nothing the establishment can do to stop it.'

'Unless they destroy the hard drive and all who know about it?' Connor surmised.

'Exactly. That's why I need you.'

'What can I do?'

'Get this damn hard drive to the Russians for their Beast Shamer site and take the money in return.'

'What's in it for me?'

'You can have 100 grand. The rest I need.'

'You can keep your 100 grand. I want the stories.'

'We don't have time and I don't have the energy.'

It was Connor's turn to remain silent.

'Tell me, did you take a copy of the hard drive?' Monahan asked.

'Of course.'

'Thank fuck. Got it somewhere safe?'

'Of course,' was all Connor would say, as he wasn't prepared to let Monahan know where.

'Will you help me get the drive to the Russians? I will make the contact and tell you where and when.'

'I need to think about it,' Connor said.

'Well, don't take too long. Time is not on our side. And it certainly isn't on mine.'

'I'll be in touch,' Connor said, concluding the conversation. He sat in silence mulling over everything Monahan had just said. He decided he didn't like what he'd heard.

79

Dee-lays

'What did you think of Monahan?' Connor asked April as he entered their broom cupboard office the next morning.

'Wouldn't trust him,' April replied.

'Why, because he was rude to you?'

'No, I'm used to that with you. I just didn't like him. All he seemed interested in was whether you had made a copy of the hard drive. When I said I didn't know, he blew me off. Only wanted to speak to you after that,' April explained.

'Yeah, asked me the same shit, then changed the conversation and started banging on about the Beast Shamer website.'

'What do you think is going on?' April asked.

'I think we're being played like an old Stradivarius. And I don't like dancing to someone else's tune.'

'What are you going to do?'

'Unfortunately, I have little choice. I need to see how this thing plays out.'

'Still got the doo-dah, I see,' April observed as Connor casually put the hard drive on the desk. Whenever April didn't know the name for a piece of tech, it became a 'doo-dah', a 'dee-lay' or a 'gizmo'.

Connor was all too aware of her IT limitations. 'It's called a hard drive, dearie,' he said condescendingly. 'You really are hopeless, aren't you? Do you still keep your PIN number by your card?'

April blushed at the memory. They had been heading for their usual breakfast at the Peccadillo when April stopped to get some cash from an ATM. The scrap of paper with her PIN had fluttered to the ground when she took out her bank card, earning her a stinging rebuke from Connor, who'd retrieved it.

'Your PIN number? Beside your bank card. What are you, ninety? Do you keep your savings under a mattress too? And do you make sure you show them to that nice man from the gas board who said he just needed to check your pipes in the bedroom?'

April had been embarrassed not only by her stupidity, but the fact she genuinely could not remember her PIN. She'd never had problems for the thirty-odd years she'd been using ATMs—then one day it was gone and she was left staring at the machine's keypad with a completely blank mind.

Connor may have been brusque with his older colleague but he could also read her like a book. 'Your fading grey matter is the least of our problems. This little black box here is worth £100 million apparently.'

'Wow,' April said in genuine amazement. 'Like a EuroMillions jackpot.'

'Yeah, although there is a very real possibility you can be executed for trying to claim the prize.'

'What about doing a story on it?'

'I don't think our editor would print it after the visit from the man in black.'

'So what are you going to do?'

'If I sit on it, they'll just come after me anyway.'

'Is there anything I can do?'

'Do you speak Russian?

'O-Grade French is it, I'm afraid,' she replied.

'It's fine, I know someone who might be able to help,' Connor said, grabbing his man-bag and heading for the door.

'Don't forget your gizmo,' April said, waving the hard drive at her colleague.

'Thanks. I have a feeling I'm going to need that,' he said, placing it back in his man-bag.

80

Anya

Connor pulled up outside the Hungry Cossacks in Glasgow's Merchant City. He had known the owner, Anya, for years after writing a series of articles about her attempts to adopt an orphan following the Chechen atrocity. The Government had initially denied her a visa for a child until the intervention of Connor and his newspaper, doing the sort of good for society that the media rarely gets credit for. Anya was finally able to adopt a baby in 2008, and Connor had kept in contact ever since, periodically writing articles on the child's various landmarks, like her first day at school.

Anya's Russian accent had gone unchanged, despite her decade and a half living in Scotland, and was so thick that Connor's ears always took a moment to adjust.

'Anya,' he said, warmly embracing her, 'how are you? And where's the star attraction?'

'I'm not your star attraction no more, Elvis?' Anya replied, pronouncing Elvis as 'Eelvis'.

'As far as I'm concerned, yes. As far as our readers are concerned, no. They just can't get enough of Katusha.'

'Hey, Katusha,' Anya hollered in the direction of the restaurant's kitchen. 'Come and speak to the reporter man.'

The girl who emerged through the kitchen doors, still brandishing a dishcloth, seemed to become more beautiful every time Connor saw her. She was blonde and taller than most girls her age, with cheekbones a supermodel would kill for.

'Katusha, you are going to break so many hearts when you're older,' Connor remarked.

'Ya, and I am going to break so many legs,' her mother replied as Katusha wandered back towards the kitchen.

Connor laughed. 'I know you're not kidding, Anya.'

'So how can I help my favourite reporter?' she asked.

'"Favourite" because I'm the only one you know?'

'This is very true. I don't have much to compare you with, but for now you're my favourite.'

'I need your translation skills. I am meeting Russians and I just want to make sure I'm not missing anything.'

'But that is not all, ya?'

'Correct. It could be dangerous. So I want you to think about it first.'

'I have thought about it: let's go.'

'What about Katusha?'

'She can come too. KATUSHA, DAH'LING. TIME TO GO,' Anya shouted in the direction of the kitchens.

'But I said it would be dangerous.'

'Not so dangerous if we bring a beautiful little blonde girl with us, I think.'

'You always think one step ahead, Anya.'

'Where I come from, it was how you stayed alive.'

'I need to fill up my car first,' Connor said.

'Let's take mine. I prefer to drive, anyway,' Anya insisted. 'And I have a nicer car than yours,' she said, grabbing the keys to her Mercedes Benz.

81

Precision

Kelly administered another dose of morphine to help with Monahan's pain. He smiled broadly as the pain reliever coursed through his veins, and closed his eyes to sleep. Kelly took her time checking his heart rate and blood pressure, then finally his temperature. Satisfied all was in order, she leaned over and gave him a small peck on the forehead and left to go and make herself some lunch.

As she closed the door to the bedroom behind her, Monahan immediately opened his eyes and retrieved his iPad from beneath his pillow. He had pre-written a set of explicit instructions with precise timings and colour coding, so everyone was in no doubt as to exactly what they had to do. Monahan had lost none of his legendary attention to detail in his weakened state. He pressed *Send* then waited for the confirmation replies, which he had demanded were sent back immediately. Only when the last one dropped into his inbox was he finally satisfied. He switched off his iPad and placed it back under his pillow and closed his eyes.

This time he would make sure he enjoyed his morphine-induced sleep, as he knew he would need every ounce of his remaining energy for the final push. With any luck he may even dream of one of his missions again. Just the thought of being in the field brought that cocky smile back to his face.

As he slowly began to drift off, the image of a dying woman filled his unconscious state.

But this time it wasn't Diana he was dreaming of, from his dim and distant past. It was a vision of the future. Monahan liked what he saw. He looked forward to his dream coming true.

82

Attack

Stevie Brett gasped for air as the rag, covered in cat hairs, was held against his nose and mouth. He tried to thrash his arms and legs to break free from his attacker, but the powerfully built man held him down on the floor of his flat, with the rag firmly in place. Whoever was attacking him had done their homework. Nothing brought on an asthma attack for Stevie Brett like his cat allergy. A cat only had to have passed through the landing of his apartment block and he could feel his chest tighten up. But now he was inhaling lungfuls of feline fur.

'Where's the copy of the hard drive?' a gruff voice demanded, removing the hairy rag to allow Stevie to answer.

'In . . . data . . . storage,' Stevie spluttered, his intakes of air becoming shorter and shorter.

'Which one?' the man demanded. Stevie gave up the name of the centre where he and Connor had made and kept a copy of the hard drive.

'Make any more copies?' the man demanded.

With no breath left to speak, Stevie shook his head.

'Good lad,' the man said, releasing Stevie's arms and stuffing the cat hair rag into his jacket pocket. 'You had better find your inhalers, then,' his attacker smirked, as he left the apartment, leaving Stevie in the foetal position on the floor.

The computer hacker dragged himself to the chest of drawers that contained his inhalers, knowing he only had seconds before a full bronchial spasm, which would close up his airwaves for good. Stevie was still half lying on the floor when he pulled open the top drawer and felt around for one of several inhalers. He clutched one, put it in his mouth, squeezed the button and inhaled as deeply as he could. But no life-saving vapour came out. He took it out of his mouth and pressed the button twice more, but didn't see the telltale cloud of mist, meaning it was empty. He threw it away and grabbed another, this time pressing the button first before trying to take a breath. But it was empty too. As was the next one and the next. Stevie's head thumped onto his wooden floor, a knowing look in his eyes. His attacker had emptied all of his inhalers.

His post-mortem would state that he died from a massive asthma attack, while an inquiry would conclude that he probably would have survived if he'd kept a closer eye on his inhalers. The official report didn't state it, but anyone reading between the lines would see that Stevie Brett died as a loner and a loser. Only Connor Presley would know that neither was true.

83

A voyage of discovery

Anya, Connor, and Katusha drove towards the west of the city on the M8, heading for the A82 and then the A83. The radio was on, with some BBC phone-in show full of old people moaning about whatever the topic of the day was.

'Every time I hear that programme it's the same old biddies complaining about the same things,' Connor remarked.

'They should come and live in my country—then they would have something to moan about,' Anya chuckled.

'Pensioners have never had it so good. Seriously. They get everything for free. Free bus pass. Free TV licence when they're seventy-five, or whatever. Yet still they complain,' Connor ranted.

'What is it kids say now? "Meh"? Everything is "Meh". So, meh, let them on your radio shows and moan. If we moaned about our Government on radio back home then they'd shut down the station. Straight away.'

'Aye, suppose you're right. Freedom of speech and all that. Just a pity it's always the same people who exercise that freedom.'

'Do you think this country has freedom? Truly?' Anya asked.

'Not truly. I mean, how come on my first day as a cub reporter I was told that Jimmy Savile was a paedophile who was being protected by the establishment? Not a word of it ever made it to print. Yet on his death it all came pouring out. The biggest serial paedophile in British history. Hundreds of victims, from kids to grannies to cancer patients. It was all there in front of us, yet again hidden in plain sight. But none of this came out when he was alive, and he lived a long, long time—right into his eighties.'

'How is this possible? How could you not report it?' Anya asked.

'I obviously didn't try hard enough. There were other journalists just like me who were desperate to go after him. But, mysteriously, all their investigations would be wrapped up with a nod and a wink and a word in the ear of the editor from some establishment figure, promising God knows what. Knighthoods, probably. All editors want to be remembered for their contribution to journalism with a knighthood.'

'And the establishment would do this? Why?' she asked.

'Because child abuse is rife in the establishment, simple as that. So it's in their best interests to cover it all up. But I may finally have proof in a black box in my bag. I haven't had time to go through it all in detail, but it appears to all be there.'

'Your chance to finally put a wrong right?' Anya asked.

'Something like that. Sadly, I believe the same still stands today. If I took this to my editor, it would never see the light of day. So I've been told to take it to some Russians, who will leak it all out. That's where you come in. I need you to be my eyes and ears. I want to make sure this gets to the right people,' Connor said, tapping his man-bag.

'No problem. Let us see if your Russians know their Russian. Katusha, tell these people we meet about your favourite kids' show, *Nu, pogodi!*. Tell me exactly what they say.'

'Yes, Mama,' her daughter replied dutifully.

• • •

They continued driving north, around scenic Loch Lomond, passing through Tarbet, swinging through the curved bay of Arrochar, before putting the pedal down to tackle the steep incline of the Rest And Be Thankful stretch of the A83. A name that, back in the day, would have perfectly summed up the feelings of any coachman making his way over the pass.

They continued towards Loch Fyne, with its famous Oyster Bar, hugging the loch as they wound down towards Inveraray.

'We'll stop for a cone, Katusha—and one for your mum too,' Connor promised.

'I will have a 99,' Anya announced. 'I love those chocolate Flakes. In Russia we did not have these chocolate Flakes.'

'I'll have a Flake too, Mama,' Katusha beamed.

They parked in the high street just down from the medieval jail, which had long since been converted from a place of misery and torture into a tourist attraction. Minutes later they left a shop with three large cones, complete with the promised Flakes sticking out of the top.

'What a beautiful day,' Connor remarked.

'Any day it doesn't rain in Scotland is a beautiful day,' Anya said.

Connor shrugged in agreement. 'This was supposed to be my big James Bond mission. But it's turned into a family day out.'

'And this is bad, why? Maybe you need more normal days in your life, Elvis,' Anya mused.

'Maybe you're right,' he said as they climbed back in the car. His mind now refocused on what lay ahead and the instructions Monahan had given him. 'Our final destination is Crinan. You'll love it there. It has locks, a harbour and even a lighthouse. It's gorgeous. We'll act like day trippers, take in the view, and see if anyone approaches. Sound like a plan?' Connor asked.

'Sounds like spy movie. James Bond, just like you said. This is exciting.'

They sat in virtual silence for the rest of the journey, only breaking it occasionally to point out sights as they passed through Lochgilphead then joined the narrow windy road that hugs the canal built in the early 19th century to connect Loch Gilp with the Sound Of Jura.

'This is the most beautiful part of Scotland I have seen. I had no idea,' Anya said.

'It's one of my favourite places. I love the way it opens up to the rugged West Coast. Stunning. I used to come here with my mum.'

'You don't mention much about your life, Elvis,' Anya said.

'There's not much to mention. Raised by my mum. We were skint. No big deal in the seventies and eighties as everyone was. Then my mum got ill. Huntington's disease. Hereditary. No cure. Horrible. She started going downhill from fifty-five. By sixty-five she couldn't speak or even recognise me.'

'Hereditary. So you can get it?'

'Yup. A straight fifty-fifty chance.'

'Are there tests?'

'Of course. Great if I'm negative. But what if it's positive? Who wants to know that in ten years' time they'll be shitting themselves and unable to speak?'

'That's heavy.'

'I tend not to dwell.'

'What are you going to do about it?'

'What can I do about it? Balance is one of the first things to go. As soon as I start falling over I'm off to Dignitas.'

'You are not serious.'

'I am deadly serious,' Connor assured Anya, killing the conversation stone-dead for several minutes.

'We're almost there, ladies,' Connor announced. 'Stay close to me and keep your wits about you.'

84

Inferno

The flames from the data storage centre could be seen from almost everywhere in Glasgow. Several incendiary devices had gone off in the mail room at the same time, having been delivered that morning by someone doubling as a courier.

Normally, the internal fire suppression systems would have activated, suffocating the flames almost instantly with a mixture of inert gases, and saving the valuable data from being destroyed. But someone had disabled the entire system when the whole surrounding area suffered a major power outage just seconds before the flames took hold.

The delivery man drove off in his courier van, smiling at the raging inferno that danced around in his rear-view mirror. Job done.

85

Cruising

Connor instructed Anya to park next to the Crinan Hotel, by the flagpole that marked where the rocks fell away to the sea below. They walked past the boathouses leading down to the harbour, where yachts glide out to Scotland's West Coast islands and beyond.

Katusha was giddy with excitement. She was also hungry. 'Can we get a sandwich, Mama?'

Connor answered for Anya. 'Of course, there's a café just down by the water.'

'What about meeting your Russians?' Anya asked.

'I'm pretty sure they'll make themselves known to me.'

They ordered a burger, sandwiches, cake, coffees, and a soft drink for Katusha, and then took a seat outside to make the most of the little sunshine Scotland has to offer. Connor made his excuses to use the rest room, which had only one cubicle. He had just finished urinating when he turned round to see a white envelope had been pushed under the door. Whoever put it there had certainly moved stealthily as he hadn't even heard the main bathroom door opening. He tore the envelope open to see three tickets for a boat cruise to the Corryvrechan, with a handwritten note saying it left in ten minutes.

He knew one little girl who would love it. He just hoped her mum felt the same after he explained they were about to visit the third largest whirlpool in the world.

'I got us tickets for the Corryvrechan tour,' Connor said as he returned to the table.

Anya looked sceptical. 'Most men just get piss on the seat when they go to toilet. But you get boat tickets?'

Connor knew he was well and truly busted. 'Okay, I was given tickets,' he said in barely more than a whisper.

Anya raised an eyebrow. 'Well, let's see what happens,' she said, placing a napkin over the pointed steak knife she'd used for lunch and deftly slipping it into her handbag. Connor looked at her in surprise, and she simply said, 'In Russia you must always be prepared.'

'I'm beginning to think that'd be a good motto for Scotland too.'

86

Wessel

The catamaran was around thirty-five feet long and seemed to have been moulded out of one piece of fibreglass. Connor chuckled at the boat's name—*Dignity*—and wondered how many vessels had been named after Deacon Blue's dismal eighties hit about a garbage man who saves up enough money to buy his own 'ship'. Given that the pop group was made up of university graduates, Connor was less than convinced that they'd known many council workers over the years. But he knew that was just the cynic in him, and millions of people had lapped up their brand of middle-of-the-road melodies.

Connor helped Anya and Katusha aboard from the jetty. The rear of the boat was covered in a canopy to protect the paying customers from the worst of the Scottish weather. But today was one of those rare days when the sea was calm and the skies clear. Connor did a quick head-count—there were twenty passengers on board including themselves. For the next few minutes Connor and Anya studied them all, looking for anyone who looked remotely Russian. But Connor found it hard to tell as they all looked like typical tourists, with their bright-coloured rain jackets and sun-tanned skins from warmer climes. He shot a quizzical look at Anya, who shrugged before whispering in his ear, 'I can spot a Russian at twenty paces, but the only Russians here are me and Katusha.'

The skipper was a tall man who did nothing to conceal his height, holding himself up poker straight. Connor took an educated guess that he was a naval man, which was confirmed by his clipped manner when he spoke.

'As you can see there is plenty of room to move about. But please don't let these lovely calm conditions fool you. The Corryvrechan is the most unpredictable lady in the world,' the skipper said, giving a well-rehearsed briefing, which he'd probably repeated hundreds of times before. 'But seriously, you never know how you are going to find her. I've been spun around 180 degrees in a split second. I know of other vessels that have been *rotated* 180 degrees. That's upside down to you non-nautical folk. We really don't want that to happen today.'

The passengers gave a nervous laugh in unison, but Connor knew the skipper wasn't joking.

'So, with that in mind, we shall all put on our life jackets when we are approaching the Corryvrechan. That'll be in about an hour's time. Now, everyone always forgets to fasten the most important part of the life jacket, which is the crotch strap. Please don't be embarrassed to be rooting about down there. It may just save your life. Oh, and if we do have to jump into the drink, please make sure you hold the collar of your jacket tightly. You'd be surprised how many people break their necks with these things—which are supposed to save you, not kill you.'

Definitely military, Connor surmised. In his experience, people in the services always speak about life and death in such a matter-of-fact way.

'Will we see any dolphins?' Katusha asked, with her hand in the air as she would do in school.

'We might see their little cousins, the porpoise, or we might see nothing at all. Nature is as unpredictable as the Corryvrechan. But it's a very flat surface today so keep your little fingers crossed. You can look out for them with these,' the skipper said, slinging a pair of powerful-looking binoculars around Katusha's neck. 'Now you hang on to those or I'll get into trouble from my missus. They were an anniversary present.' And with that the skipper returned to his cabin to start up his twin Iveco 400-horsepower engines, which sent shudders through the fibreglass hull.

The journey from Crinan was like something straight out of a tourist brochure as *Dignity* cut through the plate-glass water, heading towards the ominous gap between the Isles of Scarba and Jura, with its world-famous whisky distillery, and where the red deer population is easily three times larger than the human population.

On clear days like today the roar of the Corryvrechan in full flow can be heard ten miles away. Not that Connor could hear much over the roar of the diesel engines. With Katusha beside her mother, excitedly scanning the water's surface with the binoculars, Connor decided to have a chat with the skipper.

'How long were you in the navy?'

'That obvious?' the skipper replied. 'Too long. Twenty-eight years in total.'

'This looks like a nice little number,' Connor said, looking around the cabin, which was kept as meticulously clean and orderly as you would expect from a naval man.

'It ain't easy,' the skipper said, rubbing the back of his head. 'Sailing is only about 25 percent of what I do. The rest is admin, admin, admin. More red tape than the bloody navy. But then you get a beautiful day like today and it makes it all worth it.'

'I bet—you have a very nice office,' Connor said, gazing out to sea.

'And over there is my secretary,' the skipper said, pointing at a dot in the sky. 'That there is big Bella. A fully-grown sea eagle. There's a spare pair of binoculars in the back if you want to take a look.'

'I don't think I need them, that thing is like a flying barn door.'

'You're not far off. She has an eight-foot wingspan. And she always gives me a little flypast. She's good to the customers that way.'

'What's your name, skipper?'

'Tom MacPherson.'

'Connor Presley. But most people call me Elvis.'

'Okay, Elvis it is.' And the pair shook hands.

'Incidentally, how do you buy tickets for your boat trips? Is it done online? It's just, ours were presents,' Connor said, telling a half-truth as he went fishing for who had bought theirs.

'They need to be purchased from me on the day of the trip. I've no Internet access here. The mobile phone companies are a bloody disgrace. They promised to have 4G in 98 percent of the country, yet in Argyll and Bute our signal is stuck somewhere in 1994. Seriously, the first mobile phone I got was in 1994 and I still get the same lousy signal twenty bloody years later. As for 4G and Internet access—forget it.'

Connor checked the screen of his iPhone. It showed one bar of the most basic 2G coverage, meaning he'd be lucky just to make a simple call. He stored that information away for later as he knew it would make a rainy day news feature: highlighting the broken promises of the major mobile phone operators.

'See those shapes on the beach over there?' Tom asked, as they sailed close to the shore of Jura.

'Seals?'

'You'd think. But they are actually wild Andalusian goats. No one has a clue how they got there. Been living here for centuries. Best bet is they survived a shipwreck from the Spanish Armada. Makes sense. Could be crap, though. But it makes a good story for the tourists.'

'Just hope we don't join them today.'

'Been close a couple of times. Went through the Corryvrechan once in a Force Eight. She was a right angry bitch that day.'

Connor's journalistic curiosity had been well and truly pricked. 'So the main danger isn't always the whirlpool, then?'

'Sometimes it is. You can get huge ones, other times there's a lot of little ones. If you look over the port side you will see a nice little eddy—that's what we sailors call a whirlpool.'

Sure enough, Connor could see a whirlpool, around ten meters in diameter, swirling close to the boat. 'Don't you have to avoid them?' he asked a little anxiously.

'Most are just like potholes in the road. It does you no real harm. But an eddy over ten meters in diameter is probably best to steer clear of. Like a cyclone, there's no telling when the bottom can drop out of it and suddenly you find yourself disappearing down one huge plughole. And we don't want that.'

'I guess not.'

'But what you've really got to watch are the areas of flat calm, like that one,' Tom said, this time pointing towards the starboard side, while adjusting his course to head directly towards it.

'What the heck is that?' Connor asked, mystified. 'It looks weird. Like a duck pond in the middle of a raging sea.'

'The gulf has two tides flowing past each other: as one goes in, the other goes out. That "duck pond", as you call it, is where they cancel each other out. The currents are pulling down so hard not even the waves can pass over them without being flattened out.'

Tom took *Dignity* straight into the calm expanse of water, where the tone of his engines immediately changed. 'Hear that? That's the engines struggling like fuck.'

'Sorry, I'm unaware of your fancy nautical terms,' Connor quipped.

Tom smiled. 'It's true, though. Sometimes even 800 horsepower of engine doesn't feel enough. Right now, the currents are trying to pull this boat down. We're currently sitting about a meter deeper in the water. And please don't fall in. Even with your life jacket on you will still be sucked straight to the bottom.'

Silence fell between them as Connor took in how surreal it felt to be chugging across an area of tranquillity, while a cauldron raged all around them. 'On that sobering note, tea?'

Connor asked as he helped himself to a brew in the cabin, making one for the skipper too.

'I hate those bastards,' Tom said, taking a sip from his mug and nodding in the direction of a fast black speedboat about a hundred meters ahead that seemed to be using the waves as ramps, to launch itself high into the air. 'A rigid inflatable boat. Or RIB, to you and me. Any playboy with a hundred grand can buy one, turn the key, and all of a sudden find themselves dancing through one of the most dangerous stretches of water in the world, without a minute's training. I've lost count of the number I've dragged out of here.'

'What happens to them? Are their engines unreliable?' Connor asked.

'Nah, but their fuel is. They jump around the waves so much that any crap in their fuel tanks gets stirred up and clogs their engines. That's why I triple-filter mine. It's the sort of thing they'd know to do if they cared to read their manuals. Anyway, better get these drinks finished quick, it's about to get a lot bumpier.'

Connor took out a hot chocolate for Katusha and black coffee for Anya.

'Ah, strong. The way I like it,' Anya said, taking a sip.

Something caught Connor's eye. 'Look, Katusha. Dolphins.'

The rest of the passengers looked to where Connor was pointing before the skipper's voice boomed over the tannoy. 'And if you look starboard—that's the right hand side of the boat to you landlubbers—you will see a pod of porpoises.'

'I was nearly right,' Connor shrugged as Katusha fixed her binoculars on the fins that periodically broke the surface of the water in perfect unison.

'Wow, Mama,' she gasped, handing the binoculars to Anya.

'Ah yes, darling. Lovely animals. Very tasty.'

'Mama, you don't eat porpoise?'

'You do in Siberia.'

'And sea eagles?' asked Connor.

'Only for special occasions,' Anya smiled back.

'Mama,' Katusha said, giving her a playful nudge.

'You know, Elvis, I have studied everyone over and over again, when you have been wagging your chin with the captain. We are definitely the only two Russians on this wessel.'

'Did you just say "wessel"?' Connor teased. 'Do you mean "vessel"?'

'That's what I said. Wessel. Wessel. What's wrong with that?' But she lost her audience as Connor and Katusha descended into fits of laughter. 'Okay, boat, then. Happy?' Anya said, pretending to be hurt.

'Soon it will be time to get those life jackets on, folks, so hopefully I come back with as many passengers as I left with,' the skipper's voice said, crackling over the tannoy once more.

There was excited chatter amongst the passengers as everyone got into their life preservers, helping to tighten cords and fasten buckles. The boat was already starting to rise and drop with the increasing swell, which just added to the sense of anticipation.

Connor took a picture of Anya and Katusha on his iPhone before suggesting they try a selfie of all three of them. As he struggled to get everyone in frame, and not drop his phone overboard, a man sitting in the row next to them asked if he could help.

'I don't know about iPhone in Scotland, but in Russia it's very expensive.'

All three of them turned to look at the stranger with the strong Russian accent beaming back at them. Connor had seen him step onto the boat with what appeared to be his wife. But they looked more Spanish than Soviet, with their dark skin, brown eyes and multi-coloured clothes.

'Thank you,' Connor said, handing his device to the man. He could feel the power of Anya's stare studying the interloper.

'It's beautiful here, no?' the man continued. 'Have you been before?'

'Nope,' Connor said whilst posing for the photo. 'It's our first time. Well, certainly the first time on a boat.'

'Are you staying?' the Russian asked.

'No, we're on a day trip. And a bit of business. I'm meeting someone,' Connor said, his eyes still fixed on the Russian.

'Well, you have met someone. I am Oleg Ganichev and this is my wife, Roza.'

Connor introduced himself and they all shook hands. But there was no warmth from Anya, who was still eyeing the strangers. 'You don't look Russian,' she said, in her typical forthright manner.

'Ha, too many years in the Portuguese sunshine. It has made us soft,' Oleg said, sharing a playful cuddle with Roza. 'Would you mind if I talked with Connor for a moment?' Oleg asked Anya, who nodded slowly in response, suspicion etched all over her face.

The pair made their way to the stern, where the twin propellers kicked up great plumes of water, leaving a giant frothy trail of white water in their wake.

'I understand that you may have something for me. Something you want "out there", so to speak,' Oleg asked as quietly as he could, given where they were standing.

'I may do,' Connor replied, keeping his cards close to his chest. 'But how do I know who you are?'

'I'm afraid you'll just need to take a leap of faith,' Oleg beamed.

'I am not a religious man. I prefer proof,' Connor said, eyeballing Oleg.

• • •

Meanwhile, Roza was getting nowhere with Anya, who had taken to looking out at the scenery as the boat bumped and thumped along the rugged Jura coastline, with the waters becoming choppier by the minute. Embarrassed by the silence between the two women it was Katusha who struck up a conversation with Roza.

'Where are you from in Russia?'

'Moscow, darling.'

'Have you lived there all your life?'

'Most of my life. The last few years have been in Europe.'

'What do you do?'

'I teach. I'm a teacher.'

'What do you teach?'

'Russian, darling. I teach foreign pupils how to speak our language and understand our culture.'

'I have lived in Scotland most of my life. Mama has been teaching me Russian. I say it's my second language but she says it's my first. Mama loves Russia. I think she misses it.'

'Your mum is right to miss Russia. It is the best country in the world.'

'Do you watch *Nu, pogodi!*?' Katusha asked.

'*Nu, pogodi!*?'

'My mummy found it on YouTube. It's my favourite show.'

'Ah yes, *Nu, pogodi!*. Of course.'

'You don't know what it is, do you?' Katusha said. 'It's a cartoon, silly. Like a Russian *Tom and Jerry*. How can you come from Moscow and not know *Nu, pogodi!*?' Katusha asked.

Anya turned her head from the scenery to face Roza. 'Because this woman is not Russian.'

87

Bayushki

Connor had just shown Oleg the hard drive that was in his man-bag.

'This will make WikiLeaks look like a picnic,' the Russian said eagerly.

His comment instantly got the journalist's hackles up. 'How would you know? I haven't told you what's on it yet.'

The boat thudded over the choppy waters before they hit another area of flat calm, with the pitch of the engines changing once more. Suddenly, there was a piercing scream. Connor spun round to see Roza struggling with Anya, trying to yank Katusha free from her mother's grasp.

The captain turned to see the commotion going on at the stern, and temporarily lost the careful course he'd been plotting, with the currents violently yanking *Dignity* to the left, causing Anya to momentarily lose grip of her daughter. Roza grabbed the screaming eight-year-old and launched her overboard with all her might.

Time seemed to stand still as the passengers looked on in total disbelief as Katusha's little body hit the calm water and immediately disappeared below the surface, her life jacket doing nothing to save her, just as the skipper had predicted. Connor pushed by Roza to try to grab Katusha, but the girl was nowhere to be seen. Anya was screaming her daughter's name in terror.

The skipper struggled to regain control of *Dignity*, which had left the calm waters and was ploughing straight into the raging sea once more, with a huge wave breaking over the bow. Anya shrieked at the skipper to turn back, and everyone in the boat scanned the waters, looking for any sign of the girl. Everyone except the two 'Russians'. Connor swung around to confront their attackers, only to see Oleg stuffing the hard drive into some sort of waterproof bag, which was attached to his wrist. Connor had seen that exact type of bag before when he had retrieved the hard drive from the layby at Scotch Corner. In the blink of an eye both Oleg and Roza tipped themselves backwards off of the boat. Connor couldn't understand why anyone would throw themselves into near-certain death, until he saw the black RIB approaching rapidly . . . and then it all made sense. Everything had been set up, from the tickets to the speedboat, which would now rescue the 'Russians' escaping with Monahan's hard drive.

'There she is,' one of the other passengers shouted, pointing at the limp body in the orange life jacket that had surfaced about fifty meters behind them. The skipper spun his wheel to the left, and opened the throttle fully, the engines complaining loudly at the extra effort. Connor jumped on top of one of the seats, fixing his eyes on Katusha, willing himself not to blink, in case he lost sight of her.

Suddenly he gasped. 'Oh no.'

'Oh no, what? WHAT?' Anya shouted hysterically.

But Connor could not speak. He saw a giant eddy beginning to swirl and form between the boat and Katusha. Out of the corner of his eye Connor spotted the RIB, heading in the same direction. The boat was smaller and much faster than *Dignity*. The RIB skirted round the edge of the ever-increasing whirlpool and slowed down as it closed in on Katusha. For one grateful moment Connor thought it was going to help with the rescue attempt, before it skipped past the bobbing body of the little girl. He couldn't believe their callousness, but then it dawned on him that something had gone wrong with their mission. He could make out the shape of a very wet Oleg in the RIB—the waterproof bag with the hard drive still attached to his wrist—along with another man at the controls. But there was no sign of Roza.

Good. I hope she's fucking drowned, Connor thought.

The waters around them were gathering pace and Connor knew that any moment now Katusha would be sucked into the vortex. Skipper Tom adjusted his course, veering them slightly away from their target. Anya began screaming again. 'What are you doing? You're wasting time.'

Connor ran to the cabin. 'What's wrong?'

'I'm trying to get the trajectory right. The way we were heading, my propellers would kill her before the eddy. You'll have to try to grab her when I bring her starboard-side. We'll only get one shot at this.'

Connor returned to Anya's side and could now see that Katusha was caught up in the outer orbit of the whirlpool. Her body was gaining speed in ever-decreasing circles. Anya was now hanging half out of the boat, with Connor holding on to the belt of her jeans to prevent her joining her daughter overboard. The skipper killed his speed, throwing the engines into reverse to prevent them being sucked into the vortex. Connor reckoned that in two more orbits Katusha would be gone from them forever.

'Elvis, get ready,' Tom shouted over the tannoy.

Tom was battling to keep his boat in its holding pattern as waves crashed into them from all angles. All the time he was trying to judge the orbit of the girl's limp body. The skipper threw his throttles forward, with Connor leaning over the rear of the starboard side as far as he could go without toppling in. This time it was the turn of Anya to hold onto Connor, grasping his legs tightly. Katusha was close enough now for him to see her mop of blonde hair matted over her face, her eyes shut and her head being tossed from side to side with the movement of the waves.

Connor knew it was now or never.

Skipper Tom used all his naval experience and expertise to hold the boat as steady as he could midway into the massive whirlpool, which had now grown to almost twenty meters in diameter. Tom had judged Katusha's course correctly: she was now heading directly towards Connor and the starboard side of the boat.

Suddenly a wave jerked the boat violently, bringing the stern—and the blades of the propellors—directly into Katusha's path. Anya let out another piercing scream as surf swamped over the sides of the boat, stinging Connor's eyes. He blinked rapidly, trying to clear his vision. Katusha was just meters from the back of the boat when Connor felt the vessel shift again as Tom won the battle to bring her starboard-side again. A fortuitous wave lifted Katusha up almost level with Connor, who stretched as far as he could reach, before the wave bottomed out, pulling the girl back down and sucking her underneath the boat.

Connor practically launched himself over the side. With Anya now hanging onto his calves, he was pointing vertically down into the sea. He thrust his arms as deep as they would go as another wave engulfed him entirely, slamming his body into the boat's solid fibreglass frame and forcing any remaining air from his lungs. Connor thrashed his arms about, but could only feel the shocking, raw force of the currents trying to pull him to his death. Then he felt something pass his right hand. It was hair. He grabbed all he could and pulled hard, while swinging his left hand up to grab onto the side of the boat. He heaved with everything he had to bring in his catch. His head broke the surface and he gasped for much-needed air, then hauled again. Two older male passengers were now pulling Connor's left arm, lifting him into the boat. But he could not and would not let go of the handful of Katusha's hair. He gave one last haul, as he fought a life or death tug-of-war with the Corryvrechan.

'Katusha,' Anya screamed out as her daughter surfaced. She leaned over and grabbed at Katusha's life jacket. Connor could feel the girl's body being hauled past him, before he followed her back up onto the safety of the boat. He lay still, blinded from the seawater and unable to move from sheer physical exhaustion.

Tom swung the boat round, bringing the rear within meters of the centre of the vortex as he gave the engines everything they had. But the vessel continued her drift backwards, heading to oblivion no matter how loudly the outboards screamed in protest. Just as it seemed like their rescue attempt was in vain, the propellers started to bite, and almost through the sheer willpower of everyone on board, *Dignity* stopped moving backwards. The boat came to a virtual halt before finally beginning her slow surge forward to safety.

Connor hauled himself up to cough up seawater from his lungs before he was sick over the side. His vision cleared briefly enough for him to see the black RIB, with Oleg and the hard drive attached to his wrist, speeding off into the distance, having abandoned their own rescue attempt of Roza.

The boat was now clear of the whirlpool. Connor was about to slump back onto the deck when something orange flashed before his eyes in the water. It was Roza's lifejacket, but without Roza. He leaned over and managed to grab the collar, bringing it in. He closed his eyes and lay shivering from the cold. One of the older passengers had declared he was a doctor and was currently working on Katusha, rhythmically pumping water from her lungs. Connor heard the little girl cough then let out a loud cry.

Skipper Tom was now by the reporter's side, the boat on autopilot. 'Well done, lad. Well bloody done.'

Connor held up Roza's lifejacket.

'She didn't attach the crotch straps,' Tom said. 'The Corryvrechan would have sucked her right out of the jacket to the very bottom of the sea. Serves the bitch right.'

Connor, Anya, and Katusha moved into the warmth of Tom's cabin, where they stripped off their wet clothes and wrapped themselves in blankets. Connor began to drift off to sleep, whilst Anya cradled her daughter in her arms and softly sang an old Russian nursery rhyme:

Bayu bayushki bayu
Ne lazhisya na krayu
Pridet serenyki volckok
Y ukusit za bochok.

She then sang it in English:

Don't sleep on the edge of the bed,
Otherwise a grey wolf will come
And bite you on the side.

88

Verification of Death

Monahan checked his iPhone after receiving a text. He stared at the message before a smile grew across his face. He then gave a silent fist-pump and mouthed the word 'Yes'. It was a routine he always did at the end of a successful mission.

• • •

The doorbell went just as Kelly brought Monahan a cup of tea, to help wash down the nutrition shake.

'Should I answer it?' she asked him.

'Yeah, why not. What have we got to lose?'

Monahan could hear Kelly talking at the front door before inviting someone in. He listened to the visitor's heavy footfall. *Cop*, he thought to himself.

'An Officer McGill to see you, Malcolm,' Kelly said, introducing their guest.

'Charlie McGill. I wondered when you would turn up,' Monahan beamed.

'Shall I leave you both to get on with it?' Kelly asked.

'I'd rather you stayed,' McGill insisted. 'This concerns you too. I am here for the hard drive'.

'Straight down to business. You haven't changed much, have you, Charlie boy?' Monahan replied.

'The hard drive, Malky,' McGill said more sternly.

'Well, here's the thing, Charlie. I gave it to a reporter. You know, so we can get the truth out there. Expose all the paedos. Tell everyone what really happened to your beloved Diana.'

'You didn't give a shit about Diana,' Charlie spat, his face turning red with anger.

'That was always the problem with you, Charlie. You cared too much. All that time spent with Little Miss Doe Eyes turned you native.'

'Where is the hard drive?' McGill demanded.

'You missed your chance, Charlie. You must be getting slower in your old age. The reporter took it up the West Coast. If you had been keeping tabs on him, you would surely have known that?'

'We had a breakdown in communications,' McGill admitted.

'What is going on here? How do you both know each other?' Kelly asked.

'Sssh,' Monahan said, putting his finger to his lips. 'Charlie here is going to confess how he fucked up. So go on, Charlie. How did you miss a sitting duck?'

'We lost his mobile's location. It's the lousy signal up north,' McGill said shamefaced.

'A rookie's mistake. But surely you had his car bugged, Charlie?'

'He took a different car. They went in some Russian woman's.'

'And your men couldn't follow it?'

'I don't have any men. It's just me.'

'How can it just be you? You're a policeman,' Kelly said in amazement.

'Because old Charlie here has gone rogue,' Monahan interjected. 'Isn't that right, son?'

McGill pulled a Heckler and Koch 9mm pistol from underneath his jacket and pointed it directly at Monahan's head.

'Still using that peashooter?' Monahan laughed.

'Where is the hard drive?'

'It's in safe hands,' Monahan said smugly.

'With the reporter?'

'I said *safe* hands. He'd have tried to publish what was on it. Like you and that Russian website. Name-that-nonce-dot-com, or whatever it's called.'

'Beast Shamer,' McGill replied calmly.

'That's the one. If you hadn't started leaking the nation's secrets, there wouldn't have been any need for this whole operation.'

'Operation?' Kelly said, now totally confused.

'But you didn't have that much info, did you, Charlie son?' Monahan continued, ignoring Kelly. 'Just a few old lords who liked their young boys, and all that Jack the Ripper nonsense. But your Russian paymasters wanted more, didn't they? A lot more. That's when we let it be known that it was all on a hard drive. Every embarrassing secret and cover-up, right there, inside a little black box. And it was all up for grabs for the first person who could find it.'

'You set a trap?' Kelly asked. It was dawning on her that Monahan had been lying all along. That all this—everything— had been orchestrated by Monahan just to reel in McGill.

'You need to set a trap to catch a mole, my dear,' Monahan said smiling.

'Don't call me "dear". You used me. You put my whole family at risk. You killed my mother,' Kelly said, suddenly realising it had been Monahan who was behind the car bombs.

'All part of the show. It had to be convincing. That these secrets were worth killing for. And they are, believe me.'

'And Doctor Shabazi too?'

'Yeah, Duggie was always a dab hand with explosives. He's not bad with incendiary devices either. Basically anything that goes off with a bang, then Duggie is your man,' Monahan replied nonchalantly.

'Doctor Davies? Nurse Mackay in the neighbouring flat?' Kelly asked.

'Agents. They were keeping an eye on me in case the mole turned up.'

'And me being kidnapped in the Highlands?' Kelly continued.

'Sorry, we hung you out to dry with that one. Our friends in MI5 did us a turn. Kept you under the radar. Again, it was to make it as convincing as possible to you and our mole.'

272 | Matt Bendoris

'You took one hell of a risk putting all that info out there,' McGill said.

'It was worth it to catch you, Charlie boy. I was supremely confident it wouldn't reach the public domain.'

'Arrogantly confident more like. The reporter's computer geek friend has probably made a copy,' McGill continued.

'Correct. He had, but again, it's all taken care of. The geek is no more. Had a bad asthma attack, according to Duggie, and the copy's gone up in smoke. So you're right, I do feel arrogantly confident. That's how winners feel, Charlie. But you wouldn't know anything about that, would you now?'

'You know what they say about pride before a fall,' McGill warned.

'Ah, Charlie. The only proverb I live by is "when the going gets tough, the tough get going",' Monahan sneered.

'Are you even sick?' Kelly asked.

'Only in the head,' McGill butted in.

'Exactly.' Monahan smiled. The shot was deafening, forcing Kelly to put her hands over her ringing ears as she slumped down on one knee. Disorientated, she looked up to see Monahan was still grinning. There was a black hole in the white sheet, with a puff of smoke rising from it. She turned round to see McGill clutching his bloodied arm, his gun lying on the floor.

'I never did like you, Charlie,' Monahan said, throwing the covers back to reveal a handgun that looked a lot bigger and more powerful than McGill's. 'You worshipped the ground Diana walked on. But she was nothing but a filthy whore who'd sleep with anyone who showed her any attention . . . A bit like yourself, dear,' he said, turning his gun towards Kelly. 'Didn't take much to get you into the sack, did it? With a patient too. You should be struck off.'

'You're insane,' Kelly said, turning to attend to McGill.

'They don't call me Mad Malky Monahan for nothing. And leave him alone. Dying's too good for his type. But I *will* take his gun. Pick it up by the barrel very slowly and put it on the bed beside me. There's a dear.'

Kelly did as she was told, making sure she made no sudden movements. 'You planned all of this, didn't you?'

'Most of it. You were a bit of a Brucie bonus, in more ways than one. I improvised. When I saw you reading that Diana shite, it was too good an opportunity to miss. You were the perfect cover story. There was a good chance our mole here would have seen right through me, even with all my deathbed confession shit. But you swallowed it hook, line, and sinker. The poor nurse caught up in a massive conspiracy. It was the perfect trap.'

'Can you even hear yourself?' Kelly asked. 'You took advantage of someone who cares for terminally ill people.'

'Oh, my poor, little angel,' Monahan mocked. 'I do look ill though, don't I? I had to convince you I was really dying. My notes said I was, so why would you doubt it? The iodine drops in my eyes also gave me that lovely jaundiced look. Months of dieting helped a lot as well. Can't wait for a dirty big steak. I'll be glad if I never taste a nutrition shake for the rest of my life. Chuck in some erratic breathing and Bob's your uncle and Fanny's your aunt.'

Kelly could do no more than shake her head in disgust.

'There was just one snag. A little side effect, if you will. I have become rather accustomed to the morphine. Be a dear and reload the machine for me,' Monahan said, indicating with the barrel of his gun towards the syringe driver. 'I think I've become a wee bit opium-tolerant. I'll sort all that out once this is all over though.'

Kelly changed the empty syringe for a new one full of the yellow, powerful, pain-relieving liquid.

'And I know my dosage is thirty milligrams. So don't try to overdose me,' Monahan warned, still pointing the gun at her menacingly.

Kelly set the digital display to thirty milligrams as instructed, turning it round to show her hostile patient. 'Happy?' she asked.

274 | Matt Bendoris

'Perfect. I may as well have one last whack to celebrate. This shit is better than champagne.'

A tense moment of silence passed before Kelly asked, 'Did you really kill Diana?'

Monahan burst out laughing. 'Fucking Diana. That's all anyone wants to bloody know about. What does it matter?'

'I would just like to know.'

'I bet Charlie would too. He's spent the last two decades trying to find out. Haven't you?'

McGill groaned a response. The colour had completely drained from his face, and a dark stain was growing around where he clutched his shattered arm.

'Of course I killed the bitch,' Monahan said smugly.

'I don't think you did,' Kelly replied calmly.

'Oh yeah? What makes you so sure?'

'Psychosis. I've seen it in patients before. Yours is probably post-traumatic stress disorder. No one who has done all the things you have escapes unscathed.'

'Save me all the touchy-feely bullshit.'

'Don't get me wrong. I believe you were in the tunnel that night. But I think you were trying to *look after* Diana. You were part of her security detail. But something went wrong, didn't it? Her driver was going too fast. He clipped that Fiat Uno and crashed. Your Fiat Uno. The one you were driving. The one I saw in the garage,' Kelly said, placing her hand softly on Monahan's knee. 'But Mad Malky Monahan could never fail, could he? Your reputation relied on your 100 percent success rate, am I right? No one could know you screwed it up. So over the years, Diana became one of your hits. Another successful mission. I think you started to believe it yourself. But I understand. I truly do. You are not a well man. Your mind is in turmoil. But it wasn't your fault, Malcolm. It was just an accident.'

Kelly wanted to keep Monahan talking, but she knew it was a gamble: Monahan could so easily respond with the squeeze of a trigger. He stared silently into the middle distance, recalling events from his past. Eventually he whispered, 'The stupid cow should have worn her seatbelt.'

'Let me help you, Malcolm,' Kelly continued. 'Let me get you the treatment you need. It's time to stop the mayhem.'

Monahan turned his head towards her, his eyes now refocused and full of menace. He grinned. 'Nice try, dear. But your Florence Nightingale act won't wash with me. Yes, MI5 instigated a cover-up. It wasn't a conspiracy to murder, but to hide the fucking accident. If it wasn't for that useless French driver going like the clappers . . . he nearly took me out in the Uno before he swerved and crashed. I knew she was fucked the minute I looked at her. That's why I left that file encrypted. If something had gone wrong then I couldn't have that one slipping out on Charlie's Beast Shamer website, tarnishing my good name by being involved in the biggest fuck-up in the history of our secret services. That file will go back into the vaults forever more and my dirty little Diana secret will die with both of you.'

'I knew you were involved.' McGill said, grimacing through the pain. 'You were always too gung-ho for my liking. Your ego was too big for protection work. You had to be the centre of attention.'

'Guilty as charged, Charlie. What a total waste of my time and energy it was trying to look after your whore of a princess anyway.'

'She was a better person than you could ever hope to be.'

'Wasn't too good at picking her friends though, was she? Or her lovers. Was she, Charlie? Did you want to be her *true* friend? The man who would always protect her. Maybe even get a wee shag in return? Then she took up with a flash Arab and I bet she never looked twice at you again.'

'There's no point even arguing with you, Monahan. Kelly's right, you are insane,' McGill said as he leaned back against the bedroom wall for support, the energy seeping from him as quickly as the blood from his wound.

'And you'll be quite dead shortly, Charlie. Wonder if Elton John will write a soppy song for you as he did for your precious Di? *Like a candle in the shitter, he didn't know what had hit her . . .*'

'Go fuck yourself, Monahan.'

'So am I to get a bullet too?' Kelly asked.

'If you want. Would be quicker that way.'

'Where will it end, Malcolm? When will the killing stop?' she asked.

'I'm afraid I'll have to be in the cold, hard ground before that ever happens.' He raised the barrel of the gun and aimed at Kelly's head. 'Ah Kelly, dear. It was fun. I'll do you first before finishing off old Charlie boy here.'

Kelly and McGill braced themselves for what was coming. But nothing happened. The seconds ticked past slowly as they remained frozen to the spot, like a cast waiting for an actor to remember a line. The tension was broken when Monahan gave a small cough, followed by another, then another. Each becoming louder and more hacking, and the gun now shaking in his hands.

'I can't breathe,' he gasped, dropping the weapon onto the bed as he clutched at his throat. 'Help me,' he spluttered. 'HELP ME.'

Kelly picked up both his and McGill's guns and placed them out of harm's way, whilst Monahan began to thrash violently around the bed.

'What have you done?' he said, yanking the intravenous drip lines out of his arm. 'What's happening to me?' His gasps for air were becoming shorter and shorter.

'It's called opiate poisoning, dear,' Kelly explained calmly in her best bedside manner. 'You may experience symptoms including itching, flushing, constriction of pupils,'—she prised open one of Monahan's eyelids, to see his pupils were just pinpricks—'followed by a lowering of the heartbeat, reduced rate of respiration, failure to breathe, unconsciousness then death.'

'But I saw . . . It was thirty milli . . .' Monahan croaked, unable to find the breath to finish his sentence.

'Yes, it was thirty milligrams—but over five minutes rather than twenty-four hours. You've just had a full day's dose of morphine.'

Kelly could see panic in Monahan's eyes. 'You've killed me . . .'

She ignored his accusation. 'Doctor Shabazi had already pre-signed your VOD. That's your Verification of Death proforma,' she said, producing a triplicate A4 sheet from her nursing bag. 'He helpfully filled it in for me the first night he examined you. We always do that in advance for expected deaths with patients in the community. It is specifically for when the cause of death is known. In your case, cancer. I just have to verify it now. There will be no post-mortem. No enquiry. Nothing at all,' she said, taking the pen from her top pocket, clicking it, and adding her signature to the forms. 'Now, Malcolm, all that's left is for you to rot in hell.'

Monahan looked at Kelly, knowing in his final moments that he had broken a cardinal rule for the first time in his long military career. He had underestimated his opponent. It proved to be fatal.

89

Censored

What appeared in the *Daily Chronicle* bore little resemblance to what had actually happened. Connor and April reported that the kidnapped nurse Kelly Carter had been found safe and well and reunited with her family. April's 'world exclusive' interview with Kelly did include that fact that she ended up running for her life with her children from a shoot-out at a safe house near Stirling. But there were many gaps in the story, as a result of the *Daily Chronicle*'s lawyers going through the copy with a fine toothcomb. The final report left the readers with many more questions than answers.

There was only a passing reference to the deaths of Doctor Shabazi and Kelly's mother from two car bombs. The same could be said for Connor's contribution about an incident aboard a boat in the Corryvrechan—it was also scant on detail and concluded with the ambiguous statement that police were looking into things. Such fleeting mentions of these incidents just added to the disjointed feel of the entire article.

Of course, this was not how Connor and April had originally written it. They had told the whole story of Government secrets on a stolen hard drive, which had been leaked to catch a mole in the security services who had gone rogue since the cover-up of the Princess Diana tragedy. But the final article that made it into the newspaper didn't contain the information about an establishment paedophile ring, with many of the protagonists still in positions of power and influence. It also failed to detail the activities of a man who had played the part of a double agent—someone who pretended to be terminally ill and used an innocent nurse, killing her colleague and mother. All just to snare a mole.

There was also no mention at all of the mole himself, Officer Charlie McGill, who had disappeared from their final copy just as he had in real life. April and Connor's entire piece concluded with the death of an ex-serviceman, Malcolm Monahan, from 'natural causes'.

Connor threw the paper in disgust across the table in the Peccadillo towards April. 'And to think I honestly believed they would have the balls to print the lot. That the *Chronicle* would stand up and be counted as a source of truth and justice. Instead I can't make head nor tail of that fucking report. If it doesn't make sense to me, fuck knows what the readers will make of it.'

Connor's swearing had caused two elderly diners at a neighbouring table to look in his direction.

'Well, it's done now,' April said, trying to defuse his temper, but only managing to pour more fuel on the fire.

'Yes, it is done and newspapers are done,' he said, his voice growing louder. 'We're screwed. We've been screwed by the Internet and screwed by Leveson. Now we've been left neutered and toothless. Publish and be damned, my arse.'

April could feel other customers' stares boring into them. She wondered what it would be like to be young and fiery again. She hadn't got het up over anything in a long time.

But Connor looked like a broken man as he stared vacantly at his front page. 'I used to love newspapers. Now I can't fucking stand them.'

April finished her breakfast in silence, leaving Connor to his thoughts. She couldn't help think that her colleague was right.

90

Nanny-cam

'Got him,' the auxiliary nurse Cathy said, barely able to contain her glee when she called April using the number on the business card the reporter had left her.

'Who?' April asked, flummoxed as usual after just arriving in the broom cupboard to start her day.

'The fat bastard. Jim Drury. I've got him on camera.'

The penny finally dropped. 'Cathy?'

'Aye.'

April was pleased she had remembered her name. 'What have you got exactly?'

'Right, I don't know anything about technology.'

'That makes two of us,' April replied.

'But my son Colin does. He works in IT. Anyway, I'm telling him how one day I would love to catch that pervert abusing the patients when he says, "Get a nanny-cam, Mum." Now I haven't a clue what he's on about. But sure enough he clicks on his Internet thingy, and up comes a bedside clock that is really a secret camera. He says it's really popular in America for catching nannies smacking kids or old dears being abused in homes by their carers. Now, I thought, *I can't afford that— it'll be a fortune.* But guess what? It was only £20, including post and packaging. How can anyone make technology that cheaply?'

'I have no idea,' April said genuinely.

'Anyway, Colin buys it for me and sticks a dee-lay in it. What's that called again, Colin?' Cathy asked, bringing Colin into the background of the conversation.

'A memory card, Mum. I think your memory needs an upgrade.'

'Did you hear that?' Cathy said. 'Cheeky swine.'

'I have a cheeky swine in my office too,' April said.

'Anyway, I knew the fat bastard had taken a shine to a new patient. She was a petite wee thing, no match for that big lump of lard. I just knew he would try it on with her because I know what he gets up to. The patients tell me. They'll say that he has been touching them up. I took it to my supervisor more than once. But he said that without proof, it'll just be a mental patient's testimony against a long-serving medical professional. "Professional", my arse. The man's a pervert. He's disgusting. Can't even wash himself. Wears the same uniform all week even though his own colleagues have complained about his personal hygiene. But he plays the weight card. Got his union to say he's being picked on for his obesity. Everyone knows how to play the system these days, don't they?'

'Not everyone. I wouldn't know where to start,' April conceded.

'Aye, true. Me neither. Anyway, I plug the wee clock in and put it on the cabinet by this wee lassie's bed. Colin told me to point it in the direction where I think Fatty would be standing if he gets up to any funny business during the nightshift. The next day I start my shift at seven in the morning and this wee lassie is all agitated after he's been looking after her, so I know something's happened. I unplug the clock and put it in my bag to take home for Colin here and . . . we got him.'

'Recorded on camera?' April asked.

'Aye.'

'That should be with her now, Mum,' April could hear Colin saying. A new email appeared in April's inbox, containing not only the 'highlights' of the secret camera footage, but also some helpful freeze-frames showing the abuse, clear as day. In one of them the nurse is gripping his patient's breasts tightly.

'Like to see how he wriggles his fat arse out of this one,' Cathy said. 'Maybe he'll claim he was giving the patient CPR for a heart attack.'

'I doubt that explains grabbing her breasts,' April said in disgust, looking at the pictures.

'Well, this time I want to make sure there are no excuses. I want that bastard in jail. He's been doing this for years and getting away with it. I am giving these photos to you first, April. He is on day shift today and finishes at 7 p.m. He likes to leave bang on time, no matter what's happening on the ward. I'll even tell you what car he drives and where he parks. But tomorrow morning, I am taking these photos to the police. Deal?'

'Deal,' April said gratefully, as that meant she could front up Nurse Drury about the abuse pictures and get them in the paper before he was even arrested. The paper wouldn't be able to publish the images after he was charged as they would be deemed *sub judice*, preventing him from getting a fair trial.

'Just make sure everyone knows his face. I never want that beast to be left alone with vulnerable young girls again.'

'I shall,' April promised. 'And thank you, Cathy.'

April thought about all those high-society abusers who had gone unpunished. But now April could do her little bit for the victims. She forwarded the email to her news editor, picked up her jacket and coat and walked over to his desk. She would explain Cathy's story. Then she would meet a photographer to confront a sex offender.

91

Double-crossed

'Fucking horse-wanking, sheep-shagging, twatting arse-holes,' was all Connor heard as he answered the call from DCI Crosbie.

'Something up, Bing?' Connor asked, as bewildered as ever by the cop's profanities.

'Not to mention that little cock-sucking, double-crossing toerag.' This part of the detective's foul-mouthed rant made Connor's ears prick up.

'By which you mean Amy Jones?' the reporter tentatively asked.

'Yes, Amy fucking cow-face cunting Jones.'

Connor couldn't contain his glee. 'So the honeymoon is well and truly over?' he asked, with his fingers crossed.

'Damn twatting right it's over and so is my career. The little snitch bitch did me over.'

Connor's face dropped. 'I told you she was dangerous.'

'Aye, but you said that while I had my cock in her mouth, Elvis. No man is going to listen to rational advice while he's been sucked off.'

'What did she do?' Connor asked, trying to drive the conversation away from the detective's cock.

'She ratted on me. Started sleeping with my slippery, shit-arsed superior. His pillow talk extended to asking who her police sources were and, hey presto, up pops my name from the little fuck.'

'Have you spoken to her? Asked her why.'

'Sure did. As soon as I was frog-marched out of the call centre I called the little cunt. She said I was about to get sacked anyway so I would be of no use to her. Imagine that. She just told me straight. What a shit she turned out to be.'

'How did she know you were about to be sacked?' Connor was curious now.

'My dickhead boss must've told her.'

'So it wasn't just leaking stories. You'd done something else?' Connor asked.

'Aye. Maybe,' DCI Crosbie replied, a few octaves lower.

'Which is it, Bing? Aye or maybe?' Connor probed further.

'Aye. I was up for gross misconduct for something else. But I couldn't help myself,' the detective replied defensively.

'What couldn't you help, Bing?'

'Okay, despite what they'd all been hoping I'd do, I have never dropped one fucking swearword while speaking to a caller. Some minor muffing miracle, I know. Then there I am one day, being the professional call-handler that I am, when a call comes in from some old fucker saying he thinks someone is trying to break into his neighbour's flat. He starts banging on about his eyesight being shite or some pish, but he's pretty certain he saw someone force a window on the ground floor and disappear inside. I'm just about to get the bizzies round to bust some bollocks, when I ask for the old bastard's full name.' Crosbie had to stop talking as his voice began crackling with laughter.

'What was his full name, Bing?'

'A Mr. Ian Martin Cumming.'

'And what is wrong with that?'

'Don't you get it? Ian Martin Cumming? I.M. CUMMING. Fuck me, I couldn't speak from laughter. I was pissing myself. What do actors call it again?'

'Corpsing.'

'That's the bastard. Corpsing. So anyway I'm corpsing so bad that I failed to put the housebreaking call through, didn't I? Meanwhile Mr. Cumming is not fucking amused, I can tell you. Even when he starts asking for my shoulder number, to put a complaint in, I can't talk because I have totally lost the fucking plot by this time. So someone takes over the call. But by the time we get a unit round to his neighbour's flat, not only has the housebreaker fucked off, but he's battered the old homeowner senseless too.'

'Shit.'

'Shit, indeed,' DCI Crosbie agreed. 'But at least I was worth another story for Arsehole Amy. She's just phoned me for a comment on how I feel about laughing at an old-age pensioner reporting a crime while his elderly neighbour is being beaten to a pulp. I am well and truly fucked, Elvis.'

'You are,' Connor agreed. 'I can't even do your side of the story to counter hers, as your version is actually worse.'

'I know. Anyway, I'm suspended on full pay for the moment while they investigate a wilfully-neglecting-police-duty charge. Although I wasn't doing it wilfully, I was just literally pissing myself.'

'Not much of a defence, is it, Bing?'

'Not really. Anyway we should meet up for a beer sometime if you fancy it, while I still have some money or before they lock me up.'

'Will do, Bing. Will do.' Connor ended the call with a frown on his face. He feared his sweary detective had finally come a cropper.

92

Romeo

'Where are you off to? Got a date?' April asked as she packed her bag to head off and confront the pervert nurse.

'Just off to see how wee Kat is getting on. Going to take her up a present,' Connor said, brandishing a Hamleys bag.

April raised both eyebrows.

'Don't give me that look,' Connor said.

'I've said nothing,' April protested.

'You don't have to. Your chubby wee face says it all.'

'I just think you've been seeing quite a lot of them both. I don't know if I'd be so keen to hang around a man who nearly drowned my first-born.'

'I know. But Anya just dismisses it any time I try to bring it up. It's as if seeing your daughter being thrown into a whirlpool by a secret agent is just one of those things. Maybe it is in Russia?'

'How is Kat getting on?'

'She's got a chest infection. Something to do with the damage to the lungs from the seawater. They've got her on prophylactic antibiotics. But apart from that she's fine. You'd never know anything had happened. They're made of tough stuff these Russkies.'

'Well, give my love to her. And I hope you've got something for the mum too in that bag, Romeo.'

'No. I haven't. Thought it might seem inappropriate.'

'You nearly got her daughter killed, you skinflint. The least you can buy her is a bunch of flowers. Go into Markies on your way there.'

'I will do,' Connor said as he headed out. But he already had something else for Anya.

93

Plop

April found Nurse Jim Drury's four-by-four Jeep in the hospital's staff parking lot. It was just as Cathy had described: large, filthy, and clapped-out. *A bit like its owner*, April thought to herself. The Jeep was technically on private grounds, meaning Jack Barr would need a long lens to snatch the nurse while standing on the pavement in a public area. The reporting team wanted to make sure they did everything by the book, lest they receive a complaint via IPSO—the Independent Press Standards Organisation, which was set up in the post-Leveson era—by either Nurse Drury or his NHS trust.

April hoped Cathy would be okay. She would hate for her to lose her job, but the auxiliary nurse was a determined little soul and nothing would stop her from trying to nail the sex offender on her ward.

April perched her backside on the bonnet of her purple Daewoo, with the suspension sagging in protest. She had reluctantly taken the car into a friendly mechanic who had got her doors opening and closing again so she didn't have to use the hatchback in an ungainly fashion. Her mechanic had also urged her to buy a new car, which April thought was just a terrible waste of money as it didn't take long before all her vehicles looked as banged up as the poor old Daewoo.

She sat eating another chocolate éclair from the hospital 'restaurant' and had a caramel latte listing at a crazy angle on the bonnet beside her. Generally, she hated doing stake-outs as many were utterly useless affairs because they were often from the most erroneous tip-offs.

The éclair and the coffee helped pass the time until she saw her target lumber into view. Nurse Jim Drury walked in some discomfort, out of puff from hauling his huge frame the short distance from the ward to his car. His immense size made April feel positively skinny. She also knew there would literally be nowhere for him to run.

Drury had his keys out in anticipation as he approached his Jeep, which was inconsiderately parked over two bays. He always did that to allow himself more room to get in and out of his driver's door, even though spaces were at a premium. He kept telling himself he would apply for a blue badge for his obesity so he could park in one of the disabled spots nearer the hospital's entrance.

'Nurse Drury, April Lavender from the *Daily Chronicle*. We have been sent footage of you sexually abusing one of your patients this week and would like to give you the right to reply.'

Drury's face was already pink from the effort of walking, but it now turned puce with anger as April stood in his way, her notepad in hand. The photographer was out of sight, but was capturing the entire encounter on his camera.

'Whit footage? Whit are you talking about?' Drury said as he continued towards April and the sanctuary of his car.

'This footage,' April said, producing a large, blown-up, colour picture of Drury clearly massaging a patient's breasts.

'That's no' me,' Drury said as he barged past April, fumbling with his key fob to unlock the car doors.

'Oh yes it is, as well you know,' April said as she blocked Drury from opening his door.

'Fuck off, you fat cow,' the nurse snarled.

'I'd rather be a fat cow than a fat pervert,' she retorted. 'Now, this is your last chance for a right of reply before we go to press. Do you have anything to say?' she said, pointing her Dictaphone toward his mouth.

'Aye, take this,' Drury said as he swung a wild right hook at April. But his pathetic punch may as well have been telegraphed. The wily old hack simply sidestepped out of the way, and Drury's momentum carried him forward, tumbling to the ground. Winded, he lay sprawled on the tarmac, unable to move, his car keys landing at April's feet.

'I'm guessing that's a "no comment", then?' April said, feeling pleased with herself as she calmly picked up the nurse's keys, locked the doors with the fob, then dropped them down the drain by his head with a satisfying plop. 'You won't be needing a car where you're going. Look forward to seeing you in court.'

April smiled as she made her way back to her battered old Daewoo. The last sight the prostrate nurse was treated to was April's Dune high heels and the distinctive wiggle of her voluptuous backside as she disappeared into her car.

94

A new beginning

Connor enjoyed the walk through the bottom end of Glasgow city centre, after taking a shortcut through the lanes that link Queen Street to Miller Street and Virginia Street and beyond. This quieter route allowed him to avoid the chuggers, with their cheery smiles and clipboards, who clog the pedestrian precinct on Argyle Street. Although he was more at risk of bumping into the equally annoying junkies who ask for money, or a light—or both—in their high-pitched, nasally voices, whilst their eyes swivel about in their heads. Connor was always amazed how Glasgow changed from street to street. You had areas with working men's pubs round the corner from trendy restaurants and bistros. It all helped give the city its unique character.

He took the side entrance from Virginia Street into the food court in the basement of Marks and Spencer, where he was met with a dazzling display of bouquets. Connor had bought plenty of flowers over the years without really knowing what he was buying. He was wary of lilies though after an ex-girlfriend claimed they had nearly killed her cat. He had no idea that something so easy to buy on the high street could prove fatal to pets. But nearly killing the cat had been the death knell on yet another relationship. So how come Anya had forgiven him so readily, given that he'd placed her daughter in such danger?

Connor had a spring in his step as he strolled the short distance to the busy bars and restaurants of Merchant City and on to the Happy Cossacks. The door had the 'closed' sign on display but it was open when Connor pushed it. Inside, Katusha was already setting a table for their dinner, which they'd have before the restaurant opened to the public at six. She squealed with delight when she saw him, running to throw herself into his arms.

'Leave him alone,' Anya chided her daughter, 'he must be tired after a long day making up stories.'

'What's in the bag?' Katusha asked cheekily.

'Katusha. Manners,' Anya said, scowling.

'She's certainly as forthright as her mother. It's for you, Kat,' Connor replied, handing over the Hamleys bag.

'You shouldn't have,' Anya said softly, although she was glad he had.

'Mama, it's Anna and Elsa,' Katusha said, before tearing into the packaging.

'I don't really know what wee girls are into but reckon you can never go wrong with anything *Frozen*. And these are for you.' Connor handed over the bouquet of long-stemmed lilies to Anya.

'What are you trying to do? Kill my cat?'

'Oh no, not again,' Connor said, the colour draining from his face.

'Only kidding. We don't have a cat,' Anya replied, giving him a playful nudge. 'Only this little Kat,' she added, hugging her daughter. 'Thank you, Elvis. I presume you won't say no to beer and something to eat?'

'You're right, I won't.'

'Well, take a seat. Katusha shall serve,' she said, disappearing into her kitchen.

Connor tended, as a rule, not to date women with children. It wasn't a selfish thing but his mum had had a series of boyfriends during his childhood and he knew what it was like to have men come and go in your life. He never wanted to be that type of guy. But as the Siberian beer hit his stomach he was suddenly overcome with a warm, fuzzy glow, imagining what it would be like to be part of Anya and Katusha's life. It made him feel nice to think he might finally have a purpose.

95

The tap

The *Daily Chronicle* 'editor' was a relatively young man for such a position of power. Fraser Commons was nothing like his surname suggested, having been the product of two extremely wealthy corporate lawyers. But he was a good sort, and had landed the top job at the paper almost by default. The publication had virtually been rudderless since the departure of the previous editor, Nigel Bent. Nobody had shed any tears over Bent leaving, as his main aim during his tenure seemed to be to fill his own boots.

The news editor, Big Fergie, had taken over as acting editor for a while. But when management failed to offer the substantial wage increase his new position deserved, Big Fergie told them to get stuffed and returned to his old post. Senior executives then came up with a restructuring plan that changed all the desk heads from sports, news and features editors into 'content managers'. Each in turn would edit the paper on a rotational basis. It was being sold to them as an opportunity to expand their skill-set, but still came without any financial incentive.

Just before the new structure was to be signed off, the newspaper's American owners paid off all the senior executives, so now there was a new system in place but no editor. Fraser Commons was the most senior production figure left, and so, through default, found himself in charge of Scotland's biggest-selling daily publication. Commons had been a quiet but competent former sub-editor who had been steadily working his way up the career ladder. Although even he hadn't expected such a lofty position quite so quickly, even if he didn't have the salary or title to go with it. Sadly it proved to be something of a poisoned chalice as Fraser was expected to implement round after round of swingeing budget cuts and staff redundancies. He soon discovered his heart just wasn't in it.

Fraser approached the door of the special investigations broom cupboard with dread. He politely knocked and waited for an offer to enter, which was a mark of his upbringing and indicative of how his manners were unlike most of the other journalists at the *Daily Chronicle*.

'Ap-pril, do you mind coming to my office so that we can have a word?' Fraser stuttered. April and Connor shot each other a knowing look.

'Not at all,' April said, regaining her chirpiness. As she closed the door Connor silently mouthed, 'Good luck.'

Less than fifteen minutes later April returned to their cramped office and took her seat, wearing a haunted look. 'I need a fag,' she said, reaching for her top drawer, where she knew she had at least one left in a packet.

'And I need a passive smoke,' Connor replied, grabbing his jacket to join her. They didn't speak until they were outside. April lit up and inhaled deeply.

'Well?' asked Connor.

'Well, that's it,' she said, taking another long drag.

'What did he say?'

'He was nice about it . . . said I'd been a great servant . . . and there's money on the table.' The cigarette was trembling in her hand and her voice quavered as she spoke.

Connor knew he'd have to muster all his diplomatic skills for his colleague, who needed a shoulder to cry on in her time of need.

'You lucky bitch.'

'What?' The insult shook April from her trance-like state.

'Don't you see? You've made it, old girl. You've crossed the finishing line. What are you, sixty-something?'

'Fifty-blooming-eight—how many times do I have to tell you?'

'Yeah, but that's almost retirement age. And you're getting a golden handshake to go. You're leaving while they still have money to make people go away instead of piss them off out the door, like they'll do to me. Well done,' Connor said, with tears of joy in his eyes as he tried to get both arms in a hug around April's frame. 'Well bloody done.'

April began to laugh. 'You're right. I got away with it!'

'Eh?' Connor leaned back to look at her.

'I used to clean pub toilets for a living. Then I ended up writing for a living. No training. No nothing. And they never found me out. I got away with it,' April beamed, showing off her prized gold tooth.

Connor hugged her again.

'I just hope I've got enough to last me. I'm far too old to clean lavvies again,' April said, her mind already trying to figure out what she would do next. She'd now have the whole weekend to think about it. Or maybe the rest of her life.

96

Growler

'Guess where I've just been?' April asked as she breezed into the tiny office on Monday morning, almost an hour late. Her presence instantly made it more claustrophobic.

'Away to see about your prolapse?' Connor asked, without looking up from his screen.

'No. I've got used to that.'

'For a nip and tuck, then?'

'Nope. Although I do fancy one.'

'For an arse implant—i.e. they're using your arse for implants?'

'Wrong again. I've worked hard for this booty,' April replied as she slapped her ample behind.

'Electrolysis for your moustache?'

'Nah. Although I should book myself in,' she said, stroking her top lip.

'Your growler?'

'NO. Although, yet again . . .'

'The denture clinic?'

'These gnashers are all my own, sunshine.'

'The dementia clinic?'

'Don't be daft, thingummy.'

'The STI clinic?'

'Not for a long time.'

'Okay, I've exhausted all possibilities. Pray tell. Where were you?'

'Seeing a financial advisor,' April beamed.

'And, judging by your Cheshire Cat grin, I'd say it's good news?'

'Turns out I'm something of a financial mover and shaker. A real Warren Buffett.'

'Looks like you've seen plenty of buffets in your day.'

'You really are a cheeky wee bastard. Anyway, it turns out I'm going to be alright.'

'In what sense?'

'Financially, of course, stupid. I have nearly £400,000 in my pension pot. I can take £100,000 of that tax-free. More, if I want, and still have an income of £15,000 a year. Not to mention the income I have from the six flats I have.'

'I thought you had five.'

'So did I. I forgot about one. He says if I get into any financial problems I could always sell a flat every year without paying any extra tax, as long as the profit is less than £40,000. Or I could release some of the capital on my half-a-million pound home as that's mortgage-free.'

'And you understood all this?'

'Not really. I just nodded a lot.'

'How does a crazy old bat like you end up a paper millionaire?'

'By turning up at work for thirty-odd years, come rain or come shine.'

'That's a line from a Sinatra song, isn't it? You're not going to start singing, are you?'

'I feel like dancing.'

'Please don't,' Connor said sternly, 'I don't think my desk can take another 9.7 on the Richter scale. But well done. Seriously. Maybe you can stop living in fear now.'

'I do not live in fear,' April replied huffily.

'You do too. Any time we have a company meeting, fear is written all over your face.'

'Only in case they start talking about technology.'

'That's all in your mind too. You have an iPad and a smartphone. You're not as technologically illiterate as you think you are. But seriously, well done. You've achieved most people's life goal.'

'And for one so young too,' April said as she theatrically struck a pose, her moon face a mass of wrinkles as she put on her cheesiest Hollywood smile.

'Quite. In another twenty years maybe I'll be just like you, although hopefully without the massive weight gain.'

'All bought and paid for,' April said, rubbing her tummy.

97

Bothans

April had been given her departure date. In just four days' time Connor would be the one and only member of the *Daily Chronicle*'s special investigations desk. The situation sat heavily with him as he stabbed at his food in Peccadillos with his fork, with no enthusiasm for his full fry-up. He looked across the table at his soon-to-be forcibly retired colleague as she tucked busily into her breakfast. He would never cease to be amazed by her unwavering devotion to eating.

'Here, you can have mine if you want,' he said, pushing his completely untouched plate towards her.

'You're not hungry?' is what Connor thought she'd said, but he couldn't be too sure because her mouth was full.

'I'll just take the toast. You have the rest, my bottomless little chum.'

'No, no,' she protested feebly. 'Well, perhaps just the sausage,' she said as her hand shot across the table like a street urchin, expertly stabbing a sausage and whipping it across to her own plate in the blink of an eye.

Connor waited for April's next inevitable move.

'It'd be a shame to waste the bacon. And the black pudding too,' she said, repeating the process.

'That'a girl,' Connor smirked.

April cast a rare glance from her morning meal towards Connor, her cheeks as full as a hamster's as she continued to chomp away. Connor nibbled half-heartedly at his toast, before taking a sip of his coffee.

'You've got the appetite of a sparrow this morning,' she observed.

'At least you're still eating like a seagull at the dump.'

'I've told you before, don't take your foul mood out on me and my love of food. What's up?'

'Everything.'

'We helped save Kelly, didn't we? We nailed a perverted nurse.'

'Yeah, but we failed to get the info out there. The paedophile rings. The corruption. The cover-ups. The establishment win again.'

April stopped eating for a moment, pointing her greasy fork in Connor's direction. 'We tried our best and that's all we can do. Don't forget you also saved that little girl too.'

'After putting her in danger in the first place. And I couldn't save Stevie. He told me he didn't want any part of all of this and then I do my usual: badger away and drag him into it. I cost a man his life, and for what? Nothing at all.'

April opened her mouth to speak, but then decided against it. She couldn't think of anything else to say.

'This came for you this morning, Elvis,' the waitress Martel said, placing a brown package on the table. 'Oh, and Elvis, the boss says in future ask first before you start using us as a mailing address.'

'I didn't . . .' But he was speaking to Martel's back as she stomped off in the direction of the kitchen.

'What's wrong with her?' April asked, sending tiny flecks of whatever was in her mouth in Connor's direction.

'You know us. Always blowing hot and cold,' he explained.

'I'm guessing this is a cold snap, then? Maybe it's blown in from Siberia?'

'I guess so,' Connor said, trying not to give the game away about his new relationship with Anya. He studied the package, which was simply addressed to: *Elvis, Regular Customer, C/O The Peccadillo Cafe, Queen Street, Glasgow.*

'That's weird. Not too many people know I'm a Peccadillos regular. In fact, I'm struggling to think who I've even brought in here. There's only you and Stevie . . .'

Connor tore open the package, recalling how he'd interviewed Stevie Brett in the café the first time he'd met him after his court case many years ago. A small, black box around eight centimeters long and six wide fell into the palm of his hand. There was a piece of folded paper stuck to its base with Blu-Tack, which he carefully flattened out on the table. It read:

Hi Elvis. I guess if you're reading this, it means I'm dead. Bummer, huh? Needless to say if I am dead, I want you to know that it wasn't by my own hand. And that stash of animal porn they've no doubt found—I was only looking after that as a favour for a friend. Okay?

Connor chuckled before reading on.

Anyway by now I am sure the authorities have moved on to their next sinister mission, safe in the knowledge that they have wiped the board clean regarding the retrieval of their hard drive and its cesspit of secrets.

But they hadn't figured on Stevie Brett, unsung computer genius.

What you have in your hand is a copy of their precious hard drive. The last remaining copy, no doubt. I sent it to the cafe you once took me to—as I suspect that "They" will still be monitoring your mail. Does that sexy wee waitress still work there? She had a drink's name, if I recall. Martini, or something. She seemed to be well into you.

'Used to be, mate,' Connor said aloud.

Anyway Elvis, just remember that many Bothans died to bring you this information, so please make sure you blow up the Death Star this time.

All the best—from your No.1 geeky (ex)contact.

Connor smiled at the *Star Wars* references, although tears began to stream down his face. He hadn't cried in years and now felt he couldn't stop. He was in awe of the courage it had taken Stevie to write the letter, knowing full well he was going to die. Connor also admired his ingenuity. Sending the copy to the Peccadillo was his final masterstroke. His way of sticking two fingers up at the establishment.

April placed her hand on top of Connor's and squeezed tightly as her colleague quietly sobbed away. It had been time for him to let it all out.

'So what will you do now?' April eventually asked when Connor's crying had subsided.

'I'll get the information out there this time. And not through the *Daily Chronicle*,' he replied, before blowing his nose loudly on one of the café's paper napkins.

'Beast Shamer?' April asked hopefully.

'Yeah, why not?'

'How will you do that?' April wondered.

Connor rooted around in his suit jacket pocket before producing a crumpled plain, white business card with the name Charlie McGill on it, along with a mobile phone number.

'I retrieved it from the bin,' Connor explained. 'I figured I might need it someday. I think today's the day.'

Acknowledgements

My heartfelt thanks to Roza for all things Russian. To Hassan for the Farsi translations. To my wife, Amanda, and aunt, Sam, for their medical assistance (who'd have suspected you both could be so lethal?). To Colin for his usual geeky technical advice, and to the serving member of the British Armed Forces for his invaluable expertise. As for my now retired colleague, Yvonne, I shall never forget you, thingummy. And ScotRail, without your many delays and cancelled services, I would never have found the time to complete this book, so thanks. I guess . . .

I am once again eternally gratefully for the faith shown in me by my publisher Sara and to my editor, Craig, who really does a magnificent and thankless job making sense of all my ramblings. My gratitude also extends across the pond to Amy and Alex at Skyhorse Publishing in New York, who will hopefully help give April Lavender the US audience I think she deserves, which should keep her going in donuts for many more years to come.

Thank you, too, to my small and loyal (but hopefully growing!) band of readers. Your words of encouragement and deep love expressed for April Lavender really do drive me on. Without you, I'd just be a bloke writing stories on a train. It's nice to know someone is out there waiting to read them.

And finally, in case it's not blindingly obvious, this is a work of fiction and (hopefully) humour. As far as the conspiracy theories are concerned—Princess Diana, Lord Lucan, Jack the Ripper, etc.—I'm no more privy to what did and didn't happen than your average punter with a broadband connection and a few hours to spare sniffing out facts, lies and the downright bonkers.

About the Author

Matt Bendoris was shortlisted for the Bloody Scotland Crime Book of the Year Award 2015 for his second novel, *DM for Murder*. He is a senior journalist with the *Sun* newspaper and was named Arts/Entertainment Journalist of the Year at the 2016 Press Awards. He has also ghost-written two showbiz autobiographies, including The Krankies' *Fan Dabi Dozi* (John Blake Publishing, 2004), and Sydney Devine's *Simply Devine* (Black and White Publishing, 2005). He lives in Scotland with his wife, Amanda, and their two children, Andrew and Brooke. In his spare time he enjoys running and he's completed four marathons.